Black Ice

Also by Anne Stuart
in Large Print:

Into the Fire
Still Lake
The Road to Hidden Harbor
Night of the Phantom
Now You See Him . . .

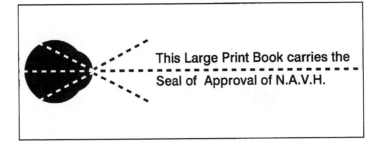

This Large Print Book carries the
Seal of Approval of N.A.V.H.

Black Ice

Anne Stuart

WHEELER PUBLISHING

Published in 2005 by arrangement with Harlequin Books S.A.

Wheeler Large Print Softcover.

The text of this Large Print edition is unabridged.
Other aspects of the book may vary from the original edition.

Set in 16 pt. Plantin by Christina S. Huff.

Printed in the United States on permanent paper.

Library of Congress Cataloging-in-Publication Data

Stuart, Anne (Anne Kristine)
   Black ice / by Anne Stuart.
      p. cm.
   ISBN 1-59722-038-8 (lg. print : sc : alk. paper)
   1. Women translators — Fiction. 2. Americans — France — Fiction. 3. Paris (France) — Fiction. 4. Illegal arms transfers — Fiction. 5. Large type books. I. Title.
PS3569.T785B57 2005
  813'.54—dc22
                                        2005012686

This was a gift book for me, one the universe delivered when I was riding in a taxi in Paris, and it comes with a sound track. Listen to Japanese Rock and Roll, French rock (Marc Lavoine, Florent Pagny) and maybe some Pretenders. Enjoy!

As the Founder/CEO of NAVH, the only national health agency solely devoted to those who, although not totally blind, have an eye disease which could lead to serious visual impairment, I am pleased to recognize Thorndike Press★ as one of the leading publishers in the large print field.

Founded in 1954 in San Francisco to prepare large print textbooks for partially seeing children, NAVH became the pioneer and standard setting agency in the preparation of large type.

Today, those publishers who meet our standards carry the prestigious "Seal of Approval" indicating high quality large print. We are delighted that Thorndike Press is one of the publishers whose titles meet these standards. We are also pleased to recognize the significant contribution Thorndike Press is making in this important and growing field.

Lorraine H. Marchi, L.H.D.
Founder/CEO
NAVH

★ Thorndike Press encompasses the following imprints: Thorndike, Wheeler, Walker and Large Print Press.

1

People might go on and on about spring-
time in Paris, Chloe Underwood thought
as she walked down the street huddled in
her coat, but there was really nothing to
compare to winter in the City of Lights. By
early December the leaves were gone, the
air was crisp and cool and enough of the
tourists had left to make life bearable. In
August she always wondered why on earth
she'd chosen to pull up stakes and move
three thousand miles away from her family.
But then winter came, and she remembered all too well.

It might have helped if she could have
abandoned the city to the tourists every
August, as all the French did, but she'd yet
to find a job that included such luxuries as
vacations, health care or a living wage. She
was lucky she'd managed to find work at
all. As it was, her presence in France was
quasi-legal, and most days she decided just
being there was blessing enough, even if
she shared a tiny walk-up flat with a fellow

expatriate who seemed to have very little sense of responsibility. Sylvia barely remembered to pay her half of the rent, she'd never swept a floor in her life and she considered any piece of furniture or flat surface a place to leave her astonishingly large wardrobe. On the other hand, she wore the same size eight that Chloe did, and she was not averse to sharing. She was also single-mindedly determined to marry a wealthy Frenchman, and in pursuit of that goal she spent most nights away from their cramped quarters, leaving Chloe with a little more breathing room.

In fact, it was Sylvia who'd found Chloe her current job translating children's books. Sylvia had worked at Les Frères Laurent for two years, and she'd slept with all three of the middle-aged *frères,* ensuring job tenure and a decent salary for translating spy novels and thrillers for the small publisher. Children's books were less of a moneymaker, and Chloe was paid accordingly, but at least she didn't have to ask her family for money or touch the trust fund her grandparents had left her. Not that her parents would encourage her. That money was earmarked for her education, and working a menial job in Paris hardly constituted advanced learning.

If she weren't hamstrung by job requirements she could have found something a bit more challenging. While her French was excellent, she was also fluent in Italian, Spanish and German, with a healthy smattering of Swedish and Russian, and even a few bits of Arabic and Japanese. She loved words, almost as much as she loved cooking, but she seemed to have a greater talent out of the kitchen. At least, that's what she'd been told when she was dismissed from the famous Cordon Bleu halfway into the program. Too much imagination for a beginner, they'd said. Not enough respect for tradition.

Chloe had never been particularly respectful of tradition, including her family tradition of medicine. She'd left all five of the Underwoods back in the mountains of North Carolina. Her parents were internists, her two older brothers were surgeons, and her older sister was an anesthesiologist. And they still couldn't believe Chloe wasn't dying to enter medical school, ignoring the fact that there was no one in this world more squeamish at the sight of blood than the youngest member of the Underwood family.

No, Chloe wasn't going to get to touch that nice little chunk of money until she gave in and went to medical school. And it was going to be a cold day in hell before she did.

In the meantime, she could do amazing things with pasta and fresh vegetables, and all the walking she did kept the carbohydrates from gathering in force, though they seemed to have developed a fondness for her rear. At twenty-three she couldn't still be built like a coltish teenager, and she was never going to look like a Frenchwoman. She just lacked the style even her roommate Sylvia, an Englishwoman, had in abundance. She could wear Sylvia's clothes, but she never could master that faintly arrogant, slightly amused mien that she longed for. She might as well have a big butt, too.

Les Frères Laurent was on the third floor of an older building near Montmartre. Chloe was the first one in, as always, and she put on a pot of the strong coffee that she loved, cradling a cup in her chilled hands as she looked out into the busy street below. The brothers kept the heat off at night, and as a junior employee she wasn't allowed to touch the thermostat, so she'd learned to keep an extra sweater in the tiny cubicle she'd been allotted. She wasn't in the mood for working

— it was a gorgeous day, with the sky a bright azure above the old buildings that surrounded them, and for some reason the adventures of Flora the plucky little ferret didn't call to her. Not enough sex and violence, she thought wistfully. Just moral lessons in a heavy-handed lecture, given by a skinny rodent in a pink tutu and the smug values of an American Republican. Just once she wished Flora would yank off her tutu and jump the rascally weasel who'd been giving her the eye. But Flora would never stoop so low.

Chloe took a sip of her coffee. Strong as faith, sweet as love, black as sin. She wouldn't be a real Parisian until she started smoking, but even to annoy her parents she couldn't go that far. Besides, the farther away her parents were, the less annoying they became.

It was another hour before anyone else would arrive at the office, and she told herself that no one would know or care if she wasted a few precious minutes before turning to the boring Flora. It was no wonder she was so irritated with the fictional character. What she needed was a little more sex and violence in her own life.

Be careful what you wish for, a little

11

voice murmured in her head, but Chloe shook it off, draining her coffee. Sex had been notable by its total absence for the past ten months, and her last affair was so lackluster that she hadn't been energized enough to look for a replacement. It wasn't that Claude had been a bad lover. He prided himself on his skills, and expected the gauche *Américain* to be suitably dazzled. She wasn't.

And she could probably do without violence, which was usually accompanied by blood, which tended to make her puke. Not that she'd encountered much real violence in her life. Her family had kept her sheltered, and she had a healthy respect for her own safety. She didn't go wandering into dangerous parts of the city at night, she locked her doors and windows and looked both ways and prayed diligently before she crossed the homicidal Parisian traffic.

No, she could look forward to another peaceful winter in the underheated apartment, eating pasta, translating *Flora the Plucky Ferret* and *Bruce the Tangerine,* though how a tangerine could have a life of its own had so far escaped her. Maybe that was why she was stalling on Flora, knowing her next task was citrus.

12

She'd find another lover, sooner or later. Maybe Sylvia would finally hit the mother lode, move out, and Chloe would find some nice, gentle Frenchman with wire-rimmed glasses and a skinny body and a taste for experimental cooking.

In the meantime, the doughty little ferret awaited her, as did the daunting task of coming up with the French equivalent of "doughty."

She heard Sylvia before she arrived — there was no mistaking the noisy clatter of her expensive shoes on the two flights of stairs, the muttered cursing from her perfectly rouged mouth. The only question was, why was Sylvia showing up at work three hours before she usually dragged herself in?

The door slammed open with a bang and Sylvia stood there, panting, not a hair out of place, not a speck of her makeup smudged. "There you are!" she cried.

"Here I am," Chloe said. "Want some coffee?"

"We don't have time for coffee, dammit! Chloe, sweetie, you have to help me. It's a matter of life and death."

Chloe blinked. Fortunately she was used to Sylvia's dramatics. "What now?"

Sylvia stopped cold, momentarily affronted. "I'm serious, Chloe! If you don't help me out I . . . I don't know what I'll do."

She'd dragged a huge suitcase all the way up the flights of stairs — no wonder she'd been making such a racket. "Where do you want to go and what do you need me to do to cover for you?" she asked, resigned. The huge suitcase that would suit most people on a two-week trip would keep Sylvia decently clothed for three or four days. Three or four days with the flat to herself and no one to pick up after. She could open the windows and let the air blow in and no one would complain about the cold. She was prepared to be helpful.

"I'm not going anywhere. You are."

Chloe blinked again. "The suitcase?"

"I packed for you. Your clothes are awful and you know it — I put in everything I thought looked good on you. Except my fur coat, but you can't expect me to part with that," she added, momentarily practical.

"I don't expect you to part with anything. And I can't go anywhere. What would the Laurents say?"

"Leave them to me. I'll cover for you," Sylvia said, looking her over. "At least you're decently dressed for a change, though I'd lose the scarf if I were you. You'll manage to fit in just fine."

A deep foreboding filled Chloe. "Fit in where? Just take a deep breath and tell me what you need and I'll see whether I can help you."

"You have to," Sylvia said flatly. "I told you, it's a . . ."

"Matter of life and death," Chloe filled in. "What do you want me to do?"

Some of Sylvia's anxiety vanished. "Nothing so onerous. Spend a few days at a beautiful estate in the country, translating for a group of importers, making scads of money and being waited on by an army of servants. Wonderful food, wonderful surroundings and the only drawback is having to deal with boring businessmen. You get to dress for dinner and make tons of money and flirt with anyone who takes your fancy. You should be thanking me for giving you such a golden opportunity."

Typical of Sylvia to turn things around in her own mind. "And exactly why are you giving me a golden opportunity?"

"Because I promised Henry I'd spend the weekend with him at the Raphael."

"Henry?"

"Henry Blythe Merriman. One of the heirs to Merrimans Extract. He's rich, he's

15

handsome, he's charming, he's good in bed and he adores me."

"How old is he?"

"Sixty-seven," Sylvia said, not the slightest bit sheepish.

"And is he married?"

"Of course not! I have some standards."

"As long as they're rich, single and breathing," Chloe said. "And just when would I be going?"

"A car's on its way to pick you up. Actually, they think they'll be picking me up, but I've called and explained the situation and said you'd be taking my place. All they need is French to English and back again, which is a piece of cake for you."

"But, Sylvia —"

"Please, Chloe! I beg of you! If I leave them in the lurch I'll never get another translating job, and I can't quite count on Henry yet. I need to do these little weekend jobs to supplement my income. You know how badly the Frères pay."

"About twice as much as they pay me."

"Then you need the money even more," Sylvia said, unabashed. "Come on, Chloe, go for it! Be wild and dangerous for a change! A few days spent in the country is just what you need."

"Wild and dangerous with a bunch of

businessmen? Somehow I can't quite see it happening."

"Think of the food."

"Bitch," Chloe said cheerfully.

"And they probably have an exercise room as well. Most of these big old houses turned conference centers do. You don't need to worry about your butt."

"Double bitch," Chloe said, regretting she'd ever expressed concern over her curves.

"Come on, Chloe," Sylvia said, wheedling. "You know you want to. You'll have a marvelous time. It won't be as boring as you think, and maybe we'll be able to celebrate my engagement when you get back."

Chloe doubted it. "When am I supposed to leave?"

Sylvia let out a little crow of triumph. Not that she'd ever seriously expected not to get her way. "That's the best part. The limo's probably downstairs by now. You'll be reporting to Mr. Hakim and he'll tell you what to do."

"Hakim? My Arabic is lousy."

"I told you, it's all French to English and back. Groups of importers are bound to be multinational, but all of them speak either English or French. Piece of cake, Chloe. In more ways than one."

17

"Triple bitch," Chloe said. "Do I have time . . . ?"

"No. It's eight-thirty-three and the limo was supposed to arrive at eight-thirty. These people tend to be very precise. Just put on a little makeup and we'll go down."

"I'm already wearing makeup."

Sylvia let out an exasperated sigh. "Not enough. Come with me and I'll fix you up." She grabbed her hand and started tugging her toward the bathroom.

"I don't need fixing up," Chloe protested, yanking her hand free.

"They're paying seven hundred euros a day, and all you have to do is talk."

Chloe put her hand back in Sylvia's. "Fix me up," she said, resigned, and followed Sylvia into the cramped little bathroom at the far end of the room.

Bastien Toussaint, also known as Sebastian Toussaint, Jean-Marc Marceau, Jeffrey Pillbeam, Carlos Santeria, Vladimir the Butcher, Wilhelm Minor and a good half dozen other names and identities, lit a cigarette, inhaling with mild pleasure. The last three jobs he'd been a nonsmoker, and he'd adapted with his usual cool acceptance. He didn't tend to let weakness get to him — he was relatively impervious to addictions, pain, torture or tenderness. He could, occasionally, be merciful if the situation called for it. If it didn't, he dispensed justice without blinking. He did what he had to do.

But whether he needed the cigarette or not, he enjoyed it, just as he'd enjoy the fine wines with dinner and the single malt whiskies that were supposed to lower his guard and make him indiscreet. And he would be, spilling just enough information to satisfy the others and advance his agenda. He could do the same with vodka, but he preferred Scotch, and he'd enjoy it along with the cigarettes and do without when this job was over.

It had lasted longer than most of his assignments. They'd been working on his cover for more than two years, and when he'd stepped into the role eleven months ago he'd been more than ready. He was a patient man, and he knew how long it took for things to be set in motion. But the payoff was close at hand, and that knowledge gave him a cool satisfaction, although he was going to miss Bastien Toussaint. He'd gotten used to him by now — the faint, Gallic charm, the sharp-witted ruthlessness, the eye for women. He'd had more sex as Bastien than he'd had for a

19

while. Sex was another indulgence he could take or leave, another pleasure to be savored if it came his way. He was supposed to have a wife back in Marseilles, but that made little difference. Most of the men he'd be meeting with had wives and children, nice little nuclear families back in the mother country. Children and wives who happily live off the profits of their mutual occupation.

Importing. Importing fruit from the Middle East. Importing beef from Australia. Importing arms to whoever could pay the highest price.

At least it wasn't drugs this time. He had never been totally comfortable with smuggling heroin. Foolish sentimentality on his part — people chose to use drugs, they didn't choose to be shot by the guns he trafficked. It must be a throwback to his old life, so long gone that he barely remembered it.

It was a cold, crisp winter day. There was a distant scent of apples on the air, and the calming sound of the garden staff raking leaves in front of the sprawling house. Most of the staff would be carrying guns under their loose clothing. Semiautomatics, maybe Uzis. Possibly ones he'd provided.

It would be damned funny if one of them killed him.

He dropped his cigarette on the ground and ground it out with his foot. Someone would come and remove the butt, someone who would just as calmly remove him if ordered to do so. And the odd thing was, he didn't really care.

The door opened behind him, and Gilles Hakim stepped out into the sunlight. "Bastien. We're having coffee in the library. Why don't you come and join us? Meet the others? We're just waiting for the translator to show up."

Bastien turned his back on the beautiful December day and followed Hakim into the house.

2

Chloe had far too much time to consider how rash she'd been. The uniformed chauffeur kept the glass screen up between them, it was too early for a drink to calm her nerves and Sylvia had been in such a hurry to get her going that she'd forgotten to bring a book with her. All she had were her thoughts to keep her company for this seemingly endless ride.

She automatically reached up to shove her long brown hair behind her ear when she remembered the miracle Sylvia had wrought in three minutes with nothing more than a handful of makeup and a brush. She might not have a book but she had Sylvia's compact in Sylvia's Hermès handbag, and she wanted one more surreptitious look. To see the stranger looking back at her out of the same calm brown eyes she'd always had, though now they were lined and smudged and gorgeous in her pale face. The long, straight brown hair no longer hung down around her face

— Sylvia had moussed and teased and fiddled with it so that in less than a minute it turned from a lank veil to a tousled mane. Her pale mouth was now plump and red and shiny, and the borrowed scarf adorning her shoulder was draped just so.

The question was, how long would she be able to carry on with the illusion? Sylvia could look like this in three minutes — it had taken her less than five to transform Chloe from a plain brown wren into a peacock. Chloe had tried to achieve the same results on numerous occasions and had always fallen short. "Less is more," Sylvia had lectured her, but more was never enough.

And she was fussing for nothing. They wanted an interpreter, not a fashion model, and if Chloe knew one thing, it was languages. She could do her job and spend the rest of the time pretending she belonged in a château instead of her tiny apartment that always smelled of cabbage. And she would eat anything she wanted.

Three or four nights in a château and then she'd be back, and Sylvia would owe her big time. And it might not be the sex and violence she was playfully longing for, but at least it would be a change. And who knows, maybe one of the boring businessmen would have a handsome young assistant with an interest in American girls. Anything was possible.

Château Mirabel had more security than Fort Knox, she thought a half hour later, as they began their journey through a series of gates, checkpoints, armed guards and leashed dogs. The deeper inside the grounds they went, the more uneasy Chloe became. Getting inside was hard enough. Getting out looked to be just about impossible, unless they were willing to let her go.

And why wouldn't they? She was being ridiculous, and when the limousine finally pulled up outside the wide front steps she'd managed to control both her curiosity and her imagination and climb out of the back of the car with a fair approximation of Sylvia's languid grace.

The man waiting for her was tall, older and dressed better than the average Frenchman, which meant he was well-dressed indeed. He was clearly of Middle Eastern origin, and Chloe gave him her most dazzling smile. "Monsieur Hakim?"

He nodded, shaking her hand. "And you are Miss Underwood, Miss Whickham's replacement. I only just found out you were coming. If I'd known, I could have saved you a trip."

"Saved me a trip? You don't need me?"

Two or more hours back to the city was not at the top of her list of things she most wanted to do, and she was even more loath to part with the promise of the money Sylvia had mentioned.

"We are a smaller group than expected, and I think we could manage to understand each other without outside help," he said in gentle, well-modulated tones. They were speaking English, and Chloe promptly switched over to French.

"If you wish, *monsieur*, but I'm sure I could be quite useful. I have nothing else planned for the next few days, and I would be more than happy to stay."

"If you have nothing planned then you will be able to go back to Paris and enjoy a nice vacation," he suggested in the same language.

"I'm afraid my apartment is not the best place for a vacation, Monsieur Hakim." She wasn't sure why she was trying to talk him into letting her stay. She hadn't wanted to come here in the first place — it was only Sylvia's wheedling that had talked her into it. That and the thought of the seven hundred euros a day.

But now that she was here she didn't want to go back. Even if it was the smarter thing to do.

Mr. Hakim hesitated, seemingly unused to argumentative women. And then he nodded. "I suppose you could be of value to us," he said. "It would be a shame for you to make such a long trip for nothing."

"It was a long trip," Chloe said. "I think the driver might have gotten lost — we passed several places more than once. Next time he should have a map."

Hakim's smile was slight. "I will see to it, Mademoiselle Underwood. In the meantime, we'll have the servants take care of your bag while you come meet the guests you'll be translating for. It shouldn't be too onerous a task, and when we're not meeting you'll have a beautiful setting in which to enjoy yourself. And, of course, the presence of such a lovely young woman can only make our work go more smoothly."

For some reason the usual French good manners sat slightly askew on Hakim, and she found herself wanting to go wash her hands. She gave him the maternal smile she reserved for the most lecherous of the Laurent brothers and murmured, "You're too kind" as she followed him up the marble steps.

A great many of the old châteaus had been turned into luxury hotels and conference centers, with the shabbier ones be-

26

coming bed-and-breakfasts. This was more elegant than any she had seen or even heard of, and by the time Hakim ushered her into a large room she was finding herself more and more uneasy.

At least she wasn't the only woman. There were eight people gathered in the room drinking coffee, and her eyes passed over them quickly. The two women had nothing in common but their good looks — Madame Lambert was tall, of a certain age, dressed in what Chloe recognized as Lagerfeld, thanks to Sylvia. The other woman was a bit younger, in her early thirties, a little too beautiful, a little too vivacious. The introductions went smoothly — there was Mr. Otomi, an elderly, dignified Japanese who fortunately spoke excellent English, and his steely-eyed assistant Tanaka-san; Signor Ricetti, a vain, middle-aged man whose handsome young assistant was undoubtedly his lover as well; and the Baron von Rutter, all to be expected, no one of particular interest except . . .

Except for him. She quickly lowered her eyes, astonished at her unexpected reaction. She didn't like men in suits, even in Armani. She didn't like businessmen — most of them were entirely without humor and intent only on the acquisition of money. There were a great many things Chloe loved about France, but the obsession with finance was not one of them. Too bad he was one of them, she thought briefly. Unfair that she be instantly attracted to someone who was out of the question.

Madame Lambert, Signor Ricetti, the Baron and Baroness von Rutter, Otomi and Toussaint.

Bastien Toussaint. At least he seemed supremely uninterested in her as he acknowledged the introduction, nodding and then clearly dismissing her from his thoughts. There was no particular reason for her reaction — he wasn't the best-looking man she'd ever seen. He was a little taller than most, lean, with a hard, narrow face and a strong nose. His eyes were dark, almost opaque, and she doubted she even registered in them. He had long, thick black hair, an anomaly, maybe even an unexpected vanity. She didn't want a vain man, did she?

Yes, she did, if it was Bastien Toussaint. She pulled her gaze away as her ears attuned themselves to a torrent of Italian from Signor Ricetti.

"What's she doing here?" he demanded furiously. "It was supposed to be that stupid British female. How do we know we can trust this one? She may not be as unobservant as the other. Get rid of her, Hakim."

"Signor Ricetti, it's impolite to speak Italian in front of someone who doesn't understand the language," Hakim said in disapproving English tones. He glanced at Chloe. "You don't speak Italian, do you, Mademoiselle Underwood?"

She didn't know why she lied. Hakim was making her nervous, and the clear animosity on Ricetti's part didn't help. "Only French and English," she said brightly.

Ricetti was not pacified. "I still think it's too dangerous, and I'm sure the others would agree. Madame Lambert, Monsieur Toussaint, don't you think we should send this young woman away?" He was still speaking Italian, and Chloe kept her expression blank.

"Don't be an idiot, Ricetti." Madame Lambert spoke Italian with a British accent, a surprise. Like Sylvia, she had somehow managed to absorb the ineffable chic of French womanhood, something that had so far eluded Chloe.

"Oh, I think she should stay," Bastien Toussaint said in a lazy voice. "She's too pretty to send away. What harm could she do? She probably doesn't have a brain in her head — she'd be incapable of reading between the lines." His Italian was perfect, only slightly tinged with a French accent and something she couldn't quite define, and his voice was deep, slow and sexy. Things were not improving.

"I still say she's trouble," Ricetti said, setting down his coffee cup. Chloe noticed that his hands were trembling slightly. Too much coffee, perhaps? Or something else.

"Well, you don't need to say it again," the baron spoke up. He was plump, white-haired, grandfatherly looking, and some of Chloe's strange forebodings lessened. "Welcome to Château Mirabel, Mademoiselle Underwood," he said in French. "We're very grateful you were able to fill in at the last moment."

It took her just a millisecond to remember that she was supposed to understand the last speech. *"Merci, monsieur,"* she replied, trying to focus all her attention on the sweet old gentleman, trying to ignore the man who stood just past her right shoulder. "I promise to do my best."

"You'll do fine," Hakim said, a faint edge to his voice. Ricetti flushed, lapsing into silence. "We've finished work for this afternoon, and I imagine you'd like to get settled. Drinks are at seven, dinner at nine, and I hope you will join us. We try not to discuss business after hours, but we all tend to have our lapses, and it would aid us if you'd make yourself available."

"How available will she be?" Bastien spoke in German this time. "I may be in need of a little recreation."

"Get your mind out of your pants, Bastien!" Madame Lambert chided him. "We don't need your womanizing complicating matters. Men have a habit of confiding all sorts of unfortunate things when they're between a woman's legs."

Chloe blinked, trying not to react as Bastien moved into her line of view. His smile was slow, secretive and impossibly sexy. "My wife tells me I fuck in total silence," he said.

"Let's not put it to the test," Hakim said. "Once we're finished here you can follow her back to Paris and screw her brains out. In the meantime we have a job to do." He switched back to English. "I'm sorry for all this conversation, *mademoiselle*. As you can guess, only half of us understand the same language, and it gets very confusing. From now on we will have no languages other than French and English. Is that understood?"

31

Bastien was looking at her from beneath his hooded eyes. "Crystal clear," he said in English. "I can always wait."

"Wait, *monsieur?*" Chloe asked innocently.

A mistake. He turned the full force of his gaze on her, and the effect was startling. His eyes were very dark, and she wondered if anything even reflected off their opaque surface. She hoped she wouldn't be in the position to find out. She hoped she wasn't entirely without common sense. The man was undoubtedly gorgeous. He was also, undoubtedly, way out of her league.

"Wait for a late supper, *mademoiselle*," he said smoothly. Before she realized what he intended he'd taken her hand and brought it to his mouth. She'd had her hand kissed before — it wasn't an uncommon occurrence even in modern-day Europe. But it had always been by polite old men, flirting without meaning anything by it. Bastien Toussaint's mouth on the back of her hand was neither polite nor meaningless, but he dropped it before she could pull it away.

"I'm certain you're hungry, *mademoiselle*," Hakim said. "Marie will take you to your room and see that a tray is brought. If you're interested in exploring the grounds you have only to ask and one of the gardeners will take you on a tour. It's a bit cold for swimming right now, though the pool is heated, and Americans are such a hardy race."

"I don't remember if I brought a swimsuit," she said, wondering what the hell Sylvia had packed for her.

"You can always go without, Mademoiselle Chloe," Bastien said in silken tones.

It should have been her first inkling that he was interested in her, though she couldn't quite figure out why he was, when he'd barely seemed to acknowledge their introduction. Maybe he'd decided she was just the best of slim pickings.

But she wasn't going to let him unnerve her. "It's definitely too cold for that," she said cheerfully. "I imagine if I want any exercise I'll just go for walks."

"You must be careful, Mademoiselle Chloe," Ricetti spoke up in heavily accented French. "It's hunting season, and there's no telling where a stray bullet might come from. Not to mention that the guard dogs roam free at night and they're quite merciless. If you want to go for a walk make sure you have someone to keep you company. You wouldn't want to accidentally wander into someplace . . . unsafe."

Was it a warning, or a threat, or a little

bit of both? And what the hell was going on here? What had Sylvia gotten her into?

Sex and violence, she reminded herself. Just looking at Bastien filled the quota for sex, and violence wasn't actually her cup of tea. Still, for a weekend it would, at the least, be entertaining, and she would be foolish to think that she was in any kind of danger. This was modern-day France, after all, and she was surrounded by staid, ordinary businesspeople. She'd been reading too many of Sylvia's translated thrillers.

"I will be very careful not to wander where I don't belong," she said.

"Of course you will," Hakim said in his distant voice. He had a peculiar air to him, slightly sinister, which must have been her tiresome imagination running amok. He was both bullying and faintly subservient, and she couldn't quite figure his position among the business partners. It was no wonder she thought something strange was going on, what with people muttering cryptic things in languages she wasn't supposed to understand, but in the end they were nothing more than a group of people locked away without any form of entertainment. "We will see you at seven."

A staid woman in a starched black uniform had appeared, more of a Mrs.

Danvers than a Mary Poppins. "If you will follow me, *mademoiselle*," she said in French that was clearly a foreign language to her, though Chloe couldn't begin to guess what her native tongue was.

She knew Bastien was watching her, and it took all her willpower not to glance back at him. She wasn't supposed to know he was a womanizer, out to bed the first new woman who'd come on the property. Besides, he was married, and that was one standard she shared with her feckless roommate. Sylvia might only sleep with bachelors in her quest for a wealthy husband, but Chloe was looking for something else. What, she wasn't quite sure. She only knew that Bastien Toussaint wouldn't provide it.

"At seven," she agreed, privately wondering what kind of condition they'd be in if they drank for two hours before dinner. But it wasn't her concern. None of it was, not even Bastien's halfhearted suggestive comments. He didn't really want her — she wasn't his type. He'd have long, leggy models, women with style and a to-hell-with-you attitude. Chloe had been nursing her go-to-hell attitude for years now, and though living in Paris had helped, it was far from a finished product.

She was going to get lost in the damned

maze of rooms, she thought, moving through the hall behind Marie's stiff figure. Her own room was at the far end of one of those hallways, and the moment she stepped inside her misgivings melted. It was a room from a museum — a beautiful green-silk-draped bed, marble floors, a luxurious sofa and the largest bathroom she'd seen since she'd left the U.S. She couldn't see a television, which shouldn't have come as a surprise, but she'd surely be able to find something to read in a place like this. There'd been several well-known, pastel newspapers laid out on the hall table — she could always filch them and work on the crossword puzzles. Crossword puzzles were a well-loved linguistic problem, and a couple of them could probably keep her busy for days. She just had to remember not to pick the Italian or German newspapers.

At that moment she wanted nothing more than to get into something more comfortable and indulge in a nice, long nap. "Where is my suitcase?" she asked.

"It's been unpacked and sent to the storage area," Marie said smoothly. "I imagine Monsieur Hakim told you, but they dress for dinner. I think the silver lace would be appropriate."

If Sylvia had parted with the silver lace then this job must be important indeed to her. She never let that particular dress out of her sight except for emergencies.

It was also just the teensiest bit too snug across her butt and her breasts, but Chloe wasn't going to tempt fate by trying to guess what else might be suitable for such an occasion. Marie would know, and if she was kind enough to volunteer the information Chloe would take advantage of it.

"Thank you, Marie." For a moment she felt a sudden panic, wondering whether she was supposed to tip her. Before she could hesitate Marie was on her way out of the room, clearly not expecting anything from a gauche American. She turned back at the last moment. "When do you want to be called? Five? Five-thirty? You want to allow enough time to get ready."

Marie must have thought such a task to be arduous indeed. "Six-thirty will give me plenty of time," she said cheerfully.

Marie had a long nose, and she looked down it with the perfect mixture of disdain and concern. "If you need any help you have only to ask," she said after a moment. "I've had some experience with hair like yours." She made it sound as if it were manure-encrusted straw.

"Thank you very much, Marie. I'm sure I'll be fine."

Marie merely raised her eyebrows, setting Chloe's misgivings into full play once more.

3

Someone had made a very grave error in sending that young woman into the lion's den, Bastien thought. She was far from the accomplished operative needed to work in such an intense situation. He'd known within seconds that she understood every language spoken in the room, and probably more besides, and she hadn't been that good at hiding it. If it had taken him mere moments, it wouldn't take some of the others much longer.

The question was, who had sent her, and why? The most dangerous possibility was that she'd come to ferret out his identity. As far as he knew no one suspected him, but one never took anything for granted. The part he was playing was a dedicated womanizer — sending a nubile young female into the mix was the perfect bait, like staking a young deer in the jungle to lure a hungry panther. If he went for her he'd be playing true to form.

She was dangerously inept. That veneer

of sophistication was wafer thin — one look in her brown eyes and he'd been able to read everything. Nervousness, shyness even, and an unwanted spark of sexual attraction. She was in way over her head.

Then again, she might be much better than she appeared to be. The hesitant, slightly shy demeanor might be all part of the act, to put him off the scent.

Had she come for him, or someone else? Was the Committee checking up on his performance? It was always possible — he hadn't bothered to hide the fact that he was weary beyond belief, no longer giving a damn. Life or death seemed minor distinctions to him, but once you went to work for the Committee they never let you go. He'd be killed, and probably sooner rather than later. Mademoiselle Underwood, with her shy eyes and soft mouth, might be just the one to do it.

And there was only one question. Would he let her?

Probably not. He was jaded, burned-out, empty inside, but he wasn't about to go quietly. Not yet.

On the surface his mission was simple. Auguste Remarque had been blown up by a car bomb last month, the work of the covert, antiterrorist organization known, by a very few, as the Committee. But, in fact, the Committee had had nothing to do with it. Auguste Remarque was a businessman, motivated by nothing more than profit, and the powers that be in the Committee could understand and adjust for that. All they'd had to do was keep an eye on Remarque and the arms dealers, keep abreast of who was shipping what to where and make their own pragmatic choices as to when to interfere. A shipment of high-powered machine guns to certain under-developed countries in Africa might lead to civilian deaths, but the greater good had to be considered, and those poor countries had little of interest to the superpowers. Or so his boss, the venerable Harry Thomason, had told him.

Of course, Bastien knew why. Those countries had no oil, and they were of little importance to the Committee and its powerful, private backers.

It had been Bastien's job to keep tabs on the arms dealers, posing as one of them. But Remarque's assassination had changed all that. Hakim, Remarque's right-hand man, had set up this meeting, and they were looking at redividing the territories and choosing a new head. Not that these were people who played well with others,

41

but the leader of the arms cartel also took care of the tiresome business details, leaving the others to concentrate on the acquisition and shipment of the most dangerous weapons yet devised.

Hakim had been in charge of the petty details, but he'd gotten a little too ambitious. He wanted to take Remarque's place, including taking his lucrative territories. And there lay the problems. Through decades of dealing, assassination and bribery, the late Auguste Remarque had controlled most weapons shipments for the Middle East, an inexhaustible market.

Areas like Chile, Kosovo, Northern Ireland and the cults of Japan might ebb and flow in their desire for weapons, but the Middle East never got enough. And since America had waded into the fray, time and time again, with bludgeoning attempts at control, things had only gotten worse.

The members of the arms cartel wanted a fair share of those lucrative profits. And Hakim was disposable.

Bastien was in no hurry to see things played out — he could spend a day or two watching and waiting. The members of the cartel had learned, one by one, that Hakim had been responsible for Remarque's assassination, and it didn't sit well. Someone would dispose of him in the next few days, and if they failed it would be up to Bastien.

It had been easy enough to subtly spread the word about Hakim's treachery. The various reactions of the main players had been interesting indeed because, in fact, Hakim hadn't been behind Remarque's death, even though he was entirely willing to benefit from it.

One of the other members of the clandestine arms cartel had been behind the hit. Someone who was here now, or had yet to arrive. That person was probably delighted that someone else had been fingered, but so far the Committee had been unable to discern who had actually done it. Conventional wisdom suggested Baron von Rutter. Beneath his jovial exterior he was a brusque, impatient man and he'd made his way more by bullying tactics than finesse. Not to mention his equal partner, his young wife Monique.

One of Bastien's fellow operatives had put her money on Mr. Otomi, the reserved, elderly Yakuza boss, and Ricetti was a good possibility as well with his Mafia connections. And one could never discount Madame Lambert.

Any of them were capable and willing,

and if any of them had ordered the hit then the Committee would not be alarmed.

But Bastien was banking on the last of their little group to arrive. Christos Christopolous was, on the surface, merely a minor player. The Greek connection had always been low-key, but Bastien was paid to be untrusting. And in the eleven months he'd lived as Bastien Toussaint he'd learned that Christos was the most dangerous of them all. He was the one who was most likely to have arranged for Remarque to be killed by the car bomb, along with his wife, daughter and three young grandchildren.

Thomason had taken his word and set the assignment. Hakim was to die — no matter who was responsible, the hit on Remarque couldn't have been accomplished without his assistance.

And if Christos was chosen to lead the cartel, he, too, must die. The others were manageable — the Greek wasn't.

Maybe Christos wouldn't get chosen, and Bastien could once more vanish into the obscurity of another name, another nationality, another mission on some other continent. Not that it mattered — they all seemed to be the same, the good guys and the bad guys interchangeable.

One thing was certain, he wasn't going to be able to do a damned thing if the innocent little newcomer stuck a knife between his ribs.

He had no illusions that he was on his own here. Signor Ricetti's young male lover was Jensen, a young British operative who'd told his wife he traveled a lot as a pharmaceutical sales representative.

Bastien had learned not to trust anyone, including his co-workers. It was always possible that Thomason had decided that Bastien himself was disposable. Jensen could take him out if that was what he was ordered to do, but he'd have a better chance of success than the girl. Anyone would. If they really wanted to get rid of him they needed someone a little more knowledgeable to do it.

Someone a little more adept than sweet Mademoiselle Underwood.

She was either there for him or for one of the others. Maybe just to gather information, maybe to dispose of an unwanted player. He had only to say something to Hakim and she would be the one they disposed of. Even if Hakim himself had hired her, she would be wiped out neatly and efficiently.

He wasn't quite ready to do that, even if

it was the safest route. He hadn't been drawn into this business by the lure of safety, and Mademoiselle Underwood might offer more value alive than dead. He would find out who sent her and why, and the sooner he found out the better. Careful planning was important, but hesitation was disastrous. He would find out what he needed to find out, then drop a word in Hakim's ear. It would be a shame to have such a promising young life snuffed out, but she would have known the dangers when she signed up for this job. And he'd lost any trace of sentimentality long ago.

He just wished to Christ that he knew why she was there.

Chloe was feeling slightly giddy. She slept deeply for a couple hours, curled up under a thin silk coverlet; she'd bathed in a deep warm bath perfumed with Chanel; she'd dressed in Sylvia's clothes and put Sylvia's makeup on her face. It was a few minutes before seven, and she'd have to slip her feet into the ridiculously high heels and glide downstairs like the soigné creature she was pretending to be.

The undergarments had begun the sensory overload. Chloe wore plain white cotton. Her taste ran to lace and satin and

46

deep, bold colors, but her pocketbook did not, and she'd spent her clothing euros on things that would be seen.

Sylvia spent a great deal of time in her underwear, seldom alone, and her wardrobe of corselets, panties, demi-bras and garter belts came in a rainbow of colors, all made to be enjoyed by both the wearer and her audience. Chloe wasn't currently planning on an audience, not here, not now. Bastien Toussaint might be distracting, but Chloe had no interest in married men, womanizers, or really anyone at all until she got back to Paris. This job was supposed to be a piece of cake, a leisurely few days in the country translating boring business details.

So why was she so damned edgy?

Probably just M. Toussaint, with his bedroom eyes and his slow, sexy voice. Or maybe it was the combined suspicion of the guests — they must be dealing with something very powerful to be so paranoid. Though in Chloe's experience most people thought their concerns to be life-altering proportions. Perhaps they held the formula for a new type of fabric. The shoe designs for next season. The recipe for calorie-free butter.

It didn't matter. She would remain in

some unobtrusive corner, translating when called upon to do so, hoping no one else was going to say anything embarrassing in a language she wasn't supposed to understand. Though it would help matters if she had her own wardrobe — Sylvia's clothes were not made to be unobtrusive.

Maybe she could just plead a headache, crawl back into bed and deal with things tomorrow. As far as she knew she wasn't on call twenty-four/seven, and tonight was supposed to be more of a social occasion. They wouldn't need her, and she didn't need to be around people who were drinking enough to be even more indiscreet than they had this afternoon.

Then again, it probably wouldn't be a bad idea to find out why they were so paranoid. If she didn't like the answer she could simply announce that she had to return home. Monsieur Hakim had insisted that she wasn't really needed, and she expected they would muddle through even without a common language. In the end, her peace of mind was more important than the generous daily stipend.

But seven hundred euros could ease a little mental discomfort, and she was seldom a coward. She would go downstairs, smile charmingly, drink just a little wine — not enough to make her indiscreet — and keep her distance from Bastien Toussaint. He unnerved her, both with his dark, unreadable eyes and his supposed interest in her. For some reason she didn't quite believe it. She was not an unattractive woman, but she was scarcely in his league — he was the type for supermodels and millionaires' daughters.

It didn't help that when she opened the door he was waiting for her.

He glanced at his thin watch. "A beautiful woman who shows up on time," he said in French. "How delightful."

She hesitated, uncertain what to say. On the one hand, the faint trace of irony in his voice was unmistakable, and Chloe knew that while she was attractive enough, beautiful was a bit too generous, even with the benefit of Sylvia's wardrobe. But arguing with him would seem coy, and besides, she didn't want to spend any unnecessary time in the cavernous, shadowy hall with him.

He was leaning against the window opposite her doorway, and the formal gardens stretched out beyond, surprisingly well lit for that hour of the night. He'd been smoking a cigarette, waiting for her, but he pushed away from the window and came toward her.

She thought she'd gotten used to how graceful some French men could be. For a moment she was distracted by his body, then mentally slapped herself. "Were you waiting for me?" she said brightly, closing the door behind her when she actually wanted nothing more than to dive back into her room and lock it.

"Of course. I'm just down the hall from you, on the left. We're the only ones in this wing of the house, and I know how turned around one can get. I wanted to make sure you didn't stumble into any place you shouldn't be."

Again, that faint hint of something wrong. Maybe she was the one who was paranoid, not Hakim's guests. "I have a fairly good sense of direction." A flat-out lie — even with a detailed map she inevitably took wrong turns, but he wouldn't know that.

"You've lived in France long enough to know that French men like to think of themselves as charming and gallant. It's hardwired into me — you'll find me shadowing you when you least expect it, offering to bring you coffee or a cigarette."

"I don't smoke." The conversation was making her more and more uneasy. Complicated by the fact that looking at him, the dark, opaque eyes, the lean, graceful body, was leaving her far from unmoved. Why did she have to be attracted to someone so . . . wrong? "And how do you know I've lived in France a long time?"

"Your accent. No one speaks that well if they haven't lived here for at least a year."

"Two, actually."

It was just the faintest of smiles. "You see? I have an instinct for such things."

"I don't need anyone to be charming and gallant," she said, still uneasy. Not only did he look good, but the damned man smelled good, too. Something subtle, luscious, beneath the lingering scent of tobacco. "I'm here to do a job."

"So you are," he murmured. "That doesn't mean you can't enjoy yourself while you do it."

He was making her very nervous. By now they were walking down the hallway, in and out of the shadows. She was used to the continental art of flirtation which was usually nothing more than an extravagant show. And she knew this man to be a womanizer — he'd said so himself in a language she wasn't supposed to understand. It was expected that he behave just this way.

Unfortunately she didn't want to play the game, not with him. He wasn't someone to flirt with and then dance away, despite the practiced charm. She couldn't rid herself of the notion that he was something else entirely.

"Monsieur Toussaint . . ."

"Bastien," he said. "And I will call you Chloe. I've never known a woman named Chloe before. I find it quite charming." His voice slid over her like a silken caress.

"Bastien," she capitulated. "I really don't think this is a good idea."

"You are already involved with someone? That doesn't need to make any difference. What happens here stays here, and there's no reason why we can't enjoy ourselves," he said smoothly.

She wasn't sure how she'd react if he were someone else. She knew how to extricate herself from unwanted situations, though they didn't crop up as much as she might have hoped. The unfortunate fact was, she was both attracted and afraid of him. He was lying to her, and she had no idea why.

She halted. They had managed to reach the more populated part of the renovated château, and she could hear the voices, an amalgam of French and English, from beyond the double doors. She opened her mouth, not sure what she was going to say, what kind of argument she could come up with, when he spoke.

"I'm very attracted to you, you know," he said. "I don't remember when I've been quite so charmed." And before she realized what he intended he'd put his hands on her, moving her back against the wall, and proceeded to kiss her.

He was very good, she thought dazedly, trying not to react. His hands were touching her, his mouth the merest whisper against her lips, and without thinking she closed her eyes, feeling his kiss brush against her cheekbones, her eyelids, then down to her mouth again, clinging slightly, then moving on, down the side of her neck.

She didn't know what to do with her hands. She ought to reach up and push him away, but she didn't really want to. The soft, feathering kisses simply made her want more, and since this was definitely going to be the only time she let him kiss her then she ought to experience it entirely.

So when he moved his hands from her waist to cup her face, and when he pressed his mouth against hers, harder this time, she opened for him, telling herself that one little taste of forbidden fruit was all right. After all, it was France. *Vive l'amour.*

But just as she was about to let herself sink into the pleasure of it, nasty little warning bells stopped her. He was, oh, so adept. He knew how to kiss, how to use his lips, his tongue, his hands, and if she were just a little bit more stupid she'd be awash with desire.

But something wasn't right. It was a performance that even she could see through. He was making all the right moves, saying all the right things, but some part of him was standing back, coolly watching her response.

Her hands, which were just about to clutch his shoulders, pushed him away instead. She used more strength than she needed to — he made no effort to force her, he simply fell back, that faint amusement on his face.

"No?" he said. "Perhaps I misread the situation. I'm very attracted to you, and I thought the feeling was mutual."

"Monsieur Toussaint, you are a very attractive man. But you're playing some kind of game with me, and I don't like it."

"Game?"

"I don't know what's going on, but I don't believe you've developed a sudden, uncontrollable passion for me." Sylvia was always chiding her for being so outspoken, but she didn't care. Anything to upset the smooth, beguiling lies of the man who was still standing too close to her.

"Then I'll have to work harder to convince you," he said, reaching for her again.

And fool that she was, she might have let him, but the door to the drawing room opened and Monsieur Hakim appeared, glowering.

Bastien stepped back, in no particular hurry, and Hakim's expression darkened further. "We wondered where you were, Mademoiselle Underwood. It's half-past seven already."

"I had trouble finding my way here. Monsieur Toussaint was kind enough to guide me."

"I'm certain he was," Hakim grumbled. "The baron is waiting for you, Bastien. And behave yourself — we have work to do."

"*Bien sûr,*" he said, flashing an ironic smile in her direction as he moved past Hakim.

Chloe started to follow, but Hakim put a strong hand on her arm, halting her. "You need to be warned about Bastien," he said.

"I don't need to be warned. I know his type very well." Not true, she thought. He was trying to convince her he was a certain kind of man — sophisticated, charming, flirtatious and totally without morals. And he was that kind of man — she had no doubt of that. There was just something more, something darker inside, and she couldn't figure out quite what it was.

Hakim nodded, though he was clearly unconvinced. "You are very young, Mademoiselle Underwood. I feel I am in a fatherly position, and I would not like to see anything unfortunate befall you."

It was his overformal English that made it sound threatening, of course. Not any real danger. But that uneasy little shiver slid down her backbone, and she wondered if she'd made a very real mistake in taking Sylvia's place. Adventure, luxury and money were all very nice things, but not at too high a price. And remembering the feel of Bastien Toussaint's practiced mouth against her, she was afraid she'd already gotten herself into too much trouble.

Because she wanted to see what it would be like if he really kissed her. Not a performance, meant to dazzle her. But something he wanted as much as she did.

And she was out of her mind, she thought, moving past Hakim into the library, in time to see Bastien in close conversation with one of the women she'd seen earlier. The baron's wife, who seemed far too friendly with someone who wasn't her husband, with her beautifully manicured hand on his Armani-clad arm, her perfectly made-up face tilted toward his. Chloe took a glass of sherry from the waiter and moved to a seat by the open doors, looking out over the brightly lit gardens, away from Bastien and his more amenable partner. The jumble of languages was at first indecipherable, and she didn't want to listen. It was like eavesdropping, and she was already uncomfortable with what she'd overheard earlier.

But then she realized they were politely speaking only French and English, and anything she heard was far from secret, and she relaxed back against the wing chair. Her imagination had always been her besetting sin, and she was imagining conspiracy everywhere. What could possibly be dangerous about a group of high-level grocers?

She looked up to see Bastien and the woman slip outside, into the shadows, and her attempt at rationalization vanished abruptly. Seeing him go would have been difficult enough, if he hadn't paused at the last minute to look directly into her eyes, and he gave her a faint, rueful shrug.

"Miss Underwood." The elderly baron sank down beside her, wheezing slightly. "It looks like we've been abandoned. Now why did such a pretty young thing like yourself want to spend days locked away with such tiresome old capitalists like ourselves? Surely you must have had better things to do in Paris? Some young man waiting for you?"

She smiled at him, willfully forgetting the couple who had just disappeared. "No young man, *monsieur*. I live a very quiet life."

"I don't believe it!" he said. "A young girl as pretty as you are? What has happened to young men nowadays, that someone like you should be unattached? If I were forty years younger I'd go after you myself."

She roused herself to play the game. "Surely not forty!" she said lightly.

"I'm thirty years older than my wife, and even that is a bit of a strain. Which is why I give her a lot of room to entertain herself."

Chloe blinked. "That's very generous of you."

"Besides, what can she and Bastien do out on the terrace with so many people wandering around? An indiscreet caress, a kiss or two? In the end it only sharpens the appetite."

"I beg your pardon?"

"I saw you watching them. Bastien is fine for someone like my wife, who knows how the game is played and expects nothing but immediate gratification. He's not for an innocent like you."

He was the second man to warn her away in the last ten minutes. Little did they know that she hadn't needed the warning — her own defenses had popped up just in time. "I am here to translate, *monsieur*," she said brightly. "Not to indulge in dangerous flirtations."

"I hope you don't count me as one of those dangerous flirtations," he said. "Or perhaps I do. No one considers me very dangerous anymore." He sounded mournful.

"I'm certain you're a very dangerous man indeed," she said in an encouraging voice.

His smile was almost beatific. "You know, my child, you may actually be right."

4

There was no question, Bastien thought, as he methodically slid his fingers over Monique's firm breast. The woman hadn't come here for him. If she had, Mademoiselle Chloe would not have been so quick to push him away. Even a mediocre operative would know that sleeping with the enemy was the best way to find out what you needed to know, and most men were at their most vulnerable when they were fucking.

He wasn't most men. He had ice water in his veins, in his cock, and even in the middle of an orgasm he was a dangerous man. Chloe wouldn't know that — she was inept enough to betray her knowledge of languages within moments of arriving, and she would have taken the bait he'd dangled in front of her if he were really her target.

Which means she was after someone else. Normally that wouldn't matter to him — he had a job to do and whoever she was there to watch would have to take care of himself.

But this whole affair had been in the works for too many months, and he wasn't going to let an unexpected player destroy everything he'd worked so hard for.

He slid his hand inside Monique's silk gown. She wasn't wearing a bra, and she was hot for him, as she always was. Her husband was old and compliant, as long as she gave him details about her adventures, and he expected the old man had even watched them once or twice. It had neither excited nor bothered him. He could perform with or without an audience, and in the end his partner was unimportant if they were the means to an end.

Monique had no particular value at that point. He'd found out everything he needed from her at their last meeting, but it wouldn't do to lose interest too quickly. She would be less trouble if he pulled up her skirt and did her against the cool stone wall of the château, in the shadows.

They would be seen, of course. By security cameras, by the armed guards patrolling with such impeccable deference. Hakim would probably have them taped, and provide a copy of it to the old man, as well as anyone else with the right price.

He put his hands between her legs and

she moaned in his mouth. She wasn't wearing underwear either, in his honor, no doubt. She was groping for his zipper, and he knew she expected him to be hard. He willed it, by thinking of the look on her face when she came, and he reached for his fly with his other hand, ready to accommodate her, when he realized it wasn't her face he was envisioning. It was the inept Miss Chloe.

And suddenly he wasn't in the mood. Instead of unzipping his trousers he simply took her hand away, and with his other he made her come, instantly, so hard that she screamed as her body went rigid.

Not a good idea. He put his hand over her mouth and she bit, hard. Monique liked rough fun and games, and he knew she was trying to draw blood.

He put a stop to that, and the whimper that came from the back of her throat was like a female tiger who'd just been mounted. Monique was like a cat — ruthless, amoral, impervious to ordinary pain. A good match for him.

But he wasn't interested. He pulled away, letting her skirt fall down around her perfect legs, and she leaned back against the stone wall, mouth open, panting, her eyes glazed with satisfaction. She had blood on her mouth, the bitch. He should have paid better attention.

"That was . . . interesting," she said, her voice a husky purr. "But we've only just begun."

"We've finished," he said, and the words surprised him. He'd intended to string her along. After all, the last time he'd been with her was over four months ago, and some recreational sex would have only honed his senses.

But he didn't want her, and there was nothing to be gained by having her. There were too many unanswered questions about the nervous woman who'd arrived that afternoon and looked at him as if he were crème brûlée and froze when he touched her.

"What do you mean?" Monique demanded.

He leaned over and kissed her full, red lips, taking his own blood with it. "We've had a good time, you and I, but don't you think it's past time to find a new playmate? Your husband must be tired of hearing about me. Choose a woman next time."

As he expected, she wasn't insulted. She smiled her cat smile. "We could ask Miss Underwood to join us. It could prove very entertaining."

He kept his irritation well hidden. "She's not my type."

"And neither am I, apparently. Not any longer." She shrugged. "Too bad, but as you said, my husband was getting bored. He likes it when men hurt me, and you weren't particularly into that."

"Maybe next time," he said lightly, feeling a faint desire to wring her neck. It was a pretty neck, decked in diamonds.

"Maybe not," she said, and moved past him, reentering the living room without a backward glance.

He lit a cigarette, blowing the smoke skyward, dismissing her and moving back to more important things. Who had hired Chloe Underwood, and who was she checking up on?

And what a ridiculous name. She might as well call herself Mary Poppins. The name went well enough with her cover, but she should have gone with something a little less *jeune fille*.

His own organization might have sent her, but he doubted it. Anyone as obvious as she was would have been weeded out long ago. And who was she after? Mr. Otomi, Ricetti or Madame Lambert? Maybe Hakim himself?

One thing was certain — she hadn't

come from the most dangerous of the cozy little cartel. Christos Christopolous didn't hire any but the best, and he had little use for women in any capacity.

He wondered where the original translator was. Probably in some alley with her throat slit. Just because Miss Underwood wasn't an expert at dissemination didn't mean she couldn't accomplish wet work with the best of them. Those small, slender hands of hers could kill just as efficiently as Hakim's fists.

And why was he still thinking about her, when she'd already made it clear that this wasn't about him. Just a word in Hakim's ear and she would be gone, and he could concentrate on his job.

But then, he was tired of the job. Tired of so many lies he'd forgotten what the truth was, so many names and disguises that he'd forgotten who he really was. So many years that he no longer knew who were the good guys and who were the bad guys. And even worse, he didn't care.

For some reason Chloe Underwood piqued his curiosity. Made things a little more interesting. It would be a shame to get rid of her too quickly. This job wasn't a particular challenge — his cover had been accepted long ago, and Hakim wouldn't prove to be much of a problem. Until Christos showed up he could afford a minor diversion. And if she became an obstacle he could dispose of her just as easily as Hakim could. With more speed and mercy. Hakim liked to see them suffer.

He could watch and wait. He had an instinct for knowing when to act, and right now more could be accomplished by simply biding his time. Until Chloe Underwood decided to make her final, fatal mistake.

She'd made a fatal mistake, Chloe thought as she put her glass of wine back on the table. She should never have had so much to drink on a relatively empty stomach, not when she needed to keep her wits about her. It had been a simple enough matter to keep up with things during the long, leisurely dinner. The conversation had been purely social, and she hadn't been called upon to translate more than a few words. Which was a good thing, since they kept refilling her wineglass whenever she took a sip, until she was borderline tipsy by the time the cheese course arrived.

She probably would have been fine, even then, if she hadn't been operating on a base of two glasses of Scotch drunk in quick succession after Monique von Rutter waltzed back into the living room, her lipstick smudged, her hair tousled, her eyes slumberous.

Bastien Toussaint had kissed her in the hallway, walked into a crowded room, singled out another woman and taken her outside to have sex. There was no question about it — one look at Monique's flushed face made it crystal clear.

She should have at least waited long enough to let the color subside, Chloe had thought critically, tossing back the glass of whiskey someone had handed her. Bastien was showing more restraint, but then, Monique could have managed it with just lifting her skirts, whereas Bastien would have had to unfasten his trousers. . . .

She drained the glass and reached for another. What the hell business of hers was it? Clearly the man was going after anyone who'd hold still long enough for him to nail them. At least she'd managed to drive him off quickly enough.

She slumped down in her chair, eyeing her brie with dislike. When Bastien had sauntered back in a few minutes later, he looked as cool and composed as he had when she'd first seen him. Really, she was absurd to even think about him. There was nothing less appealing than a man who refused to let his reactions show. If someone could still look that composed after a quickie in the garden then he wasn't for her. She preferred men who weren't afraid to show emotion.

And she was making wild assumptions all over the place, she reminded herself, none of which were justified. It didn't matter whether he was her type or not, he was definitely out of her league.

He hadn't glanced at her during the interminable dinner, making it even more clear that his interest had been a moment's distraction. She sat quietly enough in her chair, translating when she needed to, saying nothing otherwise. Monique von Rutter, on the other hand, was the life of the party — witty, charming, flirting with everyone there, both male and female.

Chloe was ready to slide under the table in defeat when Hakim finally rose, signaling an end to the endless meal. "We have a great deal to accomplish tomorrow, *mesdames et messieurs*. I suggest coffee and liqueurs in the west salon, and then we retire. Those who wish to go directly to bed may, of course, be excused." He turned his small black eyes in her direction. "You won't be needed anymore tonight, Mademoiselle Underwood."

The dismissal was clear and welcome — a liqueur would have put her under the table for sure. She rose steadily enough, secure that her slightly impaired state wouldn't be noticed in the general exodus.

He was watching her. She couldn't imagine why, and she couldn't actually catch him at it, but she knew that he had been watching her all evening, while he charmed every other female present.

Maybe it would make sense in the morning when the wine had worn off and she'd had some sleep, but right then it felt confusing, disturbing, threatening. And oddly, wickedly exciting.

She'd forgotten how tortuous the halls of the château were. Bastien had led her downstairs — she wasn't about to ask for his help in finding her way back. Trial and error would work well enough.

It took her longer than expected. She should have asked for directions, but by the time she was halfway up the formal staircase there was no one in sight. She halted, slipping off Sylvia's high heels with a grateful sigh, then continued onward, reasonably certain that she'd find her room sooner or later.

She hadn't realized quite how large the château was. Even if she'd been entirely clearheaded she would have had a hard time finding her own hallway. At that hour, in the dim light, she could have wandered forever, down one tasteful hall and up another, each one familiar yet strange. It wasn't until she turned a corner that a familiar-looking door appeared, and she practically sprinted toward it, certain it led to the hallway with her rooms.

She was wrong. The smell was powerful — rot and mildew, the decay of an ancient building. The renovations had only come this far, she realized, peering into the darkness. As far as she could tell the electricity hadn't been added, but the reflected light through the dusty window illuminated a glimpse of what the rest of the château must have looked like, before someone with far too much money decided to save it. The plastered walls were crumbling, the floor was stained and buckled, and cans of paint stood as mute testimony to further renovation plans. There was another smell beneath the damp and mold, one she couldn't quite identify, something old and dark and inexplicably . . . evil. And all that wine had definitely gone to her head — in another moment she'd start imagining she was in some kind of danger. Too much wine, too much imagination. She backed out of the room, slowly, only to come up against a solid, human form.

She screamed, biting back the sound as a heavy hand clamped on her arm, spinning her around.

It was M. Hakim. Her relief was palpable — she actually started babbling. Not that Hakim was warm and fuzzy, but anyone was preferable to the unsettling Bastien Toussaint.

"Thank heavens!" she said. "I've gotten all turned around and I was afraid I'd never find my room."

"This section of the château is off-limits to visitors, Miss Underwood. As you can see, it has yet to be renovated, and it would be very dangerous to wander around in there. If you were to get in trouble no one would hear you scream."

Chloe was suddenly entirely sober. She swallowed, looking into Hakim's dark, calm face. And then she forced herself to laugh, breaking the tension.

"I think I need a map to find my way around this place," she said. "If you can give me directions to my room I'll head there. I'm exhausted."

He hadn't let go of her arm. He had

thick, ugly hands, with dark hair across the backs of his sausage-like fingers. He said nothing, and for one brief, crazy moment she thought he was going to shove her back into the deserted wing where no one would hear her scream.

And then sanity returned, and he dropped her arm, and while his smile was far from pleasant at least it was a smile.

"You should be more careful, Miss Underwood," he admonished her. "Other people might be more dangerous than I am."

"Dangerous?" She just barely managed to keep the stammer out of her voice.

"Like Monsieur Toussaint, for instance. He can be very charming, but you would be wise to keep your distance. I saw the two of you in the hall this evening, and I was most concerned. For you, Miss Underwood."

It was shadowy enough that he wouldn't be able to see the flush that mounted to her cheeks. "He was just showing me the way to the library."

"With his mouth? I'd keep out of his reach if I were you. The man is notorious. His appetite for women is insatiable, and his tastes are, shall we say, peculiar. I would feel somewhat responsible if you were to run into any trouble while you're here. After all, I'm in effect your employer, and I wouldn't want anything unfortunate to happen to you."

"Neither would I," Chloe said.

"Turn left, down two corridors then two right turns."

"I beg your pardon?"

"That's the way back to your room. Unless you prefer I escort you?"

Chloe managed to suppress her shudder of revulsion. "I'll be fine," she said. "If I get lost again I'll scream."

"You do that," Hakim said in a cool voice that somehow failed to reassure her.

But she made it back to her corridor without further mishap, and there was no one lingering, watching for her. The satyr-like M. Toussaint must have found his partner for the night, she thought, faintly disgruntled, as she pushed open her door.

Someone had been in there. There was no key, no way to keep anyone out, and the sense of violation was unavoidable. She shook her head, trying to clear the paranoia away. Why should anyone be interested in a hired translator?

The bed was turned down, one of Sylvia's diaphanous nightgowns was laid out across it, and a tray with a crystal decanter

73

and a plate of chocolates rested on the gilt table beside the bed.

"Relax, *idiote*," she said out loud, to break the hush that enveloped the room. "It was just a maid."

She got ready for bed quickly, pulling the confection of lace and silk over her head. If she had any sense at all she'd go straight to bed, but her encounter with Hakim had driven sleep right out of her mind. A snifter of brandy wouldn't hurt.

She might not have made it as a chef, but her sense of taste was excellent, and the cognac was slightly unusual. Some faint undernote that she couldn't quite recognize. Almost metallic, she would have said, but a place like Château Mirabel would never serve an inferior cognac. It must have been her imagination. It was quite deliciously warming, and she could already feel her eyes drooping. She'd sleep soundly tonight, and she wouldn't dream of anyone, certainly not Bastien Toussaint.

It was then that she recognized the barest trace of scent in the air. A subtle, distinctive cologne that brought an instinctive, warm response. Until she remembered where it had come from. The silken folds of Bastien's Armani suit. Why . . .

She tried to set the snifter of brandy

back on the tray, but it was much farther away than she had thought, way of out her reach, and it fell on the floor with the faint tinkle of shattering glass, and she followed it, sprawling out on the carpet.

She hadn't had that much to drink, she thought, trying to sit up. Surely that one sip of cognac wasn't enough to send her over the edge.

But apparently it was, and the bed was much too high to climb into. The Aubusson rug underneath her was very beautiful, and if she was careful she could avoid the broken glass, curl up into a nice little ball, and fall into a deep, blissful sleep.

Bastien stepped into her room, closing the door quietly behind him. He didn't have to be particularly discreet — he knew where the cameras were located, and he could manage his way around them without giving anything away. Besides, he was known as a dedicated womanizer, and it wouldn't be surprising if he'd managed to do every beautiful female in the area.

Except that the girl wasn't particularly beautiful. He stood over her, staring down at her curled-up body for a moment. She was pretty. Not a word he tended to use.

She had good bone structure, even features, a sweet, full mouth.

Sweet? Pretty? Maybe she was better than he thought. She certainly managed to exude an essentially harmless persona.

He slid his arms under her and laid her out on the bed. She'd washed her makeup off — maybe that was why she was looking so innocent. The nightgown she was wearing was very expensive, with tiny little satin ties down the front. He undid them, one by one, until the gown fell open around her.

A good body as well. A little more butt than many young Frenchwomen, a little more breast as well, but basically young and strong and nicely formed. No sign of the rigorous training she should have gone through. Just enough softness through the arms and belly to tell him she would be warm and welcoming in bed.

Who was he kidding? She'd cut his throat in bed, if he happened to get distracted. And fucking was marginally distracting.

There were marks on her body, beneath her breasts. Red lines, and he ran a finger along them, wondering what kind of torture she'd endured in the distant past.

And then he smiled. Not so distant past

— she'd simply been wearing a bra that was too tight.

No woman he'd ever known would wear a constricting bra unless she had no choice. He glanced down her long legs to her feet. The lines were even more pronounced — she'd been wearing the wrong shoes as well.

The drug he put in her cognac was good stuff — she'd sleep for six to eight hours and wake without a hangover, even though she deserved one after all the wine she'd drunk at dinner. His little gift to her.

He searched the room methodically, from top to bottom. She had three more pairs of shoes, all the same size, all slender high heels. She was going to be hobbling in a couple days. If she was still here.

There were no black ops clothing. Not in the room, at least, and she couldn't have hidden them anywhere on the grounds without someone finding them. No weapons, no papers of any interest. Her passport was an excellent fake — the picture inside looked like a plainer, younger version of the woman who'd walked in today. She supposedly came from North Carolina. She was almost twenty-four years old, five seven, one hundred and twenty-one pounds, and she'd entered

France two years ago on a student visa. She had a work permit, a surprise in itself. He never trusted anyone with too clean an identity.

Nothing else in terms of papers, either forged or otherwise. Not much money. No prescription drugs, nothing personal.

There were a bunch of pictures in her wallet — fakes with the young woman posing with various genial family types. Easy enough to doctor.

He put the purse back, moving around to the side of the bed. The glass had broken in large pieces, the drugged brandy seeping into the carpet. Not a bad mess for him to clean up — he'd done far worse. This time there was no blood to get rid of, no body to dispose of. Yet.

He poured the drugged brandy down the bathroom sink, then refilled it from the flask he'd brought with him. He'd brought an extra glass, just in case, and he poured a splash in it before replacing it beside the bed.

He stared down at her again. She was a real professional after all — if he couldn't find anything in his search then she'd figured something out that even he hadn't thought of.

Unless, of course, she was telling the

truth. That she actually was a twenty-four-year-old woman from North Carolina with no knowledge of who and what they were.

But then, why would she be wearing the wrong shoes, the wrong bra. Why would she lie about her knowledge of languages?

No, given the circumstances, there was no way she could be an innocent bystander. She was there to do damage, and he needed to find out what, and to whom.

He began retying the ribbons that held the silken gown together, then stopped, leaving it open below the waist. She would wonder why, but she wouldn't remember. He could really do anything he liked to her, and she wouldn't remember.

There were any number of things he would have enjoyed doing to her, but most of them would be much better if she were awake and participating. She might be inexperienced enough not to take advantage of the blatant pass he'd made at her earlier today, but he wasn't so sanguine. She'd already betrayed too much already. Get her naked beneath him, move inside her, and he'd know her better than she knew herself.

But not if she was comatose.

He sat down on the bed beside her, watching her as she slept. It would simplify matters if he killed her now. He could do it fast, neatly, and simply tell Hakim he didn't trust her. Hakim would accept that.

He put his hand on her neck. Her skin was warm, soft beneath his skin, paler against his tanned hand. He could feel the pulse beat steadily, watch the rise and fall of her chest. He tightened his fingers for just a moment, then took them away.

Afterward he wasn't sure why he did it. Uncharacteristic of him, but then, he'd been playing by different rules recently. Or ignoring the rules he'd been taught.

He stretched his body out alongside hers, his head on the pillow next to her. She smelled like soap and Chanel and cognac, an enticing combination.

"Who are you, *bébé?*" he whispered. "And why are you here?"

She wouldn't be answering for another six hours at least. He laughed, at himself, and sat up. There was time. With no weapons, her clear mission was to gather information, and he could ensure that anything she discovered didn't make it past the walls of the château.

There was time.

5

Chloe had never been one to wake up slowly. She tended to be alert immediately, and she was nauseatingly cheerful, while her sleep-fuddled siblings and parents threatened her with death or dismemberment if she didn't stop the damned humming.

That morning was no different, except when her eyes popped open she had no idea where she was.

She decided not to panic, since panic tended to be a waste of time. She lay still, unmoving, and let memory sink back in. The château, and her sucker agreement to take Sylvia's place. Too much wine last night, and Bastien Toussaint's practiced mouth.

She hadn't been kissed in months, so it was no wonder she could still feel the pressure of his lips against hers. Too bad she couldn't have just let herself go with it. So what if it had been a performance on his part? He probably performed very well indeed.

But she'd always been too picky and too stubborn, and as her friends would tell her too American to really enjoy the pleasures of casual sex. And while a roll in the hay with someone like Bastien would be memorable, she didn't really like having nothing but memories to hold on to.

She sat up slowly, putting her hand to her head in anticipation of the searing pain she absolutely deserved for drinking all that red wine, but it didn't come. She gave her head a tentative shake, preparing for the delayed blast of pain, but felt nothing.

She glanced at the bedside table. She'd had a final cognac before she'd fallen asleep — she thought she could remember that much. She hadn't been more than tipsy; it was odd that she couldn't remember more. She'd had some cognac, and she thought she remembered dropping it. Falling.

But she was lying in the big, comfortable bed, the brandy snifter was sitting on the tray with just a trace left in the bottom, and she must have drunk even more than she realized.

She pushed back the cover and swung her legs over the side of the bed. And then stopped. Her . . . or that is . . . Sylvia's nightgown was made up of silk and a row of tiny ribbons, but half those ribbons were unfastened, from the hemline to the waist. What had she been doing?

Nothing much fun, she decided after she'd showered and dressed and arranged herself in a decent repetition of Sylvia's borrowed chic. She eyed the fawn leather shoes with their pointed toes and high, thin heels, and moaned. Maybe she could tell them she had Japanese blood and needed to go without shoes.

No, that probably wouldn't fly. Much as she would have liked to have an interesting bloodline, she was depressingly, blandly WASP, and no one was going to be fooled into thinking otherwise.

She made it downstairs without getting lost, just in time for a light breakfast of coffee and fruit before the work began. The participants were seated on either side of a long conference table, and a number of them were accompanied by assistants. Except for von Rutter, who was accompanied by his sleek and beautiful wife Monique.

Hakim was at the head of the table, and he gestured to one of the empty places to his right. Toussaint wasn't in the room, she realized as she sat, setting her cup of coffee down on the burled walnut carefully. Maybe fate was going to be kind after all.

She should have known better. He appeared a moment later, with his own coffee, and took the remaining seat. Beside her.

She listened to the proceedings with only half an ear. A moment of silence for their late colleague, Auguste Remarque. She'd heard that name before, but she couldn't remember where. It would drive her crazy until she found out — maybe she could simply ask someone. Or maybe she should just keep quiet and try to blend into the background.

There wasn't much to keep her mind occupied over the next few hours. The organization of food importers were arguing about redistributing territory, and while Chloe had a great fondness for lamb and oranges and a well-cooked chicken, there was a limit to her fascination. The discussions she was asked to translate were dull to the point of madness, she'd always found numbers tedious, and units of chickens and piglets and barrels of corn couldn't even excite the failed chef inside her. The others at the table seemed to find the discussion endlessly fascinating, and given some of the numbers she was translating she could imagine why. In euros, dollars or pounds they were talking a very great deal of money. She hadn't realized grocery importers amassed that kind of wealth.

Because she was seated at the top corner of the table she had to turn to look at the speakers, and the man next to her was always just in her line of vision. Despite her hyperawareness, he seemed to have lost all interest in her, barely registering her existence. Since he spoke both French and English she wasn't required to translate for him, and she could lean back in her chair and pretend to ignore him as well while she doodled on one of the pads of paper they'd set in front of them.

There was only one moment of trouble during the long, tedious morning. There was a word she didn't know — no great surprise, though she was very fluent.

"What is *'legolas'*?" she asked, "apart from a character in *The Lord of the Rings*?"

Dead silence in the room, only the sound of a cup rattling in a saucer. They were all staring at her as if she'd asked them about their sex life or, even worse, their yearly income, and then, for the first time that day, Bastien addressed her.

" 'Legolas' is a breed of sheep," he said. "Of no particular concern to you."

Someone in the room snickered, whether at his cool dismissal or something else.

"Don't ask questions, Miss Underwood, simply translate," Hakim said. "If you're incapable we can find someone else. We don't want our progress impeded by incompetence."

Chloe had never responded well to public reprimands, and she'd already decided she didn't like Hakim very much. At that point she would have liked nothing better than to be driven back to Paris in that luxurious limousine and never see any of these people again.

Wouldn't she? She kept her glance away from the man beside her, but she knew perfectly well she wasn't going to leave before she had to.

"I beg your pardon, *monsieur*," she said in French. "If I don't need to know the meaning of a word I certainly won't ask. I just thought it might help if I had a better understanding of the subject."

"Better watch it, Gilles," Monique said with a throaty laugh. "Bastien wouldn't like it if you bullied his little pet."

Bastien lifted his eyes from the table. "Jealous, my sweet?"

"Stop it!" Hakim snapped. "We don't have time for these petty little squabbles."

Bastien turned to Hakim, and in doing so, had no choice but to look at Chloe. His smile was beatific, and he lifted his hands in a gesture of surrender. "Forgive me, Gilles. You know I've always been easily distracted when a beautiful woman is around."

"I know you're only distracted when you want to be, and so do the others. There's too much at stake to waste time with this kind of thing. This is too important."

Ducks and pigs and chickens were too important? Fortunately Chloe simply blinked. It was only natural that an importer would think that whatever he imported would affect the fate of the world. The people at the table seemed totally devoid of any sense of humor, but then, financial matters had a tendency to make people deadly serious. She would have to control her own random frivolity.

Hakim rose. "We'll break for lunch. There's nothing more we can do at this point."

"Good," Bastien said. "I overslept, and I'm hungry."

"You're not going to be eating." The other people were filing out of the room, and Chloe was doing her best to go with them, but she was essentially trapped between the two men. "I need you to do me a favor," Hakim said.

Too close. "Excuse me," Chloe interrupted, trying to sidle past him.

"You're part of the favor, Miss Underwood," Hakim said, putting a hand on her arm to stop her.

Men in France liked to touch women. For that matter, men in North Carolina did as well, and friendly touches were a matter of course.

But she didn't like the feel of Hakim's hand on her arm. Not one bit.

"Of course," Bastien said immediately, glancing at her stubborn face with palpable amusement. "What would you like us to do?"

"I have an errand for Miss Underwood, and I'd appreciate it if you'd drive her. I need some books."

"Books?" Chloe echoed.

"For my guests. They won't be working all the time, and they must have something to occupy them in their off-time. You would know what's needed, I'm sure, given your experience in the publishing business. Just get a handful in the most common languages. French, English, Italian and

German. Something light and escapist — use your judgment."

"But what about the limousine?" she stammered. "It seems a shame that Monsieur Toussaint has to waste his time on an errand like this instead of continuing with the work."

"Monsieur Toussaint is more than happy to have a chance to escape for a bit, aren't you, Bastien? Particularly in the company of such a lovely young lady. And the limousine is being serviced — it's unavailable."

Now why on earth would he lie to her? He wouldn't — there was no reason for him to trump up an excuse to get rid of her. He could simply fire her ass and have done with it.

"And the work this afternoon?" Bastien sounded completely unconcerned. "We wouldn't want to miss anything."

"Don't worry, Bastien. I'll be looking out for your best interests, you know that. We all rise and fall together. And we're far from coming to any kind of conclusion as to who will take over as head, not with Mr. Christopolous still absent. This afternoon will be simply jockeying for position. You can safely take the afternoon off and enjoy yourself. Take Mademoiselle Underwood for a nice long lunch in St. André. There's no hurry."

Chloe racked her brain for a good excuse, even a lousy one, to get out of it, but for the moment she could think of nothing. "If you're certain, Monsieur Hakim."

Gilles Hakim's smile was benevolent, and it was only her imagination that the shadows in the brightly lit room made it look faintly sinister. "I am certain, *mademoiselle*. Tomorrow morning will be time to get back to work. In the meantime, enjoy yourself."

"I'll see that she does," Bastien said. Taking the arm that Hakim had clamped down on, his pressure was only slight, but she moved with him anyway.

Not that the touch of his hand on her skin was less unsettling, she thought, letting him steer her out of the room. The feel of his skin next to hers was a different kind of threat, one that was dangerously enticing.

It was easy enough to pull free once they left the room. "If you'd lend me your car I'm sure I can find the bookstore myself," she said evenly.

"But then I wouldn't have the chance to spend some time with you," he said. "And no one drives my car but me. I'm particular that way. Why don't you go up and change into some more comfortable shoes? I'm certain you have some."

She would have given ten years off her life to have more comfortable shoes, but Sylvia hadn't thought it was necessary, any more than she'd considered the difference in their sizes to be important. It was all Chloe could do not to hobble, but she summoned her best smile.

"These are perfectly comfortable," she said. "I'm ready if you are. The sooner we go, the sooner we can get back."

"True enough," he murmured. "Though I find I don't believe you've been quite as honest about the shoes." There was a faint emphasis, as if he thought she hadn't been honest about other things. Or maybe her crazy imagination was going at it again.

He drove a Porsche. Of course he did, Chloe thought, sliding into the front seat. He'd waited long enough for her to get her purse, and she'd tried on every pair of shoes Sylvia had sent, but the other ones were even worse. In the end she grabbed a coat and went out, finding her way down-stairs without mishap this time, only to find him waiting by his tiny little car.

It was a cloudy day, so at least the top was up. Despite the lack of brilliant sun-light he was wearing dark glasses, and he was leaning against the side of the car, arms folded across his chest, calmly waiting for her. Another custom silk suit, probably Armani, with a pale silk shirt and no tie. His black hair curled behind his neck, and his face was unreadable. He opened the door for her, and the interior looked very small and cozy. Too cozy.

And she could think of absolutely no excuse not to go with him. She pulled Sylvia's Hermès bag to her shoulder, stiffened her back, and climbed into the low-slung car, avoiding his helping hand. She heard him laugh before he closed the door behind her.

The interior of a Porsche was as tiny as she'd feared. And he seemed bigger. In the château he'd seemed average size — elegant, clean lines, not too tall, not too bulky. In the car his presence was overwhelming, and his legs were a lot longer than she'd realized. He had the seat all the way back, and he peered up at the sky before putting the car into gear.

"Are you sure you don't want to bring an umbrella?" he asked. "The weather looks uncertain."

Sylvia hadn't packed an umbrella. "We'll just have to hope the rain holds off until we get back. We shouldn't have to be gone too long. I just need to choose a few novels for Monsieur Hakim's guests and then we can come back."

"What about lunch?" He started down the long, curving drive away from the château.

"I'm not hungry," she lied. "I can get something when we get back if I change my mind."

"Whatever pleases you, Chloe," he said, his voice as silken as his charcoal-gray suit, as silken as the tanned skin at his narrow wrists. His hands on the steering wheel were lean, beautiful, and he wore a wedding ring. Of course he did. Those hands looked very strong as well. "Better use your seat belt. I drive fast."

She opened her mouth to protest, then shut it again. By now she should have gotten used to the crazed speeds used in Europe, and the faster he drove, the faster this would be over with. She pulled the seat belt across her and fastened it, leaning back in the leather seat.

"I presume you don't wish to talk to me?" he asked. They were speaking in English, she realized, and had been for the last few minutes. She hadn't even noticed.

She certainly wasn't in the mood for light conversation in either French or English, since his light conversation included flirtation, and his wedding ring was plainly visible. "I'm very tired," she said, closing her eyes.

"Then I'll put on some music." The sound of Charles Aznavour filled the car, and Chloe stifled a little moan. Aznavour had always been her great weakness, and listening to the sadness of Venice made her bones melt.

She could always lose herself in the sound of his voice, forget who she was with. Except that Bastien wasn't easily ignored. Without speaking he still filled her senses — the subtlety of his very expensive cologne teased at her, the gentle sounds of his breathing serenaded her.

The cologne was insidiously appealing. She ought to ask him what the name was, so she could buy some for her brothers. On second thought that might not be so good an idea. She would never smell that particular scent without thinking of Bastien Toussaint, and the sooner his presence — his very married, womanizing, undeniably seductive presence — was out of her life, the better.

It was her own damned fault, Chloe thought, as Aznavour's voice surrounded her like a swathe of rough silk. She'd been longing for adventure, a little vicarious sex and violence to shake things up. She'd had the vicarious sex, and that was already more than she'd bargained for. And it had been nothing more than a kiss. She could only hope that fate hadn't decided to toss a little violence her way as well.

I was only kidding, God. She cast her thoughts skyward, still trying to feign a nice, deep sleep. *A nice, comfortable, boring life in Paris is all the adventure I want.*

Be careful what you wish for. She opened her eyes just a crack, to take a surreptitious look at Bastien. His attention was focused on the narrow road ahead of them, his hands draped loosely, confidently on the small steering wheel as he sped through the countryside. For some silly reason she thought spying on him when he didn't realize she was looking might tell her something about him. He looked the same, the high, strong nose, beautiful mouth, the calm, slightly amused demeanor. As if he found the world to be nothing more than a joke of the blackest humor.

"Change your mind about lunch?" he asked, not turning. So much for spying — he'd known she was watching him and as usual he'd given nothing away.

She closed her own eyes again, closing

him out. "No," she said. And beneath the sound of Charles Aznavour her stomach growled.

He knew the minute she actually fell asleep. Her hands had been in her lap, clutching the leather handle of her bag, and they'd relaxed. Her breathing had slowed, too, and her pretty mouth was no longer a narrow, nervous line. He should have told her to take off her shoes, at least until they got there. But then, she would refuse to admit they hurt her.

What other lies would she tell? It would be interesting to see, and if all went well he'd have time enough to find out. First he had to get to a pay phone and call Harry Thomason, see if the Committee knew anything about exactly who Chloe was. As well as see what they were going to do about the shipment of Legolas sheep to Turkey. Because they weren't sheep, they were very powerful weapons with infrared sites and smart bullets capable of doing a very great deal of damage by even the most inept of marksmen. He had little doubt what the Committee wanted him to do. Let them deliver the weapons, let innocent people die while the Committee went in search of bigger fish to fry. Collateral damage was their mantra, and Bastien had long ago stopped caring.

He glanced at his sleeping companion. She wasn't going to last long, not with her ineptitude. But in her case it wouldn't be collateral damage, it would be the fortunes of war.

He just hoped, for some odd reason, that he wouldn't have to be the one who killed her.

6

Chloe woke with a start, just as the car pulled up outside a small sidewalk café. She had no idea how long she'd slept, and she still couldn't believe she'd been able to do so when trapped inside such a tiny space with Bastien Toussaint. Maybe it had been self-preservation.

"Here you go," he said, making no effort to turn off the car. "This is the remarkably boring little town of St. André. There's a small bookstore around the corner, and if you change your mind you can get yourself some lunch at the café. I'll be back in a couple hours."

"You'll be back? Where are you going?"

"I have some business to attend to. If you were counting on my company I'm sorry to disappoint you, but there are certain things that demand my attention. . . ."

"I'm not disappointed," she said, feeling oddly grumpy. She glanced through the windscreen. The sky was dark, overcast, and the town looked small and depressed.

"Are you sure the bookstore will have what I need? The town is very small."

"It doesn't matter. Hakim doesn't care about the books — he just wanted to get rid of you for a few hours. Me as well. I doubt he'll even look at what you bring back."

She stared at him. "I don't understand."

"What's to understand? This way he kills two birds with one stone." His hands were draped loosely over the steering wheel. Beautiful hands. Even with the plain gold band.

She opened the door and slid out of the low-slung car. The temperature had dropped, and the wind was picking up, sending leaves scudding across the narrow roadway. "Two hours?" she asked, looking at her watch.

"Probably." And he pulled away the moment she'd closed the door, disappearing down the narrow road as fast as he could.

It was after one — given the speed he was driving they could be halfway to Marseilles by now. She should have brought an umbrella — the weather was looking more threatening by the moment.

It was just as well that he'd left. He made her unaccountably nervous, and she wasn't used to that. Men were basically predictable creatures — what you saw was what you got. But Bastien was a different matter altogether. She wasn't sure of one thing about him — his nationality, his business, even his on-again, off-again interest in her. The only thing she was sure of was that he drove too fast. And smelled too good.

She headed for the bookstore first. Among other things, she certainly couldn't count on Hakim's errand being spurious, and she was a conscientious employee, no matter what the circumstances. The place was hard to find — she had to ask directions from a sour-faced old woman who probably wouldn't have answered her in English even if she understood it. Fortunately Chloe knew her accent was very good, the result of starting French in kindergarten at the private girls' school her parents had sent her to. She sounded more like a Belgian than a Frenchwoman, but that was much more acceptable than a lowly American.

The bookstore was just the disaster she'd expected. It was filled with the discards from some professor's old library, and some of the titles were so esoteric even she couldn't translate them. All in French, of course, and not a dust jacket in sight. They'd probably all been published before the war.

She found a couple of novels and bought them anyway. If they wouldn't do for Hakim's French-speaking guests then she'd read them herself. And then she headed back toward the café. Maybe there'd be a newsstand around — glossy magazines would probably serve just as well for bored grocers in their off-hours.

But there was no newsstand, not even a newspaper to be had at the dingy little café. But at least there was food, and by that point Chloe was ravenous.

She had a baguette and brie for lunch, washed down with strong coffee instead of the wine she usually would have ordered. At that point she didn't plan to go any-where near alcohol for the duration of this peculiar little job Sylvia had conned her into. And the sooner she was done, and back in her tiny apartment with a fistful of euros, the happier she'd be.

She lingered as long as she could over her meal, checking her watch every now and then. It was almost two hours — surely Bastien would appear at any mo-ment. Hopefully before the rain.

She paid her bill and went outside, peering down the street for some sign of the Porsche. The streets were empty, the wind was whipping her skirts against her legs, and when she turned back to the café the door was firmly closed, with *Fermé* displayed on a sign in the window.

At that moment the first fat raindrop hit her, followed by another. She considered going back to the café, banging on the door, but they'd probably ignore her. They hadn't seemed too happy to have a customer in the first place, and they were probably long out of hearing range by now. Or they'd pretend to be.

She headed back toward the bookstore as quickly as she could, but that, too, was closed and locked. She ducked under the portico, shivering slightly, pulling her coat around her as the drops of rain began to turn into a light mist. The town was so small there were no other public buildings that she could see. The post office would close midday as well, and if there were other shops they were nowhere in sight.

What was in sight was the old church. Chloe stifled a pang of guilt — getting in out of the icy rain was a poor reason for finally setting foot in a church, but she had little choice. The church was on the corner of the main square — she could keep an eye out for Bastien more easily, and it would be warmer than standing outside.

She was halfway to the church when the

rain let loose its full fury, soaking her to the skin. The too-tight high heels were making it slow going, and she paused long enough to pull them off before sprinting the rest of the way to the carved wooden doors of the old church.

They were locked as well. What the hell kind of town was this, where they locked the church? What if she were some poor sinner in need of absolution or a moment of meditation?

Well, she was a poor sinner by the church's standards, though she hadn't had the chance to sin nearly enough over the past few months. But clearly this small town didn't have much call for daytime sanctity. She plastered herself against the door, trying to keep as much of her body out of the rain as she could, and watched the water beat down on the street, running in rivulets through the cobblestones that should have been charming but had nearly broken her ankle. The temperature was dropping, and she wrapped her arms around her body, shivering. And then she realized that somewhere along the way she'd lost the books she'd purchased.

"Son of a bitch," she muttered, then stopped herself when she remembered where she was. It only needed this to make the day complete. Bastien had been gone for hours, and with her luck he wouldn't return. She'd be stuck in this unfriendly, nameless town, die of pneumonia, and Sylvia would have to find a new roommate.

Headlights speared through the rain, illuminating her as she huddled in the doorway. The Porsche pulled up in front of her, and she stood unmoving as he rolled down the window. "Sorry I'm late," he said, sounding not the least bit sorry. "I told you you should have brought an umbrella."

"Fuck you," she muttered, finally reaching her limit as she snatched up her discarded shoes and stepped out into the driving rain once more. She climbed into the passenger seat, and proceeded to shake her soaking hair in her best impression of a wet dog.

He didn't complain, which would have been half the fun. "Sorry," he said again. "Where are the books?"

"Lost them."

"You're a mess," he said, eyeing her critically. "That outfit is ruined."

The thin silk shirt was plastered to her chest, to the bra that was slightly too small for her, and she plucked it away from her skin. Sylvia had always loved that shirt —

it would serve her right for getting Chloe into this mess in the first place.

"You're cold," he said.

Chloe thought of several responses, most of them along the lines of "duh," but she resisted the temptation. "Yes, I'm cold," she said, shivering as she reached for the seat belt. Her hands were shaking too much to fasten it, and eventually she gave up, sitting back in the leather seat and hoping she'd ruin that as well.

Bastien hadn't put the car into gear — he was looking at her. Or at least she assumed he was. The interior of the car was very dark in the driving rain, and he hadn't switched on a light. "Do you want to go to a hotel and get out of those wet clothes?" He might have been asking if she wanted an ice-cream cone, so casual was his voice.

"I think not," she said in a caustic voice. "Just turn on the heat and I'll be fine."

He put the car in gear and started along the road at the same suicidal speed he'd driven before, but this time in the dark and the pouring rain, and she wasn't wearing her seat belt. The Porsche might be a glorious car but its heating system left something to be desired, and a half hour later she was still cold, fumbling with the lap belt because if Bastien was going to over-turn them in his Le Mans haste then she wanted a fighting chance at surviving.

It was pitch-black by now, not just from the rain but from the hour, and Chloe tried to huddle into her seat, hoping he'd forgotten about her presence, faintly annoyed that he had, when he suddenly pulled the car over, the tires skidding on the wet pavement until it came to a stop by a row of hedges.

It was too narrow a road to park on, but they hadn't passed another car the entire time. Which actually added to her sense of insecurity, when she thought about it. She was alone on a dark road with a man she didn't know, and she didn't trust him.

This time he flicked on the dashboard light, and the shadows it cast in the tiny space were harsh and unforgiving. Bastien no longer looked so smooth and charming. He looked dangerous.

"What the hell are you doing?" he demanded.

"Trying to fasten my seat belt." Unfortunately her voice shook slightly with the cold. "You drive too fast."

"*Idiote,*" he muttered under his breath, and reached for something behind the seat. His body brushed against hers as he did so, and she held her breath until he sat back again. He had a white shirt in his hand, and before she could figure out what he had in mind he'd caught her chin in one strong hand and began drying her face with the soft cloth.

"You look like a raccoon," he said in a dispassionate voice. "Your makeup is all over your face."

"Great," she muttered. She reached for the shirt. "I can manage."

He pulled it out of her reach. "Sit still," he said, dabbing around her eyes with surprising care. The shirt smelled like him. Like the elusive scent he wore, like the cigarettes he shouldn't be smoking, like the indefinable smell of his skin. And how would she already know what his skin smelled like?

He dropped the shirt in her lap but didn't release her face. "There," he said. "Much better. Now you simply look mysterious and smudged. They will think we spent the afternoon in bed. Which is probably what we should have been doing, if you weren't so American."

She tried to jerk her face away, but he was holding her with more force than she'd realized. "We didn't."

"Such a shame. Are you disappointed?

We could take a little detour on our way back — Hakim won't be expecting us until he sees us."

"No, thank you," she said, as polite as she'd been bred to be.

He didn't move. Didn't release her chin, and his dark, almost black eyes looked into hers, an almost speculative expression in the blank depths. She could see nothing in his eyes, and yet her breath suddenly caught, and she knew what was going to happen.

"This is a mistake," he said quietly.

And before she could ask what, he kissed her, his long fingers holding her face still as he covered her mouth with his.

They didn't call it French kissing for nothing, Chloe thought in her last coherent moment. He was an absolute master at it, starting with just a featherlight brush against her lips, followed by his tongue, just touching them gently. She knew she should push him away, but she opened her mouth anyway, knowing she was being beyond foolish.

But what harm would a kiss do? Especially from someone as gifted as Bastien. There wasn't much more they could accomplish in the tiny cockpit of the Porsche, and once they were back in the château she could keep out of his way if she made an effort. So there was no reason she couldn't just sink back against the leather seat and let him kiss her, slowly, using his teeth now, a tiny, erotic tug on her lower lip that somehow made her utter a quiet moan.

He lifted his head, his eyes glittering down in the darkness. "You like that, Chloe? You could always kiss me back."

"I — I th-thought we agreed this isn't a w-wise idea," she stammered. She decided to blame it on the cold, when in actuality she was beginning to burn inside.

"No, it isn't," he agreed, pressing his lips against the curve of her jaw. "But wise ideas are so boring."

He kissed her harder this time, no longer just a sweet seduction. He was making demands now, demands she wanted to meet.

His hand was on her thigh, moving up under the ruined silk skirt, and his touch was like flame, licking at her. She put her hands down to stop him, but she couldn't move him. All she could do was press him against her thighs, which was hardly an improvement.

He pulled away again, catching his breath, as she caught hers, and she tried to rein in her fast-departing sanity. "Why are you doing this?" she demanded in a whisper.

"Stupid question. Because I want to. Because I want you. And all you have to do is say 'no.' But you're not going to. Because you want this just as much as I do, no matter what you tell yourself. You want to taste my mouth. You want my hands on you. Don't you?"

She wanted to deny it, to tell him how delusional he was, how conceited, mistaken, arrogant, wrongheaded . . .

"Kiss me back, Chloe," he whispered. And she did.

She liked kissing. Loved kissing, in fact. But with Bastien it was bordering on orgasmic, and he didn't have to move his hand any higher under her skirt to bring her almost to the point of exploding. All he needed was his mouth — moving, touching, tasting — hers — deeper, harder — and she could feel a dark shiver run from her throat to her womb. She reached out her hands to touch him.

The car came out of nowhere, headlights spearing into the windscreen, horn honking, tires sliding on the narrow road. It narrowly avoided hitting the parked Porsche, and then it drove off. But Chloe had jumped back, from him, from temptation, moving as far away from him as possible.

She wished the light wasn't on, that she didn't have to see him. But then, if they were in the dark maybe they wouldn't have stopped. He was looking at her with a calm, speculative expression, seemingly unmoved by the last few minutes. "If you move any farther you'll be hanging out the window," he said.

"Maybe that would be a good idea."

His smile was faint. "Not in this rain. Sit back and relax. I told you I wouldn't touch you if you didn't want me to. All you have to do is say so."

"I don't want you to touch me." It was an out-and-out total lie. Or at least it was a lie of the flesh. Her body wanted him. Longed for him. Her brain still realized how bad he was for her, but it was fighting a hard battle against her melting body.

"If you say so, *petite*," he said easily. "Fasten your seat belt."

If she'd been clumsy from the cold it was nothing compared to how shaken she was now. He watched her fumble, making no effort to help her, as if he wanted to find out just how much he'd managed to disturb her. Finally he reached out and did it for her, his long fingers brushing against her stomach, so that she jumped nervously.

"Not unless you ask, Chloe," he said in a soothing voice, flicking off the overhead light and putting the car into gear again. The heat had finally come on, at a time when Chloe was already feeling overheated despite her wet clothes, but she didn't complain.

At least they hadn't gone any further, though God knew what else she might have given in to, if she'd had half a chance. She could still feel the imprint of his hand on her thigh, the long fingers against the soft skin, so unbearably close to the center of her. She needed to drive that from her mind, wipe the taste of his mouth from hers, bring a wall of ice between them, one that wouldn't melt in the heat of her body.

"You're very good at this, Monsieur Toussaint," she said in an admirably cool voice after they'd driven for a few minutes. "I don't know why you bother. I imagine it's simply a matter of male pride or too much testosterone. It must be unbearable to think that a woman doesn't want you."

She could see his profile from the lights on the dashboard, but he was giving nothing away. "Are you wanting to convince me that you aren't attracted to me? I know women, *chérie,* and I know when they're interested and when they're not. I don't understand your hesitation, but I am always one to accept my dismissal gracefully. There are other women. There are always other women."

This wasn't going the way she had planned. But then, nothing with this strange man had gone the way she wanted it to.

"And I'm sure they'll be a lot easier to seduce." Her voice was scathing.

"Oh, I imagine I could seduce you fairly easily if I set my mind to it."

For some reason she found that insulting. He couldn't be bothered to make a real effort? Why? Was she that unattractive?

She didn't show her reaction. "You can believe anything you want," she said. "But next time you want to seduce someone you ought to pick a better place than the front seat of a Porsche. It's hardly the right venue for sex."

He smiled at her. "Let me assure you, Chloe, that I could have fucked you very well indeed in the front seat of this car. I've done it before."

So why would such an insulting statement be erotic? She must be suffering hypothermia. "Just take me back to the château," she said in a low voice, giving up. He was better at this than she was, and the truth was, she probably did want him as much as he thought she did. Probably more than he wanted her — she wasn't even sure she believed him on that score. He was the type of man to go for an exotic butterfly like Monique von Rutter or a ruthlessly chic Englishwoman like Madame Lambert. Gauche little American girls were hardly his type.

But whether he really wanted her or whether it was just an automatic response, as long as she kept her distance she would be fine. She'd seen it happen last night — it had taken him less than five minutes to disappear with Monique von Rutter. He'd find someone else to distract him once they got there.

He drove too fast, in complete silence the rest of the way. He pulled around to the back of the sprawling building, and she glanced at her expensive little watch, half expecting it to have stopped working.

It was only half past six, and a long night lay ahead of them. And all Chloe wanted to do was take a long, hot bath and crawl into bed.

Somehow she didn't think that was

going to happen. He stopped the car, leaned over and unfastened her seat belt. "I thought you'd prefer a different entrance. This is the door closest to your rooms, and you can take a shower and change before anyone sees you and asks questions."

"What's wrong with questions? I wasn't anywhere I shouldn't have been, I didn't do anything I shouldn't have done." The moment the words were out of her mouth she regretted them. Kissing Bastien had been a very unwise move, and she would have done a lot worse if something hadn't stopped them.

"Really?" he murmured. "In that case I can come up with you and finish what we started."

She almost called his bluff. Fortunately she still had an ounce of sanity left. "No, thank you. I think we've already finished."

"Do you indeed?" When he smiled that slow, annoying smile she wanted to hit him. He leaned toward her, and she was terrified he was going to kiss her again. But instead he simply opened the door for her. "I'll see you at dinner."

She grabbed the ruined shoes, the drenched leather purse and her dignity, and stepped out into the courtyard. The rain had changed to a fine mist, but the air was turning colder, and her clothes felt clammy. She looked back at the Porsche, but she couldn't see Bastien in the dark interior. Just as well.

"Thanks for the ride," she said, and slammed the door with a little too much force.

And before he drove away, she thought she heard him laugh.

7

Bastien didn't like to be wrong about things. He'd been observing human nature, sussing out people for longer than he could remember, and his instincts were usually infallible. And now he was beginning to have second thoughts about Chloe Underwood.

Logic dictated that she was a dangerous operative. It would be absurd to think that there was any other possibility. And she was either very, very good or very, very bad. He just couldn't figure out which.

She came down late to dinner, no surprise, and he kept out of her way. She was acutely aware of him — anyone with half a brain would have noticed, and there was no one in the room who was mentally deficient. She sat quietly, ate little and looked everywhere but in his direction. Under different circumstances he might have found it amusing. But right then nothing was particularly funny.

She didn't look quite as polished as when she'd first arrived. Her dark hair was

curly from the rain, her makeup more min-
imal, her mouth red and slightly swollen.
He hadn't kissed her that hard, had he?
Maybe he had, but she'd kissed him back
with equal enthusiasm, until the fucking
headlights had interrupted them.

He could have found out a great deal
once he got inside her. He still could.

Monique von Rutter had honed in on
Chloe with the instincts of a great white
shark, just looking for a limb to tear off.
Bastien watched in silence as she focused
in on her, chatting with Chloe in the most
charming of voices that would have fooled
no one but a complete innocent. Chloe
was looking at her warily, answering
Monique's provocative questions in mono-
syllables, and she didn't touch her wine.
Too bad — he'd been counting on alcohol
making his task easier.

But then, he wasn't the kind of man who
looked for the easiest way out.

"I find French men utterly tedious, don't
you, Miss Underwood?" Monique was
saying. "They're more interested in their
own performance than in a woman's pleasure. And vain! Take Bastien, for example.
Only a very shallow creature would dress
that well."

Chloe's eyes darted in his direction, then

focused back on her barely touched plate, and she didn't answer. Not much fun for Monique, Bastien thought lazily, twirling his wineglass in one hand. Maybe he should help her out.

"But you're missing the point, Baroness," he drawled. "A man who is fixated on his sexual performance is devoted to pleasing his lover. If he were more interested in his own pleasure it would be one thing, but if his pride insists that he be a great lover then that can only be to a woman's benefit, is that not so?"

There was a faint stain of color on Chloe's cheeks as she stared into her plate, a stain that everyone around the table noted.

But Monique was in full flower. "Unless, of course, the woman realizes she's nothing more than a prop for her lover's vanity. That her pleasure is simply a reflection of his prowess, not real desire on his part."

Bastien shrugged. "What does it matter? As long as she is pleased."

"And you are so good at pleasing women," Monique cooed. And then added with a touch too much haste, "Or so I've been told."

Bastien was no longer amused. Everyone at the table knew he'd been fucking her, including her voyeuristic husband. Including innocent Miss Chloe. They were all scheduled to leave in less than forty-eight hours, and as far as he could tell very little had been accomplished. They had gotten no closer to choosing a new leader, and Christos had yet to arrive. But then, he had probably sent Chloe on ahead to do the groundwork. The rest of them were fools not to realize how tenuous the situation was. And how unlikely their substitute translator was.

The cartel, whose success depended on strict secrecy, had the dangerous presence of an unknown in their midst, and Monique's jealous little games weren't helping matters. She needed someone else to focus on, to leave him and Chloe alone, but there was no one else available. Hakim preferred young boys, Madame Lambert was fastidious, Ricetti gay and Otomi a devoted family man. Which only left her husband, and Monique had grown tired of him long ago.

"We should work tonight," Hakim broke in, and it was clear he was equally annoyed with Monique's behavior. "We're behind schedule and we can't afford to wait for Mr. Christopolous any longer. We have too many things to decide in too short a time — the redivision of territories, our new leader and what kind of response we should make to Remarque's assassination. These are things of monumental importance, and we can't waste any more time."

Ah, Chloe, Bastien thought. She'd turned to look at Hakim in surprise, and he could read what was going on in her mind. Why should the importation of grocery products and livestock be of monumental importance? Why was their leader assassinated? She was either impossibly gauche or incredibly clever.

"So we'll work," the baron said.

"Those of us who need to. Miss Underwood, your services will be dispensed with tonight. We can manage without you."

Chloe took that as the dismissal it was, and she rose. "I'm sorry I forgot the books," she said.

"What books?"

"The ones you sent me to buy."

Hakim waved a dismissive hand. "Unimportant. We'll be working in the conference room — I'm sure you'll be most comfortable in your own rooms."

It was as clear a directive as possible, a warning, but Chloe was still performing her artless act. "I wondered if there's a computer around I might use? I wanted to check my e-mail."

Dead silence, and Bastien leaned back, wondering how Hakim planned to deal with it. To his surprise Hakim nodded. "In the library just off the stairs on the first floor. Feel free to browse all you want."

"Just my e-mail," she said, rising from the table. The rest stayed put — no courtesies for the hired help, Bastien thought, resisting his own urge to rise. And if she only wanted to check e-mail then he was the prima ballerina with the Ballet Russe. But would she be smart enough to cover her tracks?

The door closed behind her, and conversation broke out immediately. "I don't think having the woman here was a very good idea," von Rutter said in German. "We could have muddled along well enough without a translator. Why bring a stranger into the place?"

"The woman I originally hired was an airheaded blonde with just the marginal skills to make things easier and the self-absorption not to notice anything unusual," Hakim replied in the same language. "I'm not so sure of this one."

"Not sure?" Monique said sharply. "I never thought you were the kind of man who left things to chance, Gilles. You should get rid of her, immediately."

"If necessary," Hakim said. He wouldn't like being told what to do — he thought his time had come and he was ready to sit at the power table. "You know I have no qualms about doing what needs to be done. But I never act rashly. If an American disappears without a trace there might be too many questions. I need to be convinced that either no one would miss her, or that her presence was too incriminating. I'm not sure of either. As soon as I am, Miss Underwood will cease to be an issue."

"English or French, please, if you can't speak Italian," Ricetti grumbled. "What are we talking about?"

Monique turned and smiled sweetly. "We're discussing whether Miss Underwood is a danger, and if so, how we can neatly dispose of her?" She spoke in her flawless Italian.

"Kill her and set up a fake auto accident," Ricetti said.

"Perhaps," Hakim responded. "But she's traveling with my chauffeur, and I'm not sure I want to give up my Daimler just to cover an execution. I would have a hard time replacing my driver as well."

"Just kill her and stop fussing about it," Mr. Otomi said. "If you are too squeamish I can have my assistant take care of it. We are wasting our time arguing when we have more important things to do. I want to know how we are going to transport the four dozen Legolas weapons into Turkey without anyone noticing."

"That's your problem, Otomi-san," Bastien said smoothly. "I want to know where the money's coming from before I put my goods on the table. And trust me, they're very impressive. The finest that American military research can come up with."

"No one trusts you, Bastien," Madame Lambert said. "None of us trusts each other. That's why we work so well together. Between us, we control the selling and buying of illegal weapons throughout most of the world. Trust would simply interfere with things."

"Most of the world," Bastien echoed. "But not all of it. Where the hell is Christos? I don't like this delay — it makes me edgy. Shouldn't we be worrying about him, not a hapless young woman with the guile of a rabbit?"

Monique laughed. "She is a bit of a bunny, isn't she? All big eyes and twitching little nose. We just don't know if that's an act or not. And I, for one, don't propose we endanger our enterprise by waiting around to find out. If Christos were here he'd say the same thing."

"Christos isn't here, and we're wasting too much time on the girl," Hakim said, clearly displeased. "Bastien, go after her, see what you can find out. I don't want to attract any official attention, but neither do I want to waste our time squabbling about her. We'll start with Ricetti's proposal for redividing our Middle East customers — that should give you enough time to make a determination. If she's a danger, kill her. If not, come back to the table and we'll get some work done."

Bastien raised an eyebrow. "And why do I get charged with this little assignment?" he demanded. "I already spent the whole damned day with her and didn't find out anything."

"You didn't push hard enough. You're the one who's spent the most time with her — you'll have the best chance of finding out what's going on."

"Besides," Monique purred, "she has a crush on you. Any fool can see that."

He didn't bother denying it. Any fool could see that she was almost hypersensitive to his presence. He drained his wine-glass and pushed away from the table. "My pleasure," he said lazily.

And he strolled from the room, hands shoved in his pockets, entirely at ease with his task.

There was no sign of her in the upstairs library, but the computer was out of sleep mode, proving she'd just been there. She'd made an inadequate attempt at covering up her Internet snooping, but it didn't take much to find her footprints. She'd been looking up Legolas, and she'd found the right site to tell her just how very dangerous and illegal those weapons were. She'd also looked up half the people in the room, including him.

He didn't bother to check — he knew exactly what she would and wouldn't discover in her clumsy tripping through the Internet, about the others and about him. Bastien Toussaint was thirty-four years old, married, no children, rumored connections with various terrorist organizations, never proven, suspected to be an international dealer in illegal weapons and drugs. Connected to the murder of three Interpol agents. Considered to be a very dangerous man.

She would have read that, but then, it

should be nothing new to her if she'd been properly briefed. If it was news to her he was going to have a hard time getting any closer to her, to find out exactly who and what she was.

And he was going to find out just how hard to get she was. And exactly how good his performance, as Monique termed it, was. No more graceful little dance. The time had come to find out why she was really here.

And then to do something about it.

Chloe was scared shitless. Sitting in the middle of her elegant room, crying. Her freshly applied makeup would be running down her face, she thought, and she'd look like a raccoon all over again. And this time Bastien wouldn't be there to mop up the mess with one of his soft, clean shirts. He wasn't going to get anywhere near her.

She had to get out of here. How in God's name had she managed to land in such a nest of vipers? She should have realized something odd was going on, but her parents had always told her she had an overactive imagination, and she'd decided they were right. An addiction to thrillers and fantasy novels probably hadn't helped.

But this was no imaginary danger. These weren't grocers, and why the hell she'd ever thought they were was a total mystery. Did Bastien Toussaint look like a chicken importer? Did Baroness Monique von Rutter buy her designer clothes and magnificent diamonds with the proceeds from soybeans?

"Idiote!" she said aloud. She needed to get the hell out of there, fast, before they decided she was a liability. She'd left the dining room immediately, not even pausing when she heard her name in the midst of a German sentence. Getting to the Internet before anyone could catch her was too important. Baron von Rutter was a sweet old man — he wouldn't allow them to harm her. Unless, of course, he was equally ignorant of what was actually going on here.

Her suitcase was in the bottom of the armoire. She dragged it out and began throwing Sylvia's clothes into it, including the ruined silk blouse and shredded stockings. It was simple enough — she would tell Monsieur Hakim that she'd received an e-mail from her roommate informing her that her grandmother was desperately ill and she needed to fly home to her family immediately. She could even tell them her

128

ticket on Air France was already booked, and she was due to fly out in less than twelve hours. Just enough time to get back to Paris, throw a few things in a bag and fly home. For the first time in her adult life she was actually frightened.

She was hardly set for travel. She'd picked the plainest dress Sylvia had sent — a clingy black wrap dress that showed too much cleavage, though she'd managed to pin it closed. Beneath it were black French lace underthings that belonged on a rich man's mistress, and if she had to put another pair of too-small heels on she'd cry.

But she did have to, if she was going to get out of here alive. She could hide her panic — she'd never been a very good liar but the stakes had never been so high. Just think of it as an act, she told herself. Like Blanche Dubois in *A Streetcar Named Desire* . . . No, someone more self-sufficient! She wasn't going to find any strangers with kindness to rely on in her situation.

The suitcase was a jumbled mess, and she didn't care. She went into the tiny bathroom, swept the toiletries in the embroidered satchel Sylvia used, and went back to toss it into the suitcase before she closed it.

"Going somewhere?" Bastien Toussaint drawled from the open doorway.

8

Chloe Underwood stared at him as if he was an axe murderer, Bastien thought lazily. She was in a panic — a tear-streaked, mindless panic, which seemed one more bit of evidence that she was a complete innocent who'd accidentally got caught up in this mess. Except that Bastien didn't believe in accidents.

It was like looking into a hall of mirrors, he thought. You couldn't tell where the original began, and what was merely a reflection of the real thing. Was she an innocent? An inept agent? A very good agent pretending to be an innocent? Pretending to be inept?

Time was running out, and there was only one way to get to the truth of the matter. Hurting her would get him nowhere — she'd be trained to withstand pain and she'd give up nothing she didn't want to give up.

But there were other, much more pleasurable ways of finding out what he wanted to know. He kicked the door shut behind him, watched the alarm in her eyes grow.

He knew where the security cameras were — he'd scoped them out last night when he'd searched her room. They covered almost the entire room, including the bed and the bathroom, and he had little doubt that if they didn't have an avid audience they were at least being taped for posterity. He was going to need to put on a good show — Hakim and company wouldn't be easily fooled.

That didn't mean he had to have an audience. There was a corner of the room that was mostly out of range of the cameras, a little foyer with a gilt Louis XV chest. Probably a genuine Louis XV. It would do.

She was standing in the middle of the room, unmoving, but when he came toward her she moved back nervously. She thought she knew who he was, what he was capable of. She didn't know the half of it.

He opened the armoire, exposing a television set, and turned it on. Turned the sound up, loud, and then switched channels until he came to what he wanted. Hakim would have hard-core pornography running twenty-four/seven, and the moans of simulated pleasure filled the room.

"What are you doing?" Chloe demanded, aghast, averting her gaze from the low, wide television screen. Two men were servicing one woman, not his favorite fantasy, but the sound was enough to drown out most of their conversation.

He stood there, saying nothing as he stripped off his jacket, tossing it onto a chair. He was just out of range of the camera, and the sounds emanating from the television would muffle anything they said. "Come here," he said.

He might as well have suggested she jump off a building. She shook her head stubbornly. "I don't know what you're doing here, but I want you to leave."

"Come here."

She wouldn't have started to move if she didn't want to. He'd laid the groundwork well — she was mesmerized by him and he knew it. It was a good thing he hadn't finished what he started in the car — he still had a major advantage. She was afraid, and yet her body still felt the power of her arousal. And that was almost stronger than her fear.

She stopped short of him, still in camera range. "I don't enjoy watching porn," she said. She was clearly hoping for a cool voice, but it came out strained anyway.

"I didn't think you would. After all, Americans tend to be squeamish about sexuality."

"I'm perfectly healthy when it comes to sexuality," she snapped, momentarily forgetting her fear, as he'd wanted her to. "I'm not some repressed little American virgin, no matter what you might think."

"Then come here."

She hadn't noticed that he'd been moving back, drawing her out of range of the camera. Then again, she might have no idea there were cameras in the room, in every room in this renovated château.

She came right up to him, shoulders squared, like someone going into battle. "I'm not afraid of you," she said.

"Of course you are, my pet," he said. "That's half the fun." He slid his hand behind her neck, under her heavy fall of hair, and drew her face up to his. She was looking up at him, her eyes wide and panicky, and he almost felt . . . something. Pity? Reluctance? Mercy? There was no room for any of those emotions.

He kissed her. He remembered the taste of her mouth, the soft, sighing sound she made, the way her lips moved against his. Remembered, and wanted it. He was suddenly very glad that he'd decided to do this, been forced into it. Otherwise he would have had to find some other excuse.

He deepened the kiss, putting his arm around her waist and lifting her. She was clinging to him, and he swung her over to the alcove, pressing her up against the mirrored wall as he reached for her breasts.

She'd pinned the dress closed. He drew back for a moment, breathing heavily. "What the hell did you do with that dress?"

She didn't try to escape. "It was too loose. I pinned it."

"It's supposed to be loose. Undo it."

She blinked, her only sign of hesitation. And then she reached up and unfastened the tiny safety pin.

"Now open it," he said.

He thought she was going to balk. But she didn't. She pulled the silk wrap dress open, and he recognized the silk and lace underwear beneath it. From the most expensive lingerie store in all of Paris, they were the sort of thing no mere translator could afford, the sort of thing bought to entertain wealthy lovers. Another lie.

Then again, hadn't he already figured out she was wearing the wrong bra size? Her soft skin looked pinched against the black lace, and he wanted to take it off her. But time was running out.

So he simply kissed her again, pulling her up tight against him, her nearly nude body hot against his open shirt, and she kissed him back with enough enthusiasm that he believed it when she said she was no tremulous virgin. Even though she was shaking in his arms.

The moans were coming from the television, loud and heartfelt, punctuated by screams and grunts. It didn't matter what kind of sound they made — no one would be able to tell the difference between the film and the real thing.

Her skin was hot to the touch, soft as silk against his hands. She had her arms around his neck now, holding on to him as if she might blow away in a strong breeze, and he liked that. "Take off your underwear," he said.

Her eyes, which had been half-closed in dreamy delight, shot open. "What?"

"What do you think we're doing, Chloe? Take off your panties. You can leave the bra on if you insist."

She had frozen, and the color had drained from her face. "Get away from me," she said, shoving at him.

But it was too late. It had been too late

since he'd set foot in her bedroom. Perhaps it had been too late from the moment he'd first seen her.

The upscale underwear was meant to be easily disposed of. He reached between them and caught the lace in one hand, yanking hard, and the ties tore.

"No," he said. Merciless, he reminded himself, as he pulled her up against his body. This was a job, something he had to do. He kissed her again, and while her hands tried to push him away her mouth answered his.

And then it was too late. He picked her up, moved her to the antique chest and set her down on it, moving between her legs. He didn't know if she realized what was going to happen, or if she was capable of rational thought. It didn't matter.

She was wet, as he thought she'd be. It took him only a moment to unfasten his pants, and then he was inside her, deep inside, and he felt the unmistakable shock of a tiny orgasm ripple through her before she was able to stop herself.

She was going to cry, going to push him away from her, and he wasn't about to let that happen. He stopped her mouth before she could protest, wrapped her legs around his hips and began to move, not releasing her mouth until he knew he had her with him, that she was trying to get closer to him, wanting to thrust back but unable to because of her seat on the chest of drawers. He could feel the shivers building, knew that whatever her consciousness was telling her, her body had overruled it, and all she wanted was completion. Satisfaction. Him.

And he pulled out, almost completely, drinking in her anguished cry like the honey it was. "Who are you?" he whispered in her ear. "What are you doing here?"

She clawed at him, trying desperately to bring him back, but he was much stronger than she was, and he held her still, his hands pinning her hips to the gilded top of the dresser. "Who are you?" he demanded again, his voice as cold as his body was hot.

Her eyes were dazed, her mouth a soft wound. "Chloe . . ." she said in a choked voice.

He thrust into her, hard, then withdrew before she could stop him. She cried out again, but he was without remorse. "Your clothes don't belong to you," he whispered, and in the background the noise from the television increased in intensity, matching his own ruthless arousal, "you speak languages you pretend you don't. You're here for a reason, and it has nothing to do with translating. Are you here to kill someone?"

"Please!" she cried.

Again he thrust, and he could feel her hovering on the edge, ready to explode, helpless as he knew he could make her, knew that he needed to make her. "What do you want, Chloe?" he whispered, knowing that he'd finally get the truth from her.

Her eyes were swimming with tears, and she was shaking. "You," she said. And he believed her.

He stopped thinking then. He pulled her off the table, wrapping her legs around his hips, burying himself deep inside her, and the climax hit her so hard she cried out, louder than the voices on the television, a strangled cry of helpless pleasure.

He wasn't ready — he was tired of playing games. He thrust inside her, slowly, deliberately, leaning up against the mirrored wall for support, holding her hips, fucking her slowly, sweetly, until it took him over as well, and he poured himself into her, losing everything, drowning in her hot, sweet flesh, her soft, sweet mouth.

He waited until he caught his breath, waited for the tremors to finish washing over his body, and then he withdrew, supporting her limp body against the wall until her legs could support her. He held her up for a moment, and he could see his face in the mirrored wall, dark and ruthless. He looked like the bastard he was, and there was nothing he could do about it. He'd accepted the fact long ago.

He stepped back from her, fastening his clothing. She was looking up at him as if he were a ghost, and he wanted to pull her into his arms, to comfort her. She looked so bereft. For all her claims of sophistication she was clearly not used to what he'd just put her through, and she looked disoriented, lost.

But he couldn't. He closed his eyes and leaned his forehead against hers, pulling the dress back around her body and tying it at the waist. He couldn't keep her out of sight of the cameras any longer, but he could keep it from being too easy for them.

When the logical answers get ruled out, you have no choice but to believe the impossible. Chloe Underwood was exactly what she claimed she was. An innocent, caught in a maelstrom far too powerful for her to even understand. And oddly enough, it was the so-called good guy who had done the most damage. Up to this point.

He was going to have his work cut out for him, distracting Hakim from his own suspicions. He needed to get back to that computer, erase little Miss Busybody's virtual fingerprints and convince the others they had nothing to fear from her.

But first he had to finish with her. He kissed her on her mouth, lightly, carelessly. "*Eh bien,* sweetheart," he murmured. "That was very nice. Too bad we don't have time for more."

She stared up at him, lost for a moment. And then she reached out and slapped him, using all the shattered strength in her body, and it jarred his head.

Regret was useless, remorse an unknown emotion, and his body was still humming with satisfaction. He gave her a crooked smile, picked up his discarded jacket and walked out of the room, closing the door quietly behind him.

Chloe leaned against the wall. Her legs felt weak, barely able to support her, and she slid down, slowly, ending on the beautiful parquet floor. She began to shake — it started slowly, as nothing more than a faint vibration that grew until she was shivering uncontrollably. She wrapped her arms around her body, but she couldn't get warm. She closed her eyes, but the television was still on, the moans a staccato accompaniment to her confusion, and she opened them again. The torn lace underwear lay on the floor in the little foyer, in front of the antique chest of drawers that had probably never seen such usage in its long, elegant life. Then again, this was France.

She wanted to throw up. There was no question about it — she was horrified and sick inside at what had happened, and she still couldn't understand why.

She hadn't said no. There was no way she could avoid that simple truth — she hadn't told him no. Whether he would have taken that for an answer was beside the point. She'd let him do that to her.

And the awful, sickening thing was, she'd liked it.

No, that was the wrong word. Like had nothing to do with it. She hadn't liked being manipulated, intimidated, tormented and used.

But he'd managed to make her climax anyway, despite it all. Or, most horrifying of all, because of it?

No. She had no hidden, dark need to be punished, humiliated, used and discarded. There were no dark shadows hidden in her past, no twisted self-loathing that begged to be treated with carelessness.

So why had she let him? Why had her mind screamed no as she'd kissed him back? Why had she clung to him, knowing who and what he really was? Why had she come?

She could tell herself it was simple biology. Her family, if she had ever been insane enough to discuss it with them, would tell her it was a normal, physiological reaction. Nothing to be ashamed of, nothing to horrify and sicken her.

The problem was, she knew, deep inside, what was shameful, what was horrifying, what was sickening. Not that she'd managed to have the most powerful orgasm of her life under such unloving circumstances.

But that she wanted to do it again.

9

Bastien was back at the computer, moving through the history file with rapid keystrokes. He had always had the remarkable ability to compartmentalize his thoughts, his life, his emotions. It started when he was a child, following in his globe-trotting mother's wake, barely able to keep up with her.

If you sent your mind to a separate place you didn't feel pain. You didn't hear the rage, or the screams of the dying, or smell the blood, or count the dead. You turned your mind in a single direction, and everything else fell back into its own neat space, unable to touch you.

He was good at computers, fast and decisive, and he knew he didn't have much time. The big question was whether someone was doing real-time electronic surveillance as well as monitoring them on security cameras. It could work either way — someone might be in one of the hidden rooms, watching everything he was doing on the computer, having already taken note of Chloe's ham-handed searches.

Or they could simply search through the computer's history on a regular basis, in which case he'd be safe wiping out Chloe's tracks.

Either way, he'd do it — if Hakim and the others found any record they still wouldn't know who'd cleared it. He could do that little for her, and not much more without compromising his position. Besides, there were always civilian casualties in every war. She was just at the wrong place at the wrong time.

He was just about to hit the Delete button when he heard a noise behind him. He didn't have to turn — he had an almost preternatural sense of who was approaching, and his cool, dispassionate self took over. It was Hakim, and his arrival couldn't be accidental.

Bastien let his hand rest on the mouse. One click, and it was gone. One click, and she would have a fighting chance at survival.

"So what have you discovered about little Miss Underwood, Bastien?" Hakim inquired, lighting one of his thick, Cuban cigars.

His fingers hesitated. "She's an innocent," he said. "No one sent her, she has no agenda. She is who she says she is."

"How unfortunate. For her, that is. Would you like to tell me how much she suspects?"

Bastien stared down at his hand. He moved it away from the mouse, and turned the monitor slightly so Hakim could see it. "Everything," he said in a deadly calm voice.

Hakim leaned forward, peering at the screen. He nodded. "Too bad," he said. "For her, that is. But I suppose it's to be expected. I'll take care of her — I'm quite good at it. I should tell you that the baron was most displeased that you and the girl were out of range of the cameras. I know you well enough to know that wasn't an accident. Really unfair of you, Toussaint. The baron likes his little pleasures, and they do no one harm."

"I wasn't in the mood to perform for the old man."

"You've done it in the past, with his wife. Don't try to deny it, or say that you didn't know there were cameras. You always know when there are cameras. So what made tonight different?"

The question was random, almost lazy, but Bastien wasn't fooled. "Fucking his wife was one thing — if he wants to watch and she wants to be watched then who am I to argue?"

"And why didn't you want him to see you do Miss Chloe? Were you protecting her? Do you have a soft spot for her in that ice cube of a heart?" Hakim purred.

Bastien turned to look at him, cool and unflappable, and Hakim shrugged. "Stupid question, Toussaint. Forgive me. I of all people should know that you don't come equipped with any tender emotions. Do you want to watch me kill her?"

Bastien hit the Delete button then, and all trace of Chloe's tampering vanished. "Not particularly. Are you sure that's the best way to deal with her? When an American disappears without a trace there can be a great many awkward questions."

"There's no way to avoid it. Too bad for Miss Underwood, but she shouldn't have been so nosy. Curiosity killed the cat, as they say in her country. And she won't disappear without a trace. I'll have my people set something up — a car crash, a tragic accident of some sort."

"Won't that cramp your style? I know your fondness for fire and metal, and they leave marks. Not the sort of thing that turns up in a simple car accident."

"Kind of you to worry about me, *monsieur*, but I have everything under control. If I accidentally mark her too badly then we can always set the car on fire, have her body burned just to the point of recognition and no further."

"Very practical," Bastien said.

"And you're certain you don't want to join me in this? I'm more than happy to share."

"I already enjoyed what I wanted from Miss Underwood," he said without emotion. "The rest is up to you."

He joined the others for coffee and liqueurs in the drawing room, flirting lightly with Monique. The baron gave him a disgruntled glare or two, but beyond that his earlier absence wasn't even noted. No one seemed to notice that Hakim was gone as well, Bastien thought as he lit Monique's cigarette for her. But then, as Hakim had said, curiosity killed the cat. And the members of their elite little trade organization were experts at self-preservation, and knowing only what they had to know. They knew they could count on Hakim to keep things discreet, as he always had. That was all that mattered.

He glanced at his watch. He'd left

Hakim about an hour ago — would Chloe be dead yet? He supposed he ought to hope so. Hakim was an inventive sadist, and he could make it last for hours, even days if he so chose. He didn't have that kind of luxury, but he suspected that mercy and brevity were unknown to him.

Monique would come to his room tonight — she made it more than clear, ignoring his previous dismissal. The baron would insist on it, having been deprived of his vicarious entertainment. And Bastien would service her, letting technique fill in where interest waned. If he were Hakim the thought of Chloe's suffering would excite him. But he wasn't Hakim, and all he could hope was that she died quickly.

He lingered in the drawing room as long as he could, not wanting to head back upstairs. He just wanted it over with — there had been nothing he could do to protect her, not without compromising his own position. And in the end, what was one innocent life compared to the thousands, hundreds of thousands that might be saved if this arms ring was shut down? Assuming that would ever happen — Thomason and his ilk seemed more interested in simply keeping tabs on it. But then, life was full of ugly equations, he'd accepted that long ago, and he wasn't going to waste his time bemoaning it.

It didn't help that his room was next to hers, the only two inhabitants in that wing. The maids were cleaning it out when he went back to his room, and he strolled over to the open door with the properly casual air. No signs of violence — he must have done her elsewhere.

The maids were stripping the bed. "Where's Miss Underwood?" he asked, curious to see what kind of excuse Hakim had come up with.

"She had to leave early, Monsieur Toussaint," one maid replied. "A death in the family, Monsieur Hakim said. She left so quickly she didn't take her luggage. We'll have to send it after her."

A death in the family, all right. Her own. The suitcase was still by the door, and he considered warning the maid that she'd be better off not noticing discrepancies like that one. Not if she wanted to live.

But he wasn't in the business of saving innocents, so he said nothing, simply nodded, and went back to his room.

He was in the shower when he thought he heard her scream. He shut off the water immediately, but there was nothing. No noise, no cries. If by some cruel twist of fate she was still alive she would hardly be within hearing distance. Hakim would have taken her into the old part of the building, the wing that looked as if it had yet to be remodeled, yet was fitted up with state-of-the-art electronics and sound-proofing. He wouldn't hear her if she screamed. Besides, knowing Hakim, it would be long past the time when she could make any kind of noise at all, even a whimper. He simply had to put it out of his mind — it wasn't in his nature to have regrets, or second thoughts, or even compassion.

He dressed quickly, in black. Comfortable pants and a shirt pulled over his head. He tied his long hair at the back of his neck, shoved his feet into a pair of boat shoes and went to the door.

A little after midnight. Monique would come in search of him before long. He'd considered disabling the surveillance cameras in his room, just to spite the baron, and then thought better of it. He could only push things so far, and the man he was pretending to be, the man he had become, would appreciate an audience.

He opened his door into the empty hallway. The servants were gone from the room next door, and the door was open.

All traces of Chloe Underwood had vanished from the Château Mirabel, gone as if she had never existed. Gone from his mind as well, another casualty easily forgotten. And for the first time in years he made an irrational, even emotional decision. Except that he had no emotions.

He was going to find Chloe.

He closed the door behind him and started toward the closed-off wing of the building. If she wasn't dead yet at least he could hurry Hakim along. Sentimental or not, he didn't want her to suffer. Saving her was out of the question, but he could spare her suffering. Perhaps he had that much humanity left.

He found her huddled in a corner of the room Hakim preferred for interrogation, and she was weeping. Still alive, though she wouldn't be for long, Bastien thought dispassionately as he closed the door behind him. Hakim turned to look at him, a startled expression on his face.

"What are you doing here, Toussaint? You told me you weren't interested in playing with Miss Underwood. I'm not sure I want you to change your mind."

He'd shed his jacket and tie, rolled up his sleeves and unbuttoned his shirt. His thick, hairy chest was damp with sweat, and he was clearly in a state of sexual excitement as he held the thin stiletto blade over the blowtorch.

He could smell the scorched flesh. He looked back at Chloe. She was no longer wearing her fuck-me underwear — somehow she'd managed to change before Hakim had come for her. She was wearing dark pants and a shirt. Or had been. The pants' legs were slit open, exposing her long legs, and the shirt was pulled down on her arms, exposing her chest and the plain white bra she wore.

He could see the marks. Hakim had used the knife to both cut and burn, and he'd been busy making a pattern on Chloe's arms. She hadn't gone into shock yet, but it wouldn't be long. She knew he was there, but she didn't look at him, just sat huddled in the corner, her eyes closed, head back against the wall as she silently wept.

"I'm not going to interfere with your fun, Gilles," he said. "I just thought I'd watch a master at his work."

She opened her eyes for that, staring straight at him through the shadowy room. He looked back into her brown eyes, and saw himself clearly for the first time. Who he was, and what he had become.

"Feel free," Hakim said. "Unlike you, I

always enjoy an audience. She's really very pretty, isn't she?" He moved over to her, lifting a strand of thick hair with the hot knife. It sizzled against the blade, and a hank of it fell onto the floor.

"Very pretty," Bastien said, watching her. He hadn't touched her face yet — that would come later. He'd never had to stand and watch Hakim's work, but he'd heard enough stories to know exactly how it would proceed.

He could do nothing, nothing to stop him. He should never have come here, seen her there, but he'd always done what needed to be done. "The baron was asking for you," he said suddenly. "There's a problem with the Iranians."

"There's always a problem with the Iranians," Hakim grumbled. "How serious is it?"

"Serious enough. I don't know if it can wait until morning."

"Anything can wait until morning," Hakim said, drawing the knife down Chloe's arm, searing the flesh. She didn't scream. "You see how obedient she is? Very easily trained. I told her if she made too much noise I'd use the knife between her legs. She's already had you there tonight, and I'm thinking that was enough."

Bastien said nothing. She'd closed her eyes again, and he noticed how pale her face was beneath the silent, streaming tears.

"You think I might make her stop crying?" Hakim murmured dreamily. "I could cut out her eyes."

Chloe jerked, then went still again. "Maybe you should check with the baron," Bastien suggested. "After all, we're here to work, not have fun."

Hakim turned and pouted. "I suppose you're right," he said. "There'll be someone else . . . there are always pretty girls who stick their noses where they don't belong. I'll just finish her now."

Chloe couldn't have moved even if she thought it would do her any good. She'd tried to run, earlier, but he'd hurt her so badly she'd passed out, only to come awake in this horrible little room, feeling the hot blade against her skin.

She had lost the ability to think, to reason. She was going to die at the hands of a monster. A sadist exquisitely tuned to the nuances of pain. She had accepted the fact that she was doomed, that there was nothing she could do about it, when Bastien had walked into the room.

154

Not for one moment had she hoped he'd come to save her. She had no such illusions — he was as violent and evil in his own way as Hakim was. In a way he was worse, because it was hidden so deeply beneath his elegant exterior.

She watched the second piece of hair fall on the floor. A good thing they were going to destroy her body, she thought from a great distance. It would be hard to have an open casket with her hair all different lengths.

She must be going into shock, if she could think of such frivolous things. Her parents would be upset — they'd never wanted her to go to Paris. They'd wanted her to stay home and become a doctor like everyone else in the family, and she wouldn't listen. She'd been too squeamish to bear the sight of blood, and now it would be her own blood she had to watch, to smell. At least her parents would have the dubious benefit of knowing they were right.

In the end the person who'd suffer most was Sylvia. Her clothes were gone, she'd be responsible for the astronomical rent on the tiny apartment and the French police would ask her all sorts of questions about her missing roommate. Sylvia's lifestyle didn't bear too close a scrutiny, and Chloe could only think that it served her right. A little discomfort wasn't quite a fair trade for sending her best friend to her death.

Of course she hadn't — *the pain is so fucking bad I'm going to pass out, but I can't, because then he'll kill me* — hadn't meant to endanger Chloe. But if she'd simply come herself then nothing would have happened. Sylvia was never interested in much beyond her own pretty nose. She'd never end up trapped here, with a monster pressing hot steel against her skin, while another, worse creature looked on.

She wasn't going to scream. She bit down on her lip so hard she could taste the blood, but she wasn't going to scream when he drew the tip of the blade across her skin, watching the beads of blood form and begin to trickle across her skin.

"I'll finish her now," Hakim said, grabbing her hair in one fist and bringing the knife up to her throat. "You can meet me back in the library — I'll be along in a minute."

Chloe closed her eyes, bracing herself. At least it would be over, and the darkness would be a blessed release. She tilted her head back to give him better access, des-

156

perate to have done with it, and Hakim laughed.

"You see how good I am, Bastien? I make them crave it." And he plunged the knife downward.

The sound was strange, an odd sort of popping noise, and then she was smothered, weighted down, awash in blood and darkness and smelling of sour sweat. It wasn't what she thought death would be like, but at least it didn't hurt, and she held still, letting the night overtake her.

When suddenly the weight lifted and she could breathe again. She opened her eyes to see Hakim's body sprawled out on the floor, in a pool of blood that wasn't hers.

Bastien Toussaint was standing over her, his face cool and emotionless. He held out a hand to her — in the other he held a gun. "Life or death, Chloe. Make your choice."

She put her hand in his, and let him pull her to her feet.

She was able to stand by sheer force of will. Pain shot through her arms, her legs, where Hakim had marked her. But Hakim was dead, she was alive, and even if she had to turn to the person she hated most in this world, she would do it. She didn't want to die.

"There's a back stairway that will bring us out near the garage. We'll have to get past a handful of guards and the guard dogs, and you'll have to be quiet and do everything I say. Otherwise I'll shoot you and leave you behind."

She nodded, not trusting her voice. He sounded cool, unmoved, as if he hadn't just killed a man, as if he weren't anticipating killing others. Somewhere she could find the same coolness.

He kept hold of her arm, his fingers gripping tightly as he dragged her after him. She could barely manage to keep up with him — she was shaken, weak and dizzy, but asking him to slow down wasn't an option. He'd probably put the gun to her head then and there if she held him back.

She stumbled after him, down the narrow, unlit stairway, out into the frosty December night. The fresh, cold air was so powerful that she almost choked, trying to inhale huge lungsful, trying to get the taste and smell of blood and fire out of her. She wanted more, but suddenly Bastien shoved her against the wall, covering her body with his until they both disappeared in the shadows.

His body was pressed up against hers,

plastered against hers, she noted absently. He was very strong — she'd realized that, hadn't she? She might hate him with a shocking ferocity, but when it came to being rescued it was good to have her rescuer be strong.

Chloe heard the muffled growl from a guard dog, followed by a quick admonishment. The guards were making their rounds, but they hadn't yet realized something was wrong.

"I may have to shoot them. Don't make me shoot you as well." The words were only breathed in her ear, just a whisper of sound, but she nodded.

The guards had moved past them, but they would be back. "Just promise me one thing," she whispered, a little louder than Bastien's silent communication.

He slapped his hand over her mouth, and she fought back her cry of pain. "Be quiet," he snapped, no longer lazy or charming.

She nodded, and he pulled his hand away. The guards were halfway across the wide expanse of formal garden by that point, and while bullets might reach them, the men themselves couldn't.

Bastien pulled back from her, seemingly unmoved from having been pressed up against her. "Promise you what?" he asked finally.

"Don't shoot the dogs."

For a moment he just stared at her blankly. And then an odd expression flashed in his eyes, what she might have called, in another man, in other circumstances, amusement. But there was no room for amusement in a life-or-death situation. "I'll do my best," he said. "Come on." And gripping her hand, he started to run.

10

The night had ceased to be real. Hakim had ensured the place was well-lit, and they had to dodge from shadow to shadow as they crossed the wide strip of lawn. Bastien seemed to have a preternatural instinct as to where to move, and she followed by sheer, iron will, refusing to think about the things she had seen, the things that had been done to her. Reality was long gone, and if this were a Hollywood movie she'd wake up in her own bed, sweating and horrified over the incredibly real-seeming nightmare.

She'd survived so far, but it was no dream, it was reality in all its ugliness and terror. She'd left home, left the family tradition because she couldn't stand death and pain and the sight of blood. And now she was covered with the blood of a dead man.

Bastien left her twice, and she stayed in the shadows, numb, obedient, waiting until he returned to drag her after him. His Porsche was parked near the curving drive, and their final sprint used up the last ounce of her energy. He had to stuff her into the passenger seat like she was a dead body herself, and she sank into the leather, closing her eyes, feeling the darkness beginning to take over like a curtain being drawn across a stage.

He was beside her in the driver's seat, and she heard the click of the seat belt, and she wanted to laugh. Such a careful man, who kills silently and always wears a seat belt. He leaned over and fastened hers, and the touch of his hands made her flinch as the knife hadn't, but she stilled herself, keeping her eyes closed, hunting for that oblivion she so desperately needed.

He was driving very, very fast on the dark, moonless roads, running for their lives, and yet he reached over and turned on the radio. It was a hit song from a few years back — she has revolver eyes, she kills with her glance, she shoots. Shooting, killing, guns.

The oblivion held off. She turned to look at him. "You killed a man tonight," she said.

He didn't even spare her a glance. "I killed two men tonight. You didn't see me cut the throat of one of the guards. I promise I didn't hurt any of the dogs, though."

She stared at him in horror. "How can you joke about it?"

"It was a joke that you didn't want me to kill the dogs? It would have made things simpler if I had, but I decided to defer to your tender sensibilities." He took the corner with the speed and skill of a race-car driver, only giving her a quarter of his attention.

She didn't know which was worse: a man like Hakim who killed with pleasure, or a man like Bastien who felt nothing at all.

"Go to sleep, *ma petite*," he said. "We've a long drive ahead of us, and you've already had a busy night. I'll wake you when I stop for food."

"I don't ever want to eat again," she said in a faint voice, shuddering. She could smell the blood, and something else basic and foul.

"Suit yourself. American girls are too fat anyway."

She couldn't even summon a trace of outrage. If she didn't know better she'd think he'd said it for the simple purpose of bringing her out of her dazed, deadened state, but it seemed unlikely he'd care. She ought to ask him where he was taking her, but she couldn't summon the energy or the curiosity. He'd take her wherever he wanted, do whatever he wanted. She could only hope that if he decided to put his hands on her again it would be to kill her. She would rather be dead than have sex with this cold-blooded monster.

"Go to sleep," he said again, in a gentler voice, even though the very notion of gentleness was absurd. But the song on the radio was soft and soothing as he sang of love and killing. *C'est foutu.* Everything's fucked, he sang, and she could only agree, as she closed her eyes and let the darkness come.

Bastien glanced over at her once he was certain she'd drifted off. She was a mess — her arms were crisscrossed with shallow cuts and burns, her face was pale, tear-stained, her makeup giving her raccoon eyes. She looked very fragile, but he knew she was tougher than she seemed. She was still alive, a miracle in itself. She'd somehow been able to withstand Hakim long enough.

Hakim had a rhythm to his work — he'd been a man of method. He told them not to scream, and then worked on them until they did, like a lover trying to bring a reluctant woman to orgasm. Once they started to scream he moved faster, but Chloe had managed to keep silent. She had blood on her mouth and her lips were swollen from biting down to keep the screams at bay. Or maybe it was from his own mouth on hers. He'd certainly been no tender lover.

He'd found out what he needed to know, and that had been what mattered. And then he'd gone and screwed everything up by sticking his nose where it didn't belong, interfering with Hakim's fun and games instead of accepting that every war had its casualties.

Maybe he was just tired of all the collateral damage. Maybe he wanted to save one life instead of taking it. Maybe he was so burned out that he was courting death, screwing up important assignments on a whim.

She looked pretty messed-up for a whim. He needed to get them somewhere safe, where he could clean the wounds on her soft, pale skin, where he could figure out what the hell he was going to do now, both with her and with himself.

She was easy enough. He'd patch her up, calm her down and put her on the next plane back to the United States. She must weigh about one hundred and twenty-five pounds — it would be easy enough to give her just enough drugs to make her calm and pliant but still able to get herself on and off a plane.

It wouldn't be before tonight. First he had to get to one of his safe houses, clean her up and reassess the situation. Maybe the Committee would decide to terminate him after such a royal cock-up. He'd outlived his usefulness, and he was starting to act on impulse, which made him a liability. His employers weren't the kind who gave second chances.

Hakim was expendable, but it had happened much too soon. And here he was, on the run, abandoning his mission before the main target had even showed up. Thomason would be livid. It didn't matter. He was ready for this to be over. He no longer cared about anything or anyone, even his own worthless hide. As soon as he made sure Chloe was safe they could come and get him.

She was stronger, more resilient than he could have hoped. By the time the sun had risen across the French countryside her color had improved, and she slept more peacefully. He'd driven north, heading toward Normandy, and then circled back, coming toward Paris from the northwest rather than the south. It wasn't much to throw his pursuers off, but he was hoping it would take a number of hours before someone found Hakim's body and figured out who was missing.

He considered dumping the car, stealing a new one to cover his tracks a little better, but for some reason he was loath to disturb Chloe when she was sleeping so soundly. He had plenty of places to hide the car in the city — he just had to count on his luck holding for the next few hours. Long enough to get her safely on a plane.

He stopped in a small town just outside the city, leaving the car running while he went into a small store to get a few necessities. He lucked out — they had shoes in what he guessed was her size, they had Diet Coke and premade sandwiches that would taste like a cardboard baguette, but by then he wasn't picky. Neither of them could afford to go without food, though he expected he'd have to hold her down and force her to eat. And while that vision was undeniably erotic in a pleasantly kinky way, he didn't have time for it.

The coffee was the way he liked it — strong and sweet — and he drove one-handed through the morning streets of

Paris, dodging the kamikaze traffic with expert ease, weaving in and out of the trucks and taxis like someone on a motorcycle, even taking a bit of the sidewalk at one point. Driving so fast no one would have time to notice anything but a blur. The usual Paris gridlock was nothing to him, and by the time he made it safely into the underground garage at the western-style hotel he was reasonably sure no one had followed him. They were safe for the next few hours.

It was an American hotel, bland and expensive and unremarkable, and he kept one of their better rooms, using it for the occasional cover, the occasional downtime. As far as he knew, no one was aware of its existence, but he knew that wouldn't last long. As soon as they started looking for him they'd be able to track the extended room rental, and then he'd be shit out of luck.

But that much would take hours, and he was willing to take the chance. Chloe needed bandaging, neatening up, something to eat and as close to brainwashing as he could manage without the right sort of drugs. He hadn't decided exactly what he was going to tell her. He wasn't going to be able to convince her it was all a dream, not with those marks on her arms and her hair hanging around her face in odd lengths. Her face was pale, and there was a bruise beneath her eye that would benefit from ice.

He pulled into his allotted parking spot and turned off the car. That level of the garage was deserted at that hour — too early for the idle rich to move about, too late for the working stiffs. He could get her up to his room with the minimum of witnesses.

She had opened her eyes, staring at him dazedly. She'd pulled her shirt around her, but she hadn't fastened it. Maybe it hurt too much to move her arms. He reached toward her, to fasten the buttons, but she flinched away, as if he were about to hit her.

"I was going to button your shirt," he said. "You can't walk through a hotel looking like that, not when we're trying not to be noticed."

"Where are we?"

"The MacLean Hotel. I keep a room here for times like these."

"Times like these? You've been through something like this before?"

"Yes." It was only half a lie. He'd been in messes, with his cover compromised, with innocent people caught in the middle. In the past, he'd escaped and covered his own ass, leaving the casualties where they lay, but he hadn't left this one behind.

The front of her shirt was in shreds — Hakim must have cut it open with his knife. He reached behind the seat and grabbed his shirt, watching with mild annoyance as she jerked away from him. She should realize by now that he was the least of her worries.

"Put this on," he said, "and button the cuffs. It'll make it harder to clean up, but we don't want the world seeing Hakim's marks."

At the mention of his name Chloe shuddered. "I can pull it around me. Besides, people are more likely to notice I'm barefoot."

"I stopped and bought you some shoes. You can't run for your life in bare feet or someone else's shoes. They're in a package in the back as well." He pulled the key from the ignition, reached under the front seat for his gun, two of his passports and a well-hidden wad of cash. She hadn't moved.

He climbed out of the car. "The longer we wait around here the more dangerous it is," he said. "Change your shirt or I'll do it for you."

He should have turned away while she carefully pulled her ruined shirt off, but he was beyond such polite considerations. Her white bra wasn't nearly as erotic as the sexy underwear she'd been wearing only a few hours ago, and she moved awkwardly, painfully, pulling on his shirt, then the shoes with the distaste of someone dressing in discarded rags. He watched her, refusing to react.

She followed him to the elevator, moving slowly, and he let her take her time, keep her distance as long as no one was around to watch, to interfere. The elevator was small and smelled of exhaust and garlic, and the doors closed around them, leaving her staring down at her feet as it moved upward.

He looked at her feet as well. The simple black flats seemed to fit well enough, and the shredded cloth of her trousers flapped around her calves. Her hair smell liked burnt wool, and she was bleeding through the long, loose sleeves of his white shirt.

"Merde." The elevator stopped short of his floor, the doors opening to let someone else on. He moved quickly, backing her into the corner, shielding her with his larger body, tucking her face against his shoulder. She tried to jerk away, but he

tightened his hand around her wrist, causing just enough pain to make her behave without crying out. "Pretend we're lovers," he whispered in her ear, in German.

As he expected, she understood him perfectly, an anomaly that still needed explaining, but now was not the time. The middle-aged businessman who'd gotten onto the elevator averted his eyes with polite discretion, and Bastien moved closer to Chloe, pressing his hips up against hers like a passionate lover not yet satisfied.

She jerked her eyes upward, looking at him in shock. She must have felt his erection, and known what a sick son of a bitch he was. The thought was mildly amusing.

He was tempted to kiss her, just because she would have been so disgusted, but he was smart enough not to push it. Not when there were witnesses.

The man got off, and even before the doors had closed again she'd pushed him away, shuddering visibly. "Don't touch me again," she said in a low voice.

"Don't be childish," he replied. "I'm trying to save your life, though I haven't quite figured out why. Just be quiet, do as I say and follow my lead. If I need to fuck you standing up in the middle of Notre Dame with half of Paris watching you'll do it without objection. Understand?"

"Over my dead body."

"Exactly." They'd reached the top floor, and the hallway was empty. He'd considered cutting the throat of the man who'd seen them, but with any luck he'd be long gone from the hotel by the time his enemies showed up. And disposing of the body would have caused more problems than simply letting him go. Besides, Chloe would have probably started screaming. Very impractical, these Americans.

"We're down at the end," he said, waiting for her to precede him out of the elevator. It wasn't courtesy — if he went first she might refuse to follow, and he didn't want to get into a tussle with her. She raised her head and looked at him, and in the full light of day he could see her quite clearly. See pain and fear in her rich brown eyes. See hatred aimed straight at him.

Good. It would help to keep her alive. He'd found that hatred was a very useful commodity, and igniting hers would do no harm. He had nothing to fear from her — she couldn't surprise him, hurt him, run from him. But her anger would keep her going after her body and her heart wanted to give up.

He followed her down the hallway, an anonymous corridor that could have been in a thousand different hotels all over the world. She balked when he unlocked the door, and he gave her a little nudge over the threshold. The look she gave him would have paralyzed a lesser man.

"Go into the bedroom and take off your clothes," he said.

"Go fuck yourself."

He laughed. "You've got cuts and burns all over your arms and legs, Chloe. You need them tended to, and you need to rest. Trust me, I have no interest in touching you beyond getting you in shape to leave tonight."

She didn't look like she believed him. "Leave?"

"I'll get you on a plane out of Paris, back to the States. Where are you from?"

"North Carolina."

"Is that anywhere near New York?"

"No."

"Then you'll have to figure out the rest of the way home. As long as you're out of France you'll be safe enough, but right now there are going to be any number of very talented people out to kill you."

"I would think they'd want to kill you, not me."

"Oh, they want to kill me, too. Most everyone who meets me eventually ends up wanting to kill me," he said.

"I can understand why," she said in a faint voice.

He didn't bother arguing. "Are you going to take off those ruined clothes, or would you like my help?"

"I can manage," she said stiffly. "Where's the bedroom?"

He pointed to the double doors behind him. "In there. I'll be in in a minute."

"I'm not going to sleep with you again," she said. He could see her vulnerability was lessening as her outrage grew. That would help her to survive as well.

"Again? I wasn't aware that what we did before had anything to do with sleeping."

She could blush. He watched with fascination as the color stained her face — he would have thought she'd be well past such an innocent reaction. He took pity on her. "Never mind, Chloe," he said gently. "I won't do anything but provide a little first aid. The rest of you can stay inviolate."

He could tell his frank, matter-of-fact approach was only making it worse, but at

175

that point it was the least of his problems. She needed to be patched up, fed, dressed and sent on her way, and he didn't have any time to waste. He'd be insanely lucky if they didn't find him by nightfall — his smartest plan was to keep moving. As soon as he was sure his unexpected companion was able to.

She was sitting on the bed, the sheet wrapped around her like she was at a gynecologist's office, and she was still wearing her underwear. He sat beside her on the bed, and she tried to move away. "Don't be childish, Chloe," he said.

She was looking at the dark brown bottle he held in one hand, the cotton swabs he planned to use. "What is that?" she demanded. "You didn't get that from any drugstore."

"A good thing, too. This is very expensive, very high-tech, worth more than its weight in gold. It speeds up healing. In a couple days most of this should disappear. I doubt there will even be much scarring."

"Where did it come from?"

"Trade secret," he said, putting a generous amount of the thick, translucent green stuff on a swab. "There's only one drawback." He picked up her left arm, the one Hakim had concentrated on.

"What's that?"

"It hurts like hell." And he wiped the cream against the first cut.

She jerked, and he half expected her to scream. He'd chosen this hotel for a number of reasons, one of them being its exquisite soundproofing, and he had no fears that anyone would hear her cry out, but apart from a strangled little sound at the back of her throat she said nothing, holding herself rigid to fight the pain.

He knew from experience that this was probably going to hurt worse than Hakim's ministrations. With Hakim she'd been partially numb from shock and fear, and the full effect of his handiwork wouldn't take effect until later. If she lived that long.

She was biting her lips to keep from making any sound, and her mouth was bleeding again. He kept going, trying to ignore the vibrations in her body as she fought it.

"There are better ways to deal with pain," he said calmly as he continued to paint the stripes on her arm. "The more you fight it, the more it fights back. If you let go, relax into it, you'll find it becomes almost an altered state, as if someone else is hurting. It's much better that way."

"You have that much experience with

177

pain?" She barely managed to spit out the words.

"Enough," he said. "Breathe. You know, like they do in childbirth. Deep, regular breathing, and try to relax."

"I can't," she said in a strangled voice. He could feel her heart racing against the pain.

"I could always distract you."

That got her attention. "Don't —"

"I know, don't touch you." He put one arm down and picked up the other. "Then talk to me. Tell me what you were doing at Hakim's."

"I told you! I was taking my roommate's place while she went off with her new boy-friend. I had no idea what kind of place it was, or what kind of sick creatures I was working for."

"And now you know. Which is what makes you a liability. How do you happen to understand so many languages? Most American girls can barely manage to speak English."

She shot him an angry look. She was so predictable, so easy to play. All he had to do was make a sweeping, disparaging re-mark about American women and she forgot all about her misery. He tended to like sophisticated, unpredictable women. But for some reason he liked her.

For a moment he thought she wouldn't answer. "I have a natural talent for it," she said, her voice strained as she tried to deal with the pain. "My parents sent me to a series of expensive private schools, and I started learning French in kindergarten."

"That explains why your accent is so good. Where did the others come in?"

"School. I majored in modern languages at Mount Holyoke, and my parents traveled a lot. I can even converse in Latin."

"Not a modern language. Lie back so I can work on your legs."

She was putting too much energy into dealing with the pain — there was none left over to fight him. She lay back, pulling the sheet up over her. The legs weren't as bad as the arms — Hakim had been working himself up to a proper climax and he hadn't gotten there yet.

Bastien had been between her thighs not that long ago. She had long, beautifully shaped legs — he'd been too busy to appreciate them in her suite.

"I told you, I'm good at languages. I like all of them."

"Then why do you have a shit job at a small-time publisher? Talents like yours could come in useful at any number of organizations."

"I like my life. I'd rather translate children's books than covert arms deals."

He'd finished his ministrations, and he set the bottle and swab down on the floor, then moved onto the bed beside her, crouching over her. "And that's exactly the thing you're not supposed to say, my angel. You need to forget everything you saw during the past two days. These are dangerous people we're dealing with, and you could identify most of them. You're a smart woman, despite your stupid behavior, and if you set your mind to it you could probably decipher just what we were talking about in the meetings, now that you realize it's not chickens and grain."

She didn't like him so close, leaning over her, she didn't like looking up at him, even though he wasn't touching her — he could see it very clearly. He didn't care. "Forget everything, Chloe," he said softly. "Or you might not live to regret it."

11

Chloe stared up at him. She was lying flat on her back on his bed, wearing her underwear and a sheet, and she'd had sex with him less than twenty-four hours before. Hell, maybe less than twelve — she had no idea what time it was right then.

She also couldn't bring herself to move, to reach up and shove him away. His dark, unreadable eyes were half-closed as he leaned over her, and for an insane moment she thought he was going to kiss her again.

But he didn't. He levered himself up, away from her, seemingly finished with her. "I'm going to take a shower, then I'll see what I can do about a passport for you."

"I don't need a new passport."

He shook his head. "If you travel under your own name you'll never make it home. I know what I'm doing, Chloe. Just do as I say and you might come out of this mess alive."

She stared at him. "Who the hell are you?" she said. "*What* the hell are you?"

His faint smile revealed nothing. "I don't think you need to know. Just try to sleep. You're going to need your strength to heal properly."

Doing what he said didn't exactly appeal to her, but she was too worn out to fight him. The pain had subsided to a dull throb, encompassing every inch of her body, and at that moment sleep sounded much more important than the truth.

"All right," she said grudgingly.

"What? You're actually agreeing to something? I don't believe it."

"Go to hell," she said, her voice barely audible.

"That's more like it," he murmured. "Try to sleep. You can insult me all over again when you wake up."

She would have thought sleep would come immediately, but it was frustratingly resistant. It was cloudy outside — if she tried to reconstruct the last few hours she might be able to guess what time it was, but going back in time was the last thing she wanted to do. She didn't want to think about anything that had happened yesterday, from the moment she'd gotten in the car with him. She didn't want to remember those rough, powerful moments in her room, she didn't want to relive the pain and terror and, most of all, she didn't want to remember Gilles Hakim on top of her, his body a deadweight. Literally.

He'd been hurting her, planning to kill her, and she'd wanted him dead. She'd thought she was a pacifist, willing to die rather than hurt someone else, but when it came to a matter of her own life or death, all her noble sentiments were shot to shit. If she'd had a gun she would have killed Hakim herself, and enjoyed doing it.

Maybe. At this point she didn't know what was true and what wasn't. She could hear the sound of the shower running, smell the soap and shaving cream and the faint, teasing scent of the cologne he wore. She hadn't been able to identify the components — they were subtle, nagging, almost . . . erotic. She didn't like men who wore scent.

The shower stopped, and a moment later the door opened. She looked up to see Bastien walk into the room without any clothes, not even a towel wrapped around his waist. She jerked her head to the side, closing her eyes, and heard him laugh.

"Do men's bodies make you uncomfortable, Chloe?" he said. She ignored him, keeping her eyes tightly shut as she listened to the rustle of clothing, the sound of drawers and doors being opened. She was almost asleep, miraculously enough, when she felt the bed sag beside her, and despite herself her eyes shot open.

He wasn't wearing much, but at least he was decent. He'd put on a pair of trousers, and his shirt was open around his chest. Odd. She'd had sex with him before she even knew whether he had hair on his chest.

He didn't — his skin was smooth, golden, and she closed her eyes again, trying to shut him out.

He tucked the sheet around her. "Sleep, Chloe. You need to keep that stuff on for another four hours and then you can wash it off, but in the meantime you need to just lie there and let the medicine do its job."

She considered ignoring him, then couldn't resist answering him. "There's no medicine in the world that can heal what Hakim did to me that quickly."

"Maybe not. But the physical pain will be gone. It's up to you whether you want to let it scar you emotionally."

"Up to me?" She tried to sit up, but he pushed her back down on the bed, not gently.

"Up to you," he repeated firmly. "You're young, you're strong and you're smart, despite the mess you managed to walk into. If you have the sense I think you do you'll put it behind you."

"So sensitive," she mocked him.

"Practical," he said. "He cut you. He burned you. He didn't rape you."

"No, that was you."

He swore then, words she shouldn't know, even with her command of languages, but she did. "Whatever you want to tell yourself," he said after a moment. "I must have had momentary deafness. I don't seem to remember you ever saying no."

She hadn't, and they both knew it. She said nothing, and a moment later she felt him move from the bed. She hadn't realized she'd been holding her breath, half expecting him to touch her again, and she let it out as he moved away from her. "I'll be back in a couple hours. Don't answer the door, don't answer the phone, don't go near the windows. I don't think anyone knows about this place, but you can't be too certain, and a lot of people are going to be looking for you."

She turned her head away, ignoring him. She just wanted him gone, out of there — if he said one more thing to her she'd scream.

She heard the sound of the front door closing, the click of the automatic lock, and she opened her eyes in the dimly lit apartment, to find herself alone. Finally. In his bed.

She sat up, slowly, wary of her wounds, but there was no pain. Whatever that green gunk was, it had managed to stop the pain, at least for now. She touched her arm, gingerly. The stuff had formed an almost wax-like coating over each stripe, sealing it, but it moved with her, and when she pushed the sheet off her body and stood up there wasn't even a twinge, or a pinch.

It was probably some kind of radioactive poison — it had hurt enough when he'd painted it on her, and she didn't trust him for even a moment. But she felt stronger, rather than weaker, so she could probably acquit him of that. Strong enough to get the hell out of there before he came back.

Her clothes were a shredded mess — there was no way she could walk out in public in them. She would have rather left stark naked than to put on his clothes, but she had at least an ounce of self-preservation left. If wearing Bastien Toussaint's clothes meant she wouldn't have to see him again, then so be it.

All his clothes were black. Of course —

he was as dramatic as he was monstrous. It didn't help that the only pair of trousers she could wear were a loose pair of silk pajama bottoms. Like most men, particularly the French, he had no hips, and she had at least her fair share.

Except that he wasn't French. She wasn't sure how she knew that — his accent was perfect, his manner, everything about him proclaimed him to be exactly what she'd discovered on the Internet. The son of an arms manufacturer from Marseilles — it was no wonder he'd gotten into the business of shipping them. It would have been a short move from legal armaments to illegal weaponry.

The *married* son of an arms manufacturer, she reminded herself, pulling his silk shirt over her arms, wincing in anticipation. The whisper-thin fabric barely touched her skin, and there was that inexplicable absence of pain. She moved to the window and peered outside. It was cold and rainy — it almost looked as if it might turn to flurries before long. It was a little too early for snow, but then, the world seemed to have turned sideways. She could no longer count on anything being normal.

There was no money — she searched the place thoroughly. She found a small cache of what was presumably cocaine or heroin — she didn't give a damn which, but not cash. Not a cent to get her to the opposite side of Paris. It was easy enough to orient herself, with the Eiffel Tower to her left, the Seine snaking its way through the shadowy city. It would be a hike through the back streets and alleys to her apartment in the Marais, but anything was preferable to staying here. She grabbed his coat — a long, black cashmere trench that felt butter-soft in her hands. The faint trace of his scent teased her, enough so that she almost threw it down again, rather than wrap herself in the smell and feel of him.

But now was not the time for dramatic gestures. She ran a hand through her hair, feeling the uneven lengths, the scorched ends. There was nothing she could do about it now, but when she made it back to her apartment she could get Sylvia to fix it.

He'd told her it was too dangerous to go back to her apartment, but then he'd told her a great many lies, and he was the only recognizably dangerous thing in her life. Besides, no one knew where she lived. Sylvia sublet the tiny apartment from one of her former lovers, and neither of them were on record as tenants. Chloe's mail arrived at the Frères Laurent, her cell phone was billed to the United States and there was really no way they could find her without trying very hard indeed. And she didn't think they'd consider her worth the effort.

That didn't mean she wasn't going home to America. She didn't trust Bastien for one moment, but she'd seen enough in the past twenty-four hours to know that she'd inadvertently gotten mixed up with some very dangerous people, and if he was one of the good guys she really didn't want to see the bad ones. The safest place for her was back in the mountains of North Carolina, surrounded by her overprotective family. For some reason Paris and the surrounding countryside had lost its allure.

Slogging through the cold, wet street, head down, with Bastien's coat wrapped around her, didn't do much to improve her mood. Her feet were numb from the cold, but at least the shoes fit. Funny that he'd stop long enough to buy her a pair of shoes on their escape back to Paris. She couldn't even begin to understand what went through his mind, and she didn't want to try. All she wanted to do was get far enough away from him and the others that no one could find her.

She was hungry — starving, in fact, and even remembering Hakim wasn't enough to distract her. She couldn't remember how long it had been since she'd eaten, and there was only so long she could go on nervous energy. There'd be food at her apartment, food and a warm bed. Tomorrow she'd fly home, on the first plane she could get. And maybe next time she'd listen to her family when they told her to stay put.

She was right — the rain was turning to snow. She stopped for a moment, leaning against a building to catch her breath. No one paid any attention to her as they moved quickly through the streets, their own heads down, intent on their own business. After a moment she pushed away and started forward again. It was growing dark, and even on the well-lit streets of Paris she didn't want to be out alone any later than she had to be. Yanking the coat closer to her body, she strode forward again, trying to ignore the faint scent of his cologne.

It took him longer than he'd expected. Franc had been agreeable, particularly when Bastien had demonstrated how generous he was prepared to be, and promised to have the papers ready by 6:00 p.m.

They could stop on the way to the airport and it would only take a few moments to add the right photograph. He was sending her out on Air France just before midnight, and after that he could breathe a sigh of relief, pay attention to business. Hakim was dead a little earlier than planned but that was no great disaster, and Christos hadn't even shown up. There was a good chance of salvaging the mission once Chloe was out of the way. He wasn't quite sure why he couldn't wait until then — he was seldom distracted by sentimentality. Just one more piece of unexpected behavior that he would have a hard time explaining to the Committee. Except that he had no intention of telling them the truth.

He stopped at a café and ordered a whisky and soda. The rain was coming down steadily, turning to snow, and he sat in the window, looking out into the dismal streets, waiting.

The man who sat down opposite him looked like a British civil servant — stuffy, unimaginative, middle-class and middle-aged. His name was Harry Thomason, and he was, in fact, a ruthless, soulless automaton who ran the Committee like a well-oiled machine. He shrugged out of his wet raincoat, put his newspaper on the table and ordered a cup of coffee before he finally looked at Bastien.

"What have you done, Jean-Marc?" he demanded.

Bastien lit a cigarette, his first in the last two days, milking the action of all its drama. Harry probably had as good an idea of his real name as anyone, but he went along with the Jean-Marc alias, not knowing that that particular name had come from his aunt Cecile's pet pig.

That Jean-Marc had been a very elegant pig, of course. A family with their bloodlines would have nothing less, and Cecile enjoyed carting around her Vietnamese potbellied pig into the finest hotels in Europe and Asia. An elegant, bad-tempered pig, Jean-Marc had finally disappeared while Cecile and his mother were touring Burma. He'd always wondered if he'd ended up in someone's kitchen, cosmic payback for the time he'd taken a chunk out of Bastien's backside. It had been his fault — he was twelve at the time, bored, defiant, tired of being dragged from one end of the globe to the other, an adjunct to Cecile and Marcie's renegade behavior, and as the pig received more attention and affection than he ever had, he'd decided to annoy Jean-Marc as he dozed on his fur-lined bed.

Jean-Marc had taken exception to it, and bitten Bastien on the butt, earning his grudging respect. At least the pig didn't ignore him.

Cecile had lost interest in the pig by the time he'd disappeared, just as his mother had lost interest in her only child years ago, possibly days after he'd been born. She'd made it very clear that his presence on this earth was not by her choice — her possessive lover had refused to let her abort the child until he found out that he wasn't the father, and by the time he took off it was too late. Marcie was in some quack's office begging for a late-term abortion when she went into labor, and he was born three hours later.

He always wondered why she hadn't simply strangled him and tossed him in a Dumpster or garbage can. Or not even soiled her hands by doing that much, but left him to die of starvation and cold on that November night thirty-two years ago. Maybe she'd been momentarily sentimental. Maybe it was the fact that she'd been very ill, so ill she'd almost died, so ill that they'd had to operate, removing her uterus and ovaries, making certain she'd never go through the indignity of pregnancy again. At one point he used to speculate that she'd been lying in that hospital bed, afraid of dying, and she'd made a bargain with the god she professed to believe in. If her life would be spared, she'd raise her child and be a good mother.

Well, she'd fucked that up. She'd been a lousy mother. He'd been raised, if you could call it that, by a series of hotel maids and houseboys, until he'd finally taken off at the age of fifteen, leaving with an old friend of his mother's, a woman twice his age with the body of a teenager and the heart of a . . .

Well, she had had a heart, and she'd loved him. Maybe been the very first person to do so. He'd left her in Morocco when he was seventeen — just walked away one day when she was out shopping, buying him presents. When they weren't in bed she liked to dress him in elegant clothes, and he'd learned to appreciate silk suits early on. She'd died a few years later, he'd heard, but by then he was well past any feelings of regret.

He'd been recruited in his early twenties, by a man very much like Harry Thomason. A cold-blooded, heartless son of a bitch who knew exactly what someone like

Bastien could be capable of, if properly trained. And they'd seen to his training.

Politics, morals meant nothing to him. He was ostensibly working for the good side, but as far as he could tell there wasn't a whole lot of difference between the two. The body count on both sides piled high, no one even noticed the innocent lives that got caught in between, and for that matter, neither did he. Chloe Underwood was an aberration, one he planned to take care of before people like Harry found out about her.

"So what happened at Hakim's?"

That was one of the things Bastien hated about Harry — the man wouldn't say shit if his mouth was full of it. "Things got fucked. What can I say?" He stubbed out the cigarette. He'd lost the taste for them, another annoyance.

"You can tell me what happened to the girl. Who was she?"

"Girl?"

"Don't play me, Jean-Marc. You weren't the only operative at Château Mirabel this weekend. The little American secretary — who was she working for? What happened to her?"

Bastien shrugged. "Your guess is as good as mine. I'm thinking she was on the baron's payroll, though she may have been there for recreational purposes. You know how the baron likes to watch, and he's always enjoyed Monique with another woman."

Harry wrinkled his nose with the distaste of a born celibate. "And you didn't bother to find out?"

"I did my best, boss," he drawled, knowing Harry hated being called "boss." "I couldn't get her to admit to anything."

Harry looked at him for a long moment. "If you couldn't get anything out of her then I doubt there was anything to find out. If I can say one thing about you, it's that you're the best interrogator we've got. Better than anyone on the other side, even the late Gilles Hakim. He always tended to enjoy his work a little too much. So tell me, what happened to our old friend Gilles, and what happened to the girl?"

"Dead." He lit another cigarette. He didn't want it — even Gitanes were tasteless, but it gave him something to do.

"You kill them both?"

"Just Hakim. He'd already done the girl."

"What happened to her body?"

Bastien looked at him through the drifting smoke. "There wasn't much left of her by the time Hakim got through."

"I see." Harry took a drink of his coffee. The man didn't smoke, didn't drink, didn't fuck as far as Bastien could tell. He was a machine, nothing more. Just as Bastien was trained to be. "A little premature," he continued, "but it should be salvageable, as long as there are no loose ends. Hakim was disposable, but Bastien Toussaint is not. The others will be coming to Paris to finish the discussions, and the dilatory Christos will be joining them. You'll be waiting for them."

"You don't think they'll be suspicious? Wonder why I killed Hakim?"

"They know you and they knew Hakim. Why should they wonder? All that matters is they cement the arrangements, divide up the territory and choose a new leader. They might have chosen Hakim because he was a hardworking SOB, but with him out of the picture I'm guessing that Christos has a clear shot. And you're going to stop it."

"They may be willing to overlook Hakim's death, but Christos has a great many more people in his organization. There are bound to be repercussions."

"And so you'll die," Thomason said.

Bastien didn't even blink. "Will I?"

"It's very simple — you've done this sort of thing before, and even if you hadn't I wouldn't put anything past you. Once they choose Christos you'll make a fuss, put a bullet in his head, and someone we'll already have planted will shoot you. You'll be wearing a dummy blood patch, and once you hear the gun go off you drop like a stone. Which means you only have one shot at Christos — you need to make it count."

"I've never had any trouble hitting my target."

"No, you haven't. So Bastien Toussaint will be dead and if I'm feeling particularly generous I might let you take a little vacation in the south of France until your next mission. There's a first time for everything."

Bastien lit another cigarette that he didn't want. "And the arms cartel?"

"The next obvious choice is the baron, and he'll be easy enough to control. We have no interest in putting them out of business. Someone's going to be supplying the arms to the international terrorists, and by watching the cartel we can trace the various splinter groups, tap into their plans."

"I delivered detonators to Syria last April. Seventy-three people were killed, including seventeen children." His voice was neutral, but Thomason wasn't fooled.

"Don't tell me you're still sulking about that! The fortunes of war, my boy. Casualties of the fight against terror. You never used to be so sentimental, Jean-Marc. You know the math as well as I do. Seventy-three dead, with the potential of thousands being saved. Sometimes you just have to make the ugly choice."

"Yes," said Bastien, watching through the curling smoke of his cigarette.

"I trust you, Jean-Marc. I know you'd never make the mistake of lying to me. If you say the girl is dead then I'm certain she must be. Besides, what reason would you have to lie? In all the years I've known you I've never seen you show any human emotion, any weakness. You're a machine. State-of-the-art, finely tuned, indispensable."

"Even a machine needs to rest," he said. "Let someone else do the job, and I'll just disappear. Jensen has already built up a solid cover — he can take care of Christos himself."

"Why?"

"Because I'm tired."

"People in our line of work aren't allowed to get tired. They seldom get time off, they don't get to rest. There's only one way to retire, Jean-Marc. The way Hakim did."

"Is that a threat?" he asked lazily, stubbing out his cigarette.

"No. Only a fact. The cartel will be meeting at the Hotel Denis tomorrow, with Christos arriving the next day. I leave it up to you. I have every confidence you'll do what needs to be done."

"Do you?"

"Don't annoy me, Jean-Marc. You know how much is riding on this." He rose, folding his newspaper neatly.

"The fate of the free world? Isn't it always?" He didn't bother to rise. "I think I've heard this all before. The needs of the many outweigh the needs of the few and all that crap. You've been watching too much *Star Trek*."

"I thought it was *Star Wars*," Harry said.

"I know what's at stake," Bastien said.

"See that you don't forget. Anything."

Bastien looked up at him. His time was running out, and he simply didn't care one way or the other. His luck had held far longer than he would have expected, and it wasn't going to last much longer. He'd be dead by the first snowfall. Except that it was already snowing.

But before they got to him, he just might slit Harry Thomason's throat. For old time's sake.

12

She was gone, of course. He knew it even as he rode upward in the tiny elevator, but he went anyway, just to make certain. The place was dark, and she'd left a window open. Icy air was blowing in, laced with bits of snow, and he shut it and pulled the curtains before he turned on the light. He didn't know whether they were watching, but he wasn't in the mood to take chances.

There was no sign of forced entry, no blood. Her clothes were left behind, but his coat was missing, and someone had gone through his wardrobe. If they'd come to get her they wouldn't have bothered dressing her. They wouldn't have bothered taking her — she'd be lying dead in his bed if they'd found her.

Which meant she'd left of her own accord, and she was no longer his responsibility. He'd warned her, for some crazy, quixotic reason he'd tried to save her life. Even compromised his own cover for her, whether he wanted to admit it or not.

And she'd ignored his orders and disappeared. Good riddance.

She'd searched the place pretty thoroughly, which surprised him. What could she have expected to find here? Maybe she'd managed to fool him after all, maybe she wasn't the innocent she'd convinced him she was. And then he remembered the look in her eyes when he'd made her come, and he knew she hadn't held anything back. Harry Thomason was right about that much. No one could keep the truth from him, not if he was determined to find it.

She'd found the drugs, though she hadn't touched them. He kept them as insurance — a marketable commodity for some informants who didn't need money. He pocketed them, just in case, then went through the room with quiet thoroughness, wiping down every surface. It wouldn't stop a DNA expert, but there would be no reason to go to such lengths. There were no dead bodies, no signs of a crime. Just a mysterious tenant who disappeared, leaving his clothes and toiletries behind, and not a single fingerprint.

If he'd needed to be thorough he could have torched the place. His rooms were on the top floor — most people would escape unscathed. But a fire might call too much attention. Better to just walk away, from the anonymous apartment, from the annoying memory of Chloe Underwood and her well-deserved fate.

He walked out into the damp, chilly night, pulling his jacket around him, cursing his unwanted guest who'd not only disobeyed him, but taken his coat as well. He walked, head down, leaving the car behind as well. Too many people had seen it, and there were no records that would lead back to his real life, or the Committee.

It was almost midnight when he walked into the smoky bar near Rue de Rosiers. It was the third place he'd stopped — he'd had dinner near the Opera, gambled a bit at one of the small clubs his current alter ego frequented, and now he found himself in a dingy little place in the Marais, a holdout from the gentrification that had been going on for the past few decades.

"Étienne!" the bartender greeted him as he made his way through the crowded room. "What brings you here? We haven't seen you in . . . how long is it? Two years? I thought you were dead."

"I'm hard to kill," he said, automatically switching into Étienne's guttural Marseilles accent. "How have you been, Fernand?"

Fernand shrugged. "It's a living. What can I get you? You still like that Russian vodka?"

In fact, Bastien had never been that fond of vodka, but he nodded amiably, taking a seat at the bar and pulling out his Gitanes.

"You've changed your brand, I see." Fernand nodded toward his cigarettes. "I thought you only smoked American cigarettes."

That was the kind of careless mistake that could get a man killed, Bastien thought with a faint frisson of something that could almost be called anticipation. He was getting sloppy. "I switch around," he said. "I'm not a man with strong allegiances."

"I remember." Fernand poured him a shot of vodka, and Bastien tossed it back quickly, then held it out for another hit. "You look the same. How has life been treating you?"

"Like shit, as always," he said easily. In fact, he looked very different from the Étienne he had once been. Étienne had been working class, dressed in leather and jeans, his hair had been streaked and much shorter, and he always had a couple days' stubble. It was all a matter of how he carried himself, Bastien had found. He could become Étienne, or Jean-Marc, or Frankie, or Sven, or any number of people simply by changing the way he spoke and moved, and few ever saw through it.

"You still haven't told me why you're here," Fernand persisted. "What can I get for you?"

In the past Fernand had been a purveyor of drugs, information and laundered money, but he had nothing Bastien needed.

"Can't a man come in for a drink with an old friend?" he answered easily enough.

"Not a man like you."

Bastien glanced at the street outside. The snow was still drifting down in lazy flakes, and the streets were almost empty. Those who were still awake were some-place warm on such a cold, deadly night. And he realized with real amusement what he was doing in the seedy part of the Marais at midnight when he had better things to do.

"A woman, Fernand," Bastien said with a self-deprecating smile. "I was in the area to see a woman, and I thought I'd warm myself up a bit before I face her wrath."

"Ah." Fernand nodded, immediately satisfied. "She lives around here, then? Maybe I know her?"

"Maybe. She's Italian," he said, making

it up on the spot. "Short and plump and fiery, my Marcella is. Maybe you can tell me if you've seen her in here. I want to know if she's been playing around. She swears she hasn't been, but who can trust women?"

"Who indeed? She doesn't sound familiar. Where does she live?"

Chloe shared a tiny apartment with an English girl two streets away — he'd found that out within hours of her arrival at the château. The others would know as well, but even she would have the brains to keep her distance from the first place they'd look for her. Wouldn't she?

And she was no longer his problem. Except that he'd ended up in a bar two streets away from her, for no earthly reason. And he might as well stop fighting it, go and see if she was there.

If she wasn't, he could forget about her. He should have already, but such things were easier in theory than in practice. He liked answers, and Chloe's disappearance left too much unsettled.

Fernand was looking at him with far too much curiosity. Then again, information was one of his most valuable commodities, he'd be wanting to get everything he could from Bastien for future use.

Bastien named a street in the opposite direction. "And I'd better get my tail over there before she decides to come looking for me."

"Then we'll be seeing more of you? With your girlfriend in the area?" Fernand persisted.

"This will be my home away from home," Bastien said grandly, portraying the slightly inebriated cock of the walk known as Étienne. *"'Soir!"*

He was well-hidden in the shadows by the time Fernand followed him out of the bar. The little man peered through the lightly falling snow in search of him, never realizing he was only a few feet away, hidden. Fernand swore, then moved to a corner of the building, away from the light, and pulled out a cell phone.

He was too far away for Bastien to hear more than a few words, but he heard enough to know that his death wish was drawing closer. One more mistake like this one and that would be the end of it. Too bad he couldn't bring himself to care. It didn't matter who Fernand was working for, or why. He'd have connections to half a dozen people who wanted him dead.

Fernand closed the phone, looked around one last time and spat before heading back into the bar. Bastien wondered how long it would be before reinforcements showed up.

It wasn't important — he would be long gone by the time Fernand's mysterious compatriots got there. It wouldn't take more than a moment to check the apartment. And then, unless he were completely suicidal, he would go to his house in St-Germain-des-Prés and become Bastien Toussaint again. And Little Miss Chloe would have to fend for herself.

Sylvia and Chloe shared a typically small apartment on the top floor of an old house in a poorer section of the Marais. The ground floor was let to a tobacconist, the first was occupied by an elderly couple who spent most of their time traveling and the top floor held storage rooms and the cramped little flat. The entire house was dark when Chloe finally turned the corner. Her hair was wet with snow, and the burnt edges smelled horrible. The first thing she was going to do was take a bath and to scrub her entire body, even the waxed-over wheals. It had been a lot longer than four hours since he'd spread the stuff on her. A lot longer than four hours since she'd managed to leave the hotel without anyone

209

looking twice. She'd been so muffled in his black coat that they might have thought she was Bastien. Except that duplicating his walk would be just about impossible, for her or anyone else.

Maybe, twenty years from now, she'd remember him, and wonder what fit of insanity had come over her. She'd like to think she'd been drugged, anything to take the responsibility off her shoulders, but she couldn't. She had been in an altered state of consciousness, all right, but it had nothing to do with drugs and everything to do with . . . God, she couldn't even begin to understand what had prompted her to act that way. She'd been bored, longing for romance and adventure. No, actually, she'd been longing for sex and violence, and that was exactly what she'd gotten. Be careful what you wish for — hadn't the Chinese said that? Or was it, "May you live in interesting times"? Whatever — right now all she wanted was a long bath and a warm bed, and tomorrow she'd fly home to the loving, protective arms of her family and all the boredom anyone could ask for.

It was at that moment that she realized she didn't have a key. Not to the house, not to the apartment, and she almost let out a wail of despair. Her feet hurt, her hair smelled like wet dog, her entire body ached, and even though her stomach was empty she wanted to throw up. And she was cold, even in the soft cashmere embrace.

She could go to the police, but there would be questions she didn't want to answer. She could go to the embassy, but it was probably a mile in the other direction, and she didn't think she could walk another foot, much less retrace her steps along the snow-drifted streets.

But luck was finally with her. The door leading to the upper floors was unlocked, as it often was. Sylvia usually couldn't be bothered with locking it, and no one else had been around for the past few days. She closed the door behind her, shutting herself into the dark, cold hall, and reached for the light switch to guide her way up the two flights of stairs.

And then pulled back. It was very dark, but she knew her way by heart, and there was no need to draw attention to her presence. It was highly unlikely anyone would know where she lived, but Bastien had made her nervous. If she moved through the place in the dark, like some silent wraith, she could be reasonably sure that no one would come to investigate.

The door to the flat was locked, but Sylvia always left a key on the windowsill in the hall, just in case she lost hers, which she managed to do on a regular basis. She pushed open the door, and cold air surrounded her. Sylvia must be off having a riotous time in the arms of her elderly lover.

She closed the door, leaning against it, and slowly let out her breath. In fact, she hadn't been away that long. Two nights, coming onto the third one, and Sylvia had gone off for a long weekend. It wasn't surprising that she hadn't yet returned, and probably just as well.

The moon shone in the dormer windows, illuminating the cluttered rooms enough for Chloe to make her way through them. She started the gas fire, shivering in Bastien's coat, then drew her bath. It had never been the best of arrangements. The flat consisted of one bedroom — Sylvia's — a tiny kitchen and even smaller bathroom, and a jumbled living room. Chloe slept on a mattress on the floor, stalwartly refusing to consider the possibility of insects or rodents in the ancient building.

She opened the door to Sylvia's room and peeked in, but even in the filtered moonlight she could see it looked as if it had been hit by a bomb. Sylvia must have thrown everything here and there as she packed for Chloe's magical weekend in the country. She wasn't going to be very happy at the disappearance of some of her best clothes.

It was nothing compared to Chloe's state of mind. Knowing Sylvia, she might not be back for a week or more, and by then Chloe would be long gone. Once she got back to the States she'd wire her some money to cover her share of the rent until Sylvia found someone to replace her, and an extra bit to help replace the designer clothes. While Chloe had very little money, the rest of her family had more than they knew what to do with, and they'd be so deliriously grateful that she'd decided to return home they'd probably send Sylvia enough to support herself for months.

She didn't look in the mirror as she stripped off Bastien's clothes and kicked them away. She slid into the old-fashioned tub, bracing for searing pain, but instead the hot water enveloped her like a loving embrace. She sank into it with a moan of pure pleasure and closed her eyes, at peace for the first time in what seemed like an endless nightmare.

But eventually the water grew cold, and

life had to be faced. She climbed out of the tub, catching a glimpse of her body in the mirror. She froze, staring in shock at the reflection.

The noxious, searing green gunk had done its job. The marks were still there, stripes of pain caused by fire and blade, but they looked months old, a distant memory. There were dark marks on her hips, and she peered closer, until she could make out the faint imprint of his hands on her hips where he'd held her. Bastien. It was only fitting that those marks would remain when the rest was healing.

She wrapped herself in a towel. Her wet hair was a disaster and wouldn't wait for Sylvia's leisurely return. She had no choice but to attack it herself. She found some scissors and started hacking away at it, letting the various lengths fall into the sink.

She'd been hoping for one of those movie makeovers — the dull, bespectacled secretary takes nail scissors to her mop and becomes a gamine worthy of Audrey Hepburn. Not quite. She put the scissors down before she went too far — maybe it would look better once it dried. Her mother's hairdresser would cluck in horror and then dive in, and in a few days she'd be chic and adorable. Right now she felt like a drowned cat.

The heat had managed to fill the main room, but the air was still stuffy, so she opened one of the windows a crack, searching through her clothes for her warmest nightgown, a flannel granny gown that always had Sylvia in stitches. There'd be no one around to laugh at her tonight, and she needed the warmth and comfort of the soft, enveloping fabric.

There was nothing to eat but cereal and cheese. She ate two bowls of Weetabix in the darkness, washed it down with a glass of wine and crawled beneath the duvet on her thin mattress. Tonight she could be overrun with rats and she wouldn't move. All she wanted to do was sleep.

She did, dreaming terrible dreams. The nightmares should have been the worst — Hakim's face looming over her, his soft, insinuating voice more horrifying than anger, as he lovingly drew the knife over her flesh and dared her not to cry out.

In her dreams he didn't stop. In her dreams she bled to death, with Hakim smiling down at her with gentle approval, and Bastien sitting in a thronelike chair, women draped around him as he sipped a glass of whiskey and watched.

And yet that was bearable. She knew she dreamed, and no matter how real it felt, a tiny part of her brain was aware enough to convince her it wasn't real.

But her dreams didn't give up easily. She was no longer dying, bleeding. She was lying in a white bed, covered in lace, and Bastien was on top of her, inside her, making love to her with slow, wicked intensity, and the pleasure was so exquisite she felt her body spasm in her sleep.

She was cold, she was hot, the covers were too light, then too heavy, and she could feel Bastien around her, like an embrace, his scent teasing her as she fought her way deeper into sleep. She didn't want to dream, she didn't want to remember, all she wanted was warmth and darkness.

Somewhere in the distance a church bell tolled four. She should get up and close the window, but she was finally warm, and surely she could manage to fall asleep again. In the morning, in the daylight, she could face things again. In the darkness all she could do was hide.

Something didn't feel right. Small wonder — there was very little that was right in her life, and thinking about it wouldn't help. Only time and daylight would make things better.

She shifted on the thin mattress, tugging the duvet up around her chin, reaching for Bastien's stolen coat to wrap around her as well, one more layer against the cold.

But the coat wasn't there — she'd left it lying across a chair. She opened her eyes in the darkness, only to see Bastien himself sitting on the floor beside her, leaning against the wall, watching her in utter stillness.

13

For a moment she thought she was still asleep, her nightmare come to life, and she told herself it was just a dream. When he spoke, his voice was low and calm in the darkness.

"You're lucky you're still alive," he said softly.

She wasn't going to argue with him about that, though she was tempted. She lay very still, not moving, hoping he'd just fade away. But he was distressingly real and solid, far too close to her. "How did you find me?" she finally asked. "And how did you get in?"

He didn't move from his spot against the wall. His long legs stretched out in front of him, crossed, and his hands lay in his lap. "I told you, it wouldn't take them any time at all to find you. I was faster, but it won't be long before they catch up with us."

"With us?"

He cocked his head, looking at her. "I have a tendency to finish what I started.

You've missed one plane, but I'll get you out on the next one, if I have to knock you out, tie you up and ship you in a trunk."

She reached out to turn on the light beside her bed, but he stopped her, his hand catching her wrist, and she jerked back, knocking the lamp over as she did so.

"We don't need lights," he said. "That was the one smart thing you did, leaving the lights off when you came back. When they come for you a little darkness won't stop them, but you were wise not to draw undue attention to yourself."

"Maybe I just turned off the lights when I went to bed?"

"I was here before you arrived looking like the little match girl. I decided a few hours' sleep wouldn't do you any harm. But you stole my coat — I've been freezing."

"Tough," she said. She didn't ask where he'd been, what he'd seen. There was nothing she could do about it at this point, but if he'd been watching her as she bathed, as she hacked off her hair and examined the marks on her body she wouldn't be happy. Better not to know.

He'd helped himself to her wine — the bottle and a glass sat on the floor beside him. She had no idea how long he'd been there, how long she'd been sleeping.

"Why did you change your mind?" she asked abruptly. She pulled the covers up to her chest and slid away from him to sit in the corner. And then she realized her fingers were clutching his coat, and she dropped it.

"Changed my mind?" he repeated.

"About me. I had a lot of time with Monsieur Hakim, and he enjoys talking while he hurts people. If it hadn't been for you he wouldn't have known I'd been looking on the Internet. He wouldn't have thought I was anything other than what I am."

"Anything other than what you are? And what's that?" He didn't wait for her answer. "Once Hakim decided not to trust you there was nothing I could do to stop it. Showing him your clumsy tracks through the computer only sped things up."

"So what made you change your mind and come to save me?"

"I didn't."

She was cold, so cold, but she didn't reach for his coat. "Then why were you there? Had you just come to watch?"

He shrugged. "I was surprised you were still alive. Hakim must have been enjoying himself more than usual, to have barely touched you."

"Barely touched me?" Her voice rose,

220

and he moved so fast he was a blur in the darkness, his hand over her mouth, silencing her as he held her against the wall. He'd held her against another wall, not that long ago, and she wondered what he was going to do.

"Don't raise your voice," he said, his eyes staring into hers in the darkness. So close. "Try not to be as stupid as your behavior suggests."

He moved his hand away and she was silent, looking up at him. Waiting for him to touch her. He was going to kiss her, and she wasn't sure what she was going to do about it.

But he didn't. He moved away, sitting back on the floor several feet away. "I came to find Hakim about another matter, saw you were still alive, and on a whim I killed him."

"On a whim?"

He shrugged, so very French, and yet she didn't believe he was French. "Part of my own death wish, I expect. I'm living on borrowed time as it is, and taking you out of that place only made things move a little faster. God knows when you walked out today I should have just let you go, but you annoyed me. If I'm going to that much trouble you might at least do as I say."

"I was never very obedient. I wouldn't be here in Paris if I wasn't accustomed to doing what I want."

"I don't give a damn what you want. You're going back home to the States and you're staying there. You understand me?"

At that point there was nothing she wanted more, but some inner devil prompted her to object. "And if I refuse?"

"Then I'll cut your throat and leave you here. It seems a shame, since I've already gone to so much trouble. That stuff I put on your wounds is very valuable, and I wouldn't have wasted it on you if I'd known I was just going to have to kill you a few hours later. But that won't stop me. You're a liability, a drain and a danger, and perhaps I never should have stopped Hakim, but since I did I may as well see this through. It's up to you. You want to die now and get it over with? Or do you want to get back to your family and a normal life?"

He spoke so matter-of-factly about death and killing, and she had not the slightest doubt that he would do just as he said. All she had to do was look into his dark, empty eyes. "How do I know you can keep me safe?"

"You don't. There are no guarantees in

this life. You certainly stand a better chance with me than on your own. And if I fail, I can promise I'll be the one to kill you before you get in the hands of someone worse than Hakim. I'll make it fast and painless."

Chloe swallowed. "There are worse men than Hakim?"

"Actually, the very best at torture and interrogation are usually women. Which is no surprise."

She stared at him in the darkness. "Who the fuck are you?"

His cool smile was far from reassuring. "You no longer believe I'm an arms dealer from Marseilles? It's taken you long enough."

"Then who are you? Is Bastien Toussaint even your real name?"

"Do I look like a saint to you, Chloe? And you don't need to know who I am. Suffice it to say I'm part of an international operation few people know exist, and it's better they don't. Just keep quiet and do as I say."

She stared at him, a cold, sick feeling in the pit of her stomach. "Can you tell me one thing? Are you part of the good guys or the bad guys?"

"Trust me," he said wearily, "there's not

much difference. We need to get out of here before dawn. Get out of that sexy lingerie and put some clothes on. Only Americans would dream of sleeping in such a garment."

She looked down at her soft flannel nightgown. "I'm supposed to wear a lace negligee when I'm freezing and running for my life? You've seen too many movies."

"I never go to the movies."

She crawled across the mattress, keeping as far from him as she could. Not that it mattered — he seemed to have no interest in touching her. She kept her clothes in a small chest by the window, and rose, pulling out some clean underwear, a pair of jeans and a warm shirt. She started toward the bathroom, when his voice stopped her.

"Where are you going?"

"To the bathroom. I'm going to pee and then I'm going to change in there, unless you have any objections."

"You don't need to be modest, Chloe. I have no interest in your naked body."

He'd already made that clear, but for some reason his calm statement was the final straw. She slammed her clothes down in a nearby chair and yanked her nightgown over her head, hearing it tear in her anger. She threw it at him, then picked up her clothes and stalked into the bathroom, her naked body illuminated by the moonlight.

At the last minute she remembered not to slam the door, much as she wanted to. Not enough to die for it, and certainly not enough to risk having him get up from his spot on the floor and put his hands on her again. He couldn't have been clearer — he'd used sex for one thing and one thing only. To gain information. Now that he knew everything he needed to know he had no more use for her.

She wanted a shower, but that might be pushing it. She used the toilet, then dressed quickly. Her shortened hair had dried in a messy tumble that looked better than she'd hoped, but was still a far cry from a Hollywood makeover. But then, he didn't go to the movies. And what he thought clearly didn't matter, since he wasn't interested. Thank God.

She'd do what he said, all right. She would be quiet, obedient — anything to get the hell out of France as quickly as possible. She wouldn't be safe until she did, and despite those horrifying hours with Gilles Hakim she couldn't really believe she was in that much danger. No, the most important thing was to get as far away from her mystery man, and not have to worry about him showing up again once she thought she'd escaped.

He caught the nightgown in one hand while he watched her walk from the room. Her body was pale in the moonlight, and he could see that the gunk had done its work.

He almost could have laughed. She was so offended, with little idea just how desirable she really was. He'd wanted nothing more than to strip off his clothes and crawl beneath the duvet with her, to lose himself in her body, in the darkness. He was tired, so very tired.

But he'd kept his distance, even when he read in her eyes that he could have her. He buried his face in the soft flannel, inhaling the scent of her body, her soap, her skin. She had no idea just how powerfully erotic the juxtaposition of soft, shapeless flannel covering a lithe, sexual body was. And he wasn't about to tell her.

If he were a man with any softer feelings left inside him he would have taken the nightgown as a souvenir, to remember her by. She was unlike anyone he'd ever dealt with — vulnerable and angry and surprisingly brave. But then, he didn't need a nightgown to remember her for the rest of his life. It wasn't going to be that long.

She'd torn the nightgown when she'd yanked it off — he'd been too busy covertly admiring her body to notice. The fabric was old and well laundered and very soft — it must have been in her possession for many years. She'd slept in it since she'd been no more than a girl — she wasn't that old as it was.

He didn't know why he did it. But he did. He took the fabric and yanked at the tear, ripping a piece from it. She wouldn't notice. He wasn't going to give her the chance to pack anything. He had the piece shoved in his pocket, conveniently forgotten, by the time she emerged from the bathroom, looking just as furious as she had when she went in, though unfortunately more clothed.

Nothing like telling a woman you didn't want them to really piss them off, he thought. He couldn't afford to have her start having second thoughts. The sex they'd shared had been nothing but that — short, powerful, even harsh. She belonged in a field of daisies with a tender lover. Not on the run for her life with a murderer.

He'd only begun to think of himself as that, but it fit as well as anything else. He'd killed in self-defense, he'd killed in cold blood, he'd killed by assassination and he'd killed in formal combat. He'd killed women and men, and he hoped to God that he wouldn't have to kill Chloe. But he would if he had to.

Maybe he'd tell her before she died, if it came to that. He could make it very fast, so she barely knew what was happening, but before he drove the knife up into her heart he could tell her the truth. At least she could die feeling smug.

He was getting ahead of himself. If he was forced to kill her it would be a failure, and he wasn't a man who considered failure to be an option. As long as they kept moving they'd be fine. And as long as he kept his hands off her they'd keep moving.

"Do you have a coat of your own, or do I need to let you have mine?"

"Mine's at the château. I can borrow one of Sylvia's — I've already lost some of her best clothes." She sat down in a chair and began to put on her socks and shoes. He didn't need to tell her to wear comfortable shoes — her boots were well-worn and serviceable looking, with low heels. She'd be able to run in them if she had to.

He hadn't seen her in jeans and a

sweater before. She looked even more American, and even more desirable. She got up and opened the door to the bedroom, and he recognized the smell before she did.

He tried to get there in time, but it took him a second to spring to his feet, and she'd already gone in. The room was darker than the rest, even with the early light of predawn, and she wouldn't be able to see anything. But she must have known, because she turned on the light.

His hand was already over hers, turning it off again, but not fast enough that she didn't see the woman's body lying on the floor. She hadn't been dead for more than a few hours, probably just before Chloe had arrived home. The smell would have been more noticeable if she'd been there awhile.

He'd put his arm around Chloe, clapped his hand over her mouth to silence her scream and dragged her from the room, kicking the door shut behind them, closing the body away from them. But the smell filled the room, and they had to get out of there, fast.

She was gagging, and he didn't blame her, but he couldn't afford to be gentlemanly about it. He'd come in the back way, over the roofs and through the storage room window, and he'd go back that way, taking Chloe with him, if he had to sling her over his shoulder and carry her.

She stopped trying to scream, and he let go of her mouth long enough to grab his coat from the bed before pushing her from the room, closing the door behind them.

And out into the icy dawn of the Paris streets with the stink of death still on them.

14

Chloe was in shock, the first piece of luck Bastien had had in a long while. She was past the point of speaking, of protesting, of doing anything but moving with him in blind obedience. He stopped long enough to wrap her in his coat, and then he moved on, keeping hold of her limp hand. If he let go of her she'd probably just stand in the middle of the street until they found her.

He moved fast, in and out of alleyways, backtracking. Why the hell had they killed the girl and then not come after them? Maybe it was a simple mistake — if they'd sent an outsider they might have thought she was Chloe. Or maybe they'd killed the girl as a precaution, then went looking for them, and they'd somehow managed to miss each other in the night.

That was the least likely — he didn't believe in lucky breaks. His sixth sense told him there was no one watching them as he moved Chloe through the dawn-lit streets. Maybe they thought he'd bring her in himself.

Poor little American idiot, caught up in a game that was way over her head. Both sides wanted her, and he knew his own organization well enough to know that both sides wanted her dead. She was a liability — she'd seen too much, and the sooner she was disposed of, the better.

The traffic had begun to pick up, the sun was rising over the rooftops when she suddenly froze. He knew what was coming, and he held her as she vomited into the street. Her roommate's body wasn't the first dead person she'd seen — she'd been there when he'd killed Hakim.

But her time with Hakim had momentarily inured her to reality. She'd had enough time to recover her equilibrium, to start thinking for herself, and the sight of her friend's brutally murdered body would have hit her full force.

She'd stopped, and he handed her a handkerchief to wipe her face as he hailed a taxi. One pulled up fairly quickly — despite the hour and the neighborhood and Chloe's obvious distress the taxi drivers of Paris were well trained. They could judge the cost of a patron's clothing from a block away, to know whether they were worth stopping for.

He bundled her into the cab and followed her, keeping his arms around her and her face tucked against his shoulder. The fewer people who saw her, the safer she'd be.

"Where to, *monsieur?*"

He gave an address in the fifteenth *arrondissement,* then leaned back. The driver took off, weaving through the burgeoning traffic with expert ease, but Bastien could see him watching them in his rearview mirror.

"Your girlfriend drink too much?" he asked. "I don't want her puking on my seats."

A legitimate enough concern, Bastien thought. "She's done for now. She's not my girlfriend, she's my wife. She's three months pregnant and having a hard time of it."

He felt her jerk in his arms, but he put his hand to the back of her head and held her down.

The cabdriver nodded knowingly. "Ah, that's the worst part. Don't you worry, madame, it doesn't last the whole time. My wife can't keep a thing down for the first three months, and then she can't stop eating. We've had four children, and it's always the same. Is this your first?"

So many questions, Bastien thought. "Yes," he said. "Any advice?"

That set him off, and for the next ten minutes Bastien got a lecture on everything from the food cravings of a pregnant woman to the best positions for sex when the wife is the size of a water buffalo. He listened with half an ear, making the appropriate responses, as he felt Chloe go limp in his arms once more.

The address he'd given was a modern high-rise with a basement garage — he'd spent a few weeks there several years ago with a beautiful model from Ethiopia. The last time in recent memory that he'd spent any time away from the job. She'd been warm, affectionate and sexually inventive, and he'd been very fond of her. He couldn't even remember her name.

"Could I ask you to drive us into the parking garage?" Bastien asked. "The elevator is right there and I could get my wife up to bed that much faster."

"Of course, *monsieur*." The poor man had no idea. He drove under the building, into the darkened parking garage, and pulled up to the elevator. He even got out of the taxi to help Bastien with Chloe's limp form. He never knew what hit him.

It would have made sense to kill him. Slit

234

his throat and leave him in the cul-de-sac behind the elevator, where no one would find him for days. By then Chloe would be long gone, and Bastien wouldn't care.

But at the last minute Bastien remembered the four children and the wife the size of a water buffalo, and for some reason he felt sentimental. It was probably just defiance — they had turned him into a man who would kill without compunction, and he wanted to do the opposite of what he'd been trained.

The driver had a roll of duct tape in the trunk of the taxi — it saved his life. Bastien wrapped him tightly, efficiently, stuffing the man's own handkerchief in his mouth before sealing it. They'd find him sooner or later — he figured he had at best six hours, maybe less. Chloe was still in the back seat of the cab, and he left her there, closing the door and climbing into the driver's seat. He flicked on the *Pas de Service* sign, and drove out into the early-morning sunlight, a taxi driver on his way home after a long night's work.

Too bad he didn't kill the driver — it would have given them a solid twelve hours before his wife reported him missing, maybe longer. And the disappearance of one taxi driver wouldn't be treated with much deference by the Paris police department. They would probably assume he'd gone off with a girlfriend and would return to the wrath of his wife eventually.

Another sign of why he'd outlived his usefulness, Bastien thought. Mercy was a weakness an operative couldn't afford. He glanced into the back seat. Chloe was curled up on the seat, his coat wrapped tightly around her body, her eyes open and staring. Sooner or later the shock was going to wear off, and she was going to start screaming. He needed to get her someplace safe before that happened.

He couldn't get her on a plane until that evening. For a moment he considered driving her to a smaller airport, like Tours, but then rejected it. They would be watching all the airports — he stood a better chance at Charles de Gaulle where he had a few connections even Thomason and the others didn't know about.

He found the house easily enough, though he spent a good twenty minutes circling it, alert to the possibility of surveillance. They'd stopped using the place two years ago when it had been hopelessly compromised, and while the Committee would remember to check it eventually, they would be more likely to go through the current safe houses first. Again, another few hours added to the precious horde he was building.

As far as he could tell no one was watching. It was a huge old house on the very outskirts of Paris, abandoned since the 1950s. It was sitting on a prime piece of real estate, and it was a wonder no one had forced enquiries into the ownership. On paper it belonged to the family of an old lady whose estate was so complicated it would never be resolved. In truth it had once been the home of a collaborator, the attics filled with looted treasure. That treasure had been part of the Committee war chest — whoever had owned the priceless works of art and jewelry would no longer be alive to benefit from them.

It also came equipped with a secret room where the previous owner had hidden for three weeks when the allies had liberated Paris. Bastien himself had spent several days there, and it was as protected a place as he could think of. He'd been operating on very little sleep for the past few days, and he needed just an hour or two before his brain could function properly once more. Before he could make the right decisions, instead of foolishly sentimental ones.

He drove down the narrow alleyway that

led behind the house, closed the sagging wooden gates behind them, and stashed the taxi near some bushes, hoping it might avoid aerial surveillance. He only needed a few hours.

He pulled Chloe from the back seat, and she moved like an automaton. It might be nice if he could count on her being out of it for the next few hours, but he'd already had more than his share of luck. He walked her through the empty building, up littered stairways, past broken windows and abandoned furniture, up three flights to the empty attics. Her dazed state lasted until he pushed the button hidden at the side of the old chimney and the door slid open, exposing the small room.

He was unprepared for her reaction. She went from limp obedience to full-bodied panic, lashing out at him, trying to bolt, screaming . . .

There were a number of ways to silence a person, render them unconscious. If he'd realized she was about to flip out he would have been able to do it more gently, but he had no choice but to hit her, just so, and everything drained from her terrified body.

He caught her as she fell, dragging her into the tiny room and closing the door behind them. They were enclosed in darkness, but he knew the space very well indeed. The rest of the house had no electricity, but this one room had once been very well wired. He wasn't about to check — he wasn't about to do anything that would signal their presence here. He dragged her over to the bed against the wall and dumped her down on it, lifting her legs up and pulling his coat around her. There was only one window in the place, overhead and covered with a blackout curtain that no light could penetrate.

She would be unconscious for at least an hour, maybe more. He glanced at his watch, the numbers glowing in the dark, the only light in the inky blackness. It was just after eight in the morning, and he hadn't slept for forty-eight hours. It wouldn't make sense to head out to the airport for another twelve hours, and in the meantime, even an hour's sleep would make a difference.

The bed was a narrow one, and he had no intention of doing anything to disturb her. He'd slept in worse places, and he was a creature of discipline. He took one of the thin wool blankets from the bed, covering her with the other, and stretched out on the hardwood floor. His body hurt — he felt old at thirty-two. Working for the Committee was a younger man's game — this kind of shit aged you like dog years.

He closed his eyes, willing himself to fall asleep immediately. But just as his spirit was rebelling against the Committee, his body was rebelling against its training. He lay there for five minutes, staring up into the darkness, listening to the sound of her breathing, wondering what the hell he was doing.

And then he slept.

She was trapped. Smothered in a blind darkness, the weight of it pressing down on her, stealing her sight, stealing her breath, darkness and the smell of blood all around, and she could see Sylvia lying there in a pool of red, her throat slashed, her eyes staring, her favorite dress ruined by the blood that had soaked into it. She would be furious about that. She would have wanted to be buried in that dress, she loved it so much. He'd slashed her throat — the man had *slashed* her *throat* — the same man who told her he'd kill her? And she'd let him take her, blindly, out into this darkness where she couldn't see, couldn't think, couldn't breathe, could only open her mouth to scream. . . .

240

He caught her as she flung herself off the bed, his arms like bands of iron around her body. She fought him like a crazy woman, alone in the darkness with death and blood pressing down on her, but he was much, much stronger. He put his hand over her mouth to silence her, and she bit him, as hard as she could, her teeth digging in, bit him until she could taste blood, and he didn't flinch.

"If you don't calm down I'll be forced to break your neck," he whispered in her ear as he held her tight against him. "I'm getting tired of dealing with you."

She struggled, though not as wildly, and he moved his hand from her mouth, enough to let her speak. She could barely manage to choke out the words.

"I . . . can't breathe. . . ." she whispered. "It's too dark. I . . . can't bear it. Please . . ." She didn't know what she was begging for, and she wouldn't have thought it would do her any good, but he suddenly hauled her up against him, so that they were both standing on the narrow bed, and with one arm he pushed overhead, and the darkness fell away as he opened a window in the low roof and held her up to it.

The air was cool and crisp and clean, and she drew in deep lungsful of it, drinking it like water in a desert. Slowly her panicked heart quieted its racing beat, slowly her breathing returned to a semblance of normalcy, and she looked out over the rooftops of Paris on a cold winter's morning as the first hint of calm touched her heart.

She leaned back against him as he supported her, letting the fear and tension drain from her body. "If you're tired of dealing with me then why don't you just let me go?"

He didn't answer. He simply shifted her body against his, and his face was next to hers as he looked out with her. "How long have you been claustrophobic?" he asked. "All your life? You don't strike me as someone who'd be crippled by complexes."

"Since I was eight. We own a lot of land in North Carolina, including an abandoned mine where my older brothers used to play. They didn't know I'd followed them, and I got lost there, and they didn't find me until the next morning. I haven't been able to bear dark, closed-in places ever since." She was talking too much, but she couldn't help it.

He said nothing. The air was icy cold — she could see her breath in front of her, see the mist from his mouth as well, and the two mingled in the sunlight before dissipating. She was still wrapped in his coat, but even through the layers of clothes she could feel the strength and power in his lean, elegant body.

And then the strength left her, and she sagged, and he lowered her down to the bed, reaching up for the handle on the blacked-out window.

"Please don't close it," she said. "I don't think I could stand the darkness again."

"It's cold," he warned her.

"I'll survive."

He left the window open a crack, just enough to let a narrow shaft of light into the room, as well as a few flakes of snow, and then he knelt down on the bed beside her. "The thing is," he murmured, "you have my coat. This room was cold already, but with the window open it's going to be freezing."

She tried to sit up, to pull his warm coat from her body, but he pushed her back on the bed with alarming finesse. And then he lay down next to her on the narrow bed. He covered them both with a thin wool blanket, turning on his side and pulling her back up against his chest, spoon-style. He was warm, even through the coat.

"I'll give you the coat," she offered in a

whisper. She didn't like having him so close to her.

"Screw the coat. Just be quiet and let me sleep for a few hours. We can argue about it when I wake up."

"And what if I'm not here when you wake up?"

"You will be. If you try to leave I'll shoot you. I'm a very light sleeper, and I'm not in a good mood. I suggest you try to sleep as well."

She moved her face against the threadbare mattress. Her cheekbone hurt, but Hakim hadn't touched her face. Hadn't gotten to it yet. And then she remembered. "You hit me!"

"And I'll do it again if you don't stop yammering," he said in a sleepy voice. "I did it to save your life. You were making such a fuss someone could have overheard you."

"Then why would you do it again?"

"To keep me from killing you," he said in that matter-of-fact tone that drove her crazy. "Now be quiet and let me sleep."

Clearly she wasn't going to be able to dislodge him, and any more attempts at trying would probably wind up with another enforced sleep, or possibly something worse. She shut her mouth, keeping her eyes trained on the narrow shaft of light that somehow made her able to breathe. As long as she could breathe she could survive. The things she had seen, had heard, were too horrific to even comprehend. If she stopped long enough to really feel anything but this odd, terrified numbness then she'd start screaming, and nothing would make her stop, unless Bastien snapped her neck as he'd threatened to do. She was cold, inside and out, cold and numb, and all she could do was try to survive. She took another breath, and without any warning the vision of Sylvia's body flashed into her mind and the numbness began to crumble.

She'd only seen her for a second, but that brief glimpse was forever burned into her brain. Someone had cut her throat, so deeply that Chloe could see bone. The pool of blood had been thick and viscous, and her eyes had been open and staring. Somehow that was the worst. Sylvia staring sightlessly into the world that had left her behind, and it had been Chloe's fault. She was the one who was supposed to be dead, not Sylvia. Sylvia, whose only fault was to love life too much. To prefer a good time to a weekend of work in the country.

Sylvia wouldn't have poked her nose

where it didn't belong. She would have cheerfully gone to bed with Bastien, translated and come back home with no disturbing questions. She'd always had the ability to ignore nagging discrepancies, but she'd died anyway, because her friend couldn't leave well enough alone.

"Stop thinking about it." Bastien's voice was a sleepy whisper in her ear, just a breath of sound. "There's nothing you can do about it, and brooding will only make it worse."

"It was my fault."

"Bullshit." The word sounded strange in such a quiet voice. "You didn't kill her. You didn't even lead them to the apartment — she was dead before you got there. For what it's worth, she died quickly."

"If I hadn't taken the job —"

" 'If' is a waste of time. Let her go. You can mourn her once you're safe at home."

"But —"

He put his hand over her mouth, silencing her last protest. "Go to sleep, Chloe. The best thing you can do for the girl is survive. Not let them destroy you, too. And in order to do that, you need sleep. I need sleep. Enough."

He was holding her against his body, and she couldn't turn to see his face. Instead she looked upward, through the narrow slit of light into the cold gray Paris sky. A few stray snowflakes drifted down into the room, landing on the black cashmere coat that had become almost a second skin. Drifting and melting and gone. And Chloe slept.

15

Chloe wasn't quite sure what had woken her up. She was alone in the bed, and cold, but it wasn't the dense, suffocating blackness. A small flashlight lay on the mattress beside her, the light a tiny beacon in the dark.

She sat up, slowly. Her entire body ached, her stomach was twisted in knots and her head hurt. Her best friend had been murdered because of her, and she was on the run for her life, with only an enigmatic killer to turn to.

But she was alive. Painfully, undeniably alive, despite the guilt and the fear that were tearing at her. The only question was, what would she do next? And where was Bastien?

There was always the possibility that he'd finally abandoned her. Taken her to this deserted house, dragged her up to a tiny room and locked her in there to slowly die of starvation.

But there was a window in the roof, and

she could climb out. And he had no reason to drag her all the way here if he wanted her dead.

If it was a question of simply hiding her body, then he wouldn't have abandoned her to starve or scream or fall to her death on the pavement below when she tried to escape. He would have killed her, quickly, painlessly. He'd promised her that much, and she found the notion comforting. It was a sick, twisted reaction, but she was beyond conventional thought and emotions. Everything had been stripped down to the bare minimum — survival. After seeing Sylvia's poor body she could no longer deny it. Her only means of survival was Bastien, and she wasn't going to fight him anymore. In fact, she was actually going to be glad when he reappeared in the tiny, closed-off room. Downright delirious. Though she had no intention of telling him.

She scooted over to the corner of the bed, wrapping his coat more closely around her, pulling the threadbare blanket over her as well. She was hungry, a notion that horrified her. When her nephew had died in a car accident she hadn't been able to eat for days — the very sight of food had made her nauseous. But now, even after seeing Sylvia's brutalized body, she was famished. Part of the survival instinct, she supposed. It didn't make her feel any less crass, but there it was. She wanted to survive, and she needed her strength to do it. And to be strong, she needed to eat. It was that simple.

Where the hell was he? At least he'd left her the light. She would have been screaming and climbing the walls if she'd awoken alone to total darkness.

He was right, she wasn't the sort to be crippled by complexes. She'd actually thought she'd gotten over it years ago. She had no problem with familiar places, elevators or dark basements.

It had been her fault in the first place. She'd been eight years old, tagging after her older brothers, always trying to do what the older kids did, refusing to realize her own limitations. The mines were off-limits, even to the older boys, but no self-respecting teenager would pay attention to danger warnings. They would, however, stop at bringing their younger sister on such a risky adventure, so her only choice was to sneak after them. One wrong turn too many, and she'd lost them in the warren of passageways deep below the ground.

They hadn't known she'd followed them, and no one realized she was missing for hours. Her flashlight had given out, and she'd been trapped in the darkness, in the middle of Miller's Mountain, while time lost its meaning and monsters crawled at her from every corner. By the time the search party found her she'd been in the dark for nineteen hours, and she didn't speak for two weeks after the ordeal.

Her father used to joke that after that she never stopped talking. She had a sensible family who carted her straight off to the best therapists, and by the time she was twelve she no longer had to sleep with a light on. By the time she was fifteen she could go down into the basement again, and by the time she left for college she thought she'd put it all behind her. Until last night.

It was probably just the accumulation of horrors that had suddenly made her weak and vulnerable again. She accepted that fact, grudgingly, just as she accepted she needed Bastien's help. And she might even tell him so, if he ever got his skinny ass back here.

Except he wasn't precisely skinny. She'd had a good look at his body in his apartment yesterday, whether she'd wanted to or not, and he was long and lean and smoothly muscled.

And she wasn't going to start thinking about that, even though she should have welcomed the distraction. In the end she was more comfortable thinking about being trapped in a small room with monsters trying to kill her than she was thinking about Bastien Toussaint's, or whoever he was, naked body.

She didn't even hear him approach. She didn't know whether the room was sound-proofed or he was simply very silent, but she was sitting cross-legged on the bed, staring fixedly at the tiny beam from the flashlight and trying not to think about him when the door slid open and he was standing there.

"Are you all right?" he asked as the door slid shut behind him.

She took a deep breath, trying to sound unconcerned. "I'm fine. I don't have any idea what time it is, but shouldn't we be starting toward the airport?"

He said nothing, moving into the room. She saw the spark, and a moment later he'd lit candles that she hadn't realized were there. "You're not going to be flying out tonight."

The knot in her stomach tightened. "Why not?"

"It's shut down. Most of Paris is, for that matter. The snow has brought everything to a standstill. That's why it's safe enough to light some candles. The snow . . ." He paused.

"That's all right. It's covered the roof window, hasn't it? I'm calmer now. Especially with some light."

He nodded. He'd managed to acquire a jacket somewhere, and she suspected he'd changed his clothes, though they were still all the same unremitting black. Which reminded her . . .

"I don't suppose there's a bathroom in this place?" she asked. "Otherwise I'm going to have to sample the snow first-hand."

"There is one. It's rudimentary, but it works."

She'd scrambled off the bed before he'd even finished his sentence. "Where?" Now that she knew relief was at hand it had become a great deal more urgent.

"It's on the floor below, directly beneath this. We'll have to go without light — we can't risk anyone seeing the torch."

She swallowed. She was better now, she reminded herself. Calmer. "Okay."

He blew out the candles, and in the sudden darkness she heard the door slide open. She swallowed, then jumped as she felt him take her hand.

She tried to pull away, instinctively, but he held on tight. "You're not going to find it without holding on to me," he said, matter-of-fact.

She took a deep breath, her hand still in his. "Of course," she said.

It helped, holding on to him, though she wasn't about to admit it. They walked through the cavernous darkness, down a narrow flight of stairs to a wall by an old fireplace. The door opened, and he put the tiny flashlight in her hand before giving her a little push. "Don't turn it on until the door is closed. I'll wait here."

It was utilitarian indeed, but the toilet flushed, the water ran cold from the sink, and there was even a square of mirror. She could have done without that — but curiosity got the better of her, and once she'd rinsed her mouth and done her best to wash up she took a curious look.

She'd expected hollow eyes, pale color, some kind of mark from the horrors of the last few days. Instead she looked like Chloe — practical, not unpleasant to look at, the damnably pedestrian freckles still scattered across her nose and cheekbones, the bane of her existence. Her hair was ridiculous, standing up around her face like a dark halo. But she was no saint either.

She took a deep breath, flicked off the light, and then realized she had no idea how to open the door. She rapped on it, lightly, and it slid open. She couldn't see him, but she didn't jump when he took her hand this time, and she was almost happy to be back in the safety of the little room in the attic.

She scrambled back onto the bed — the room was so small she'd bump into him if she remained standing. He lit the candles again, reached behind his coat and pulled out a gun, setting it down on the table. She looked at it like it was a poisonous snake, which it was, but it was there to help her, not kill her. She hoped.

"So what now?" she asked.

"Now we eat," he said, and she almost wanted to kiss him. "There weren't many stores open, but I managed to get us something. And don't tell me you don't feel like eating — you have to. You're not out of this yet, and you need your strength."

"I wouldn't tell you any such thing. I'm starving. What did you bring?"

She hadn't noticed the paper sack he'd

brought with him. He'd brought a couple of baguettes, some brie, two pears and two blood oranges. And a bottle of wine, of course. She wanted to laugh, but that would have been as bad as screaming. She'd never stop. Just breathe, she reminded herself.

He sat on the other end of the bed, their meager feast spread out before them. Their only utensil was his pocketknife, but he managed to open the wine with it, and they passed it back and forth to hack off pieces of bread and cheese.

The pear was divine — ripe and messy, and she wiped the juice from her mouth with the paper napkin he'd brought. And then she realized he was watching her, an odd expression on his face.

He passed her the bottle of wine. There was nothing else to drink, and no glasses, and she had no choice but to put her mouth where his had been. She took a long swallow, letting it begin to warm her, and when she passed it back to him their fingers touched. She drew back hastily, and again he smiled.

When they'd had enough he cleared the bed, putting the rest of the food on the small table next to the candle. Neither of them had touched the oranges, she noticed.

"What next?" she asked, leaning back against the wall.

"Next we sleep." He was spreading the thin blanket on the floor. There was just enough space in the tiny room for him to lie down by the bed.

"I've been sleeping for hours," she said. "Days, it seems. I don't know if I can sleep anymore."

He stared at her through the candlelit shadows. "Then what do you suggest we do?"

She had no answer to that, of course. In the two years she'd lived in Paris she'd learned a very creditable shrug, and she did just that, then stretched out on the narrow bed, staring fixedly at the candlelight while he watched her.

She had no earthly idea what he was thinking. Probably what an annoyance she was. That he should have let Hakim finish her off, or maybe that he should have killed her himself once she started fussing. But he hadn't, he was stuck with her, an albatross around his neck.

He blew out all but one of the candles, then stretched out on the floor. The hard, cold floor — she'd felt it on her bare feet.

"You don't have to sleep down there," she said suddenly, before she could regret the impulse. "There's room for both of us up here."

"Go to sleep, Chloe."

"Look, I know perfectly well you have no interest in me sexually, thank God. What happened yesterday was an aberration. . . ."

"Two days ago," he said, his voice matter-of-fact. "And it was part of my job."

That shut her up, for at least a moment, even though she'd known it. She took a deep breath. "So, clearly there's no problem with us sharing a bed. You're not going to touch me. The room is cold, and we'd both be a lot warmer if you slept up here."

She couldn't see his face clearly in the shadows. He was probably exasperated. "For the love of God," he murmured, "would you please stop prattling? You may have had too much sleep but I haven't had more than an hour or so in the last three days. I'm only human."

"I doubt that," she muttered. "Suit yourself." She turned away from him, with as close an approximation of an affronted flounce as she could manage while lying on a narrow bed, and stared at the cracked and stained wall.

"*Merde,*" he said. He rose, blew out the

candle and climbed into bed with her. "It's too small a bed not to touch you," he said in a grumpy voice.

Unfortunately true. She could feel him up against her back, his body curved around hers. If someone broke in he'd be in the way of any danger. That was the only reason why she wanted him there, she told herself. The only reason why she suddenly felt warm and safe and able to relax. It was simply a question of survival.

"I can put up with it," she replied. "But if you think that I —" His hand covered her mouth, stopping her midsentence. She could almost taste the pear juice on his fingers, an incredibly arousing sensation. She must still be hungry, she thought. But nothing under the sun was going to get her to eat a blood orange.

"Shut the fuck up," he said sweetly in her ear, "or I'll tie you up and gag you and put *you* on the floor. Understood?"

He'd probably do it, too. She nodded, as best she could with his hand covering her mouth, and he slowly moved it. She wanted to tell him that she was unwilling to share the bed after all, but he'd probably dump her on the hard cold floor if she said one more word.

His body was warm, deliciously so,

pressed up against hers. Pissed off as she was, she could still feel a heated languor spread through her body. She might be able to sleep some more after all, she thought, what with the wine and the warmth and the undeniable feeling of utter safety with his body wrapped around hers. She didn't want to — she wanted to keep awake just to spite him.

How was he going to get her out of Paris in one piece? The longer she stayed the more dangerous it became, the more likely it was that someone would find her. Would she be better off slipping into another country, leaving from Frankfurt or Zurich?

And how the hell was she going to do that with her passport back at the château? And someone must have found poor Sylvia by now. The police would have been called, they would have searched the place and found her belongings. Which meant the police would be looking for her as well.

Definitely a good thing. Even if they thought she'd somehow managed to kill Sylvia she'd rather take her chances in a French jail than running for her life, having to depend on one enigmatic man.

Everything had taken on a blessed haze of unreality. She'd seen him kill a man, and yet she could barely remember it. She'd been in such pain, and then the pain had stopped, and Hakim was lying on the floor.

He'd had sex with her. She would like to deny it, call it something else, but in truth it was sex, and he had come inside her. And to her everlasting shame, she had climaxed as well, powerfully.

But that didn't feel real anymore. Even the stark horror of Sylvia's body was beginning to fade. Maybe that would happen with everything, she thought, slowly relaxing her body against his. Maybe everything that had gone on in the last days she spent in France would wind up in a little bubble that never really touched her again. She wouldn't have to remember it, wouldn't have to deal with it. It would just be gone.

She didn't know if that was how people usually managed to get through traumatic periods in their life. All this made nineteen hours in a pitch-black cave seem like a child's prank in comparison. No one had died, no one had been hurt, no one had developed a kind of sick fascination for . . .

She didn't like the way her mind was going. She tried to inch away from Bastien's body, but his arm clamped around her waist, pulling her back. "Lie still," he muttered sleepily in her ear.

She could feel him all along her back,

the sensation of warmth and strength, bone and muscle and the unmistakable feel of him against her butt. It felt as if he had an erection, which surely couldn't be true, since he had no real interest in her and she had all the interest in the world in him.

Stockholm Syndrome, didn't they call it? When the hostage developed an unhealthy obsession with her captor. It was a normal reaction — they were in a life-or-death situation, and so far he'd managed to keep her alive. And to complicate matters, they'd had sex before she'd realized just how dangerous he was. And why couldn't she stop thinking about the sex?

Because she was lying in the shelter of his strong body, she could feel his cock against her backside and she was scared. The only thing standing between her and a painful, hideous death was his body, and she wanted it.

But he didn't want her, he'd simply been doing his job, and as he'd told her, he was very good at it. In the end his lack of interest was a very good thing. At least he wanted to keep her alive and safe and get her back home. Which was an even better thing.

Developing an unhealthy fascination for him was not unexpected. And once she was safely home everything would be back in perspective.

He was right, the bed was too small. There was no way she could move away from his body. She could turn her head just enough to see his face. He slept, which amazed her, and even her thrashing around hadn't woken him. She could barely make him out in the darkness, and she gave up trying, laying her head back down on the threadbare mattress, listening to the sound of his heartbeat against her back.

At least he had a heart — something she'd wondered about. He was human, he was warm and strong and ready to kill to keep her safe.

What more could a girl want in a man?

16

She really was the most damnable woman, Bastien thought, as her body finally stilled, her pulse slowed and she sank back into a reluctant sleep. She argued about everything, and then she looked at him with those huge brown eyes and for the first time in years he felt guilty.

He shouldn't have given in and gotten in bed with her. Yes, it was warmer with their body heat combined. Yes, the thin mattress on the bed was better than the even thinner blanket on the bare wood floor. Yes, they managed to fit their bodies together too damned well for his peace of mind. And yes, he wanted to push her over on her back, rip off her jeans and finish what he'd only begun a few short days ago.

He wondered if she'd felt his erection before she fell asleep. Probably not — she seemed totally oblivious to the effect she had on him. Which was just as well. He wasn't about to complicate this already tangled mess any more than he had to.

And making love to her would definitely complicate things.

He'd already fucked her — an entirely different matter. That should be enough. It was a normal enough response, and he knew himself well enough to try to dismiss it. Life-or-death situations brought out all sorts of primal appetites. Ugly but true. Danger aroused him.

And being in the presence of death, whether he'd been the one to kill or not, made him want to experience life on the most basic level. It made him want to fuck, and whether it was some caveman instinct about replenishing the species or a twisted fascination with sex and death, it still existed. He either acted on it or he didn't, depending on the circumstances. There were often women operatives around who shared the same reaction, and a fast, frenzied coupling usually only heightened their defenses in times of danger.

But Chloe wasn't an operative, she was ten years and a lifetime younger than he was, and a life-or-death situation would wipe all thought of sex from her mind. It would be a while before she got over the sight of her butchered friend, before she got over her hours with Hakim. She would, though. She might be not much more than a girl, but she was strong and resilient. She was back in a dark hole with him and she was sleeping, her suffocating claustrophobia at bay.

He could smell his scent on her, probably from wearing the coat that was now draped over both of them. For some reason he found that erotic. Then again, he was finding everything about her erotic.

The goddamned snow couldn't have come at a worse time. If not for that, she'd already be on her way across the Atlantic, out of his life for good, and he'd be concentrating on his assignment. His final assignment.

He had to finish what he started at the château. Find out how the territories were going to be redistributed, and who was going to take Remarque's place. Hakim had never held that much power. In fact, he'd been nothing more than a glorified administrative assistant, running things smoothly while the principals discussed disbursements. Of cabbage heads and fresh veal. Of long-range missiles and heat-seeking bullets. Of oranges and C4 and blood all around.

Christos was the big question mark. Why hadn't he bothered to show up, and when he did, what did he have planned? Because the Christos he knew never entered a situation without a very detailed plan. There would be at least one person at the château who was privy to those plans — that was the way Christos worked. It might be the baron, who wasn't nearly as harmless as he seemed, or perhaps even Monique. She was very difficult to pin down. She had a taste for pain, as well as sex, and he had yet to discover anything that made her vulnerable. It could be Ricetti or Otomi, Madame Lambert or even Ricetti's assistant. It didn't matter that the elegant young man servicing the Sicilian dealer was a Committee operative as well as Bastien. He wasn't the only one there, and anyone could change sides if the price was right.

One thing was certain. Christos couldn't be allowed to take over the leadership of the cartel, and it was up to Bastien to see to it. Thomason had been unclear as to what would happen to the rest of the dealers. Once the leader was disposed of, would they be left to reform? Probably — the Committee tended to prefer the devil they knew to the unknown, but it wasn't his responsibility. He only had to kill one more person. And then he was done. Finished. Gone.

He moved his head slightly, so that his face brushed her ridiculous tangle of hair. She looked very different as a shorn lamb. Younger, and more vulnerable. And even more desirable.

But looking like that helped remind him that she was off-limits. He had no right or reason to touch her again, and it would only complicate things.

And he needed to stop thinking about her and get what sleep he could. It didn't matter that the feel and the scent of her was all around him. He was cool enough to ignore trivial distractions like that. He closed his eyes, breathing in the scent and sound of her, and let himself sleep.

It was midday. Chloe wasn't quite sure how she knew that — the room was pitch-black, not a speck of light coming from the roof window. Her body had a natural clock — she woke up at eight-thirty every morning whether she needed to or not, and if something woke her in the middle of the night she always knew what hour it was, whether a clock was around or not.

Everything had been thrown off balance the past few days. She slept more than she'd ever slept in her life, probably a reaction to the horrors she'd seen. For all she knew she could have been asleep this time for fifteen minutes or three days.

Bastien was still with her. She'd turned in her sleep, and she lay in his arms, sprawled across him, her head on his shoulder, her hand on his chest, his arm around her. She should have yanked herself away, but she didn't. She didn't move a muscle, only her eyelids as she tried to decipher something, anything, through the darkness.

Bastien slept deeply and silently. Probably part of his self-discipline. He wouldn't allow himself to snore like most men. He slept so soundly he probably wouldn't even notice if she carefully pulled herself out of his loose embrace and turned her back on him. It was too exposed, lying like this. Too . . . confusing.

Stockholm Syndrome, she reminded herself unhappily. It had nothing to do with reality. She didn't even like the man. For now she had to stay with him, but once she was home things would be put into perspective and her momentary attraction would vanish with a dollop of self-loathing.

Well, perhaps not self-loathing. There was no denying that the man who called himself Bastien Toussaint was physically beautiful. And no denying that he saved her life, perhaps more than once, which would be bound to make her grateful.

She didn't want to think about it. She didn't want to think about anything, not the man beside her, not Sylvia, not the people who'd sat around that huge board table and pretended to talk about groceries. She would think about the snow. Thick and white and blanketing the city in stillness, drifting down in big flakes and clogging the roadways, closing the airports, trapping her in the arms of a killer . . .

"Stop thinking about it."

He hadn't moved, his steady breathing hadn't changed, but his soft voice broke the stillness like a shard of glass.

She rolled away from him, moving as close to the wall as she could. There was still no way she could keep from touching his long, lean body in such a narrow bed. "I thought you were asleep."

"I was. Until you woke up."

"Don't be ridiculous — I didn't move. I opened my eyes and that was all. Don't tell me the draft from my eyelashes woke you." Her voice was low and caustic, pushing him away as her body couldn't.

"No," he said, his voice low and sleepy, but she wasn't fooled. "Once you started thinking your blood began to move. I could feel your heartbeat speed up, your pulse race. Even though you didn't move a muscle."

"Well, aren't you special?" she said, sarcastic.

"I beg your pardon?"

Of course he wouldn't know the American reference. He might read pulses and heartbeats but he'd probably never watched *Saturday Night Live* and the Church Lady. Maybe he'd never watched television at all. It wouldn't surprise her. He'd said he never even went to movies.

What did surprise her was that even with her back safely to him she was still acutely aware of him. Still had a totally irrational longing for him. One that would lead nowhere and only embarrass and frustrate her.

"What time is it?"

"Late morning," he said. He moved then, away from her, getting out of bed, and she breathed a sigh of what she told herself was relief.

"So what do we do now? Go outside and make snow angels? I don't think I'm dressed for it." Yes, she sounded nicely cool. He wouldn't have the faintest idea how jumbled her emotions are.

He lit the candles. He had the very beginnings of a stubble, something she found oddly shocking. Throughout their long ordeal he'd never been less than perfectly groomed, whether he'd just killed someone or spent hours sitting on the floor drinking wine.

His long hair was loose and tousled around his face, and he looked rumpled and surprisingly human. Something Chloe found even more disturbing.

"I must be interfering with your personal life," she said, out of the blue, and could have bit her tongue.

He'd been rummaging in the sack of food, coming up with the rest of the baguette and the oranges. He turned to look at her, an odd expression in his dark, unreadable eyes.

"What do you mean?"

"Well, you've just sort of disappeared with me. Don't you have a partner or someone who's going to wonder where you are?" She wasn't making things better, but she couldn't seem to stop. Always her great failing, talking too much, she reminded herself.

"Partner?"

"You don't need to echo everything I say," she said, irritated and embarrassed.

"I mean a significant other. Someone you live with . . ."

"Are you talking about another man?" He cut straight to the chase, and he looked far too amused for her peace of mind. "You've decided I'm gay?"

"I was trying to be delicate about it," she said, letting her irritation show. "It just seemed likely."

"And why did it seem likely?"

She was going to borrow his knife and cut out her tongue, she thought miserably. How the hell did the conversation ever get to this point? Why hadn't she just shut up in the first place?

"That's all right, Chloe," he said, when she couldn't come up with an answer. "You think I'm gay because I don't want to fuck you. Isn't that it?"

It was getting worse and worse, and his deliberate crudeness made the color rush to her face. "I'm not that conceited."

"Aren't you? Don't you think the only reason a man doesn't put moves on you is if he doesn't like any women? And why are you so interested? I wouldn't have thought my sexual preferences would matter one way or another."

"They don't."

"Then why did you ask?"

From somewhere she found her voice. "Don't do this," she said. "It's bad enough to be trapped in a dark hole with you, don't back me against the wall verbally. I was just curious about you."

"You've already been back against a wall physically. In more ways than one," he said, and she remembered all too clearly those moments in the château, with his body inside hers, the dark, convulsive pleasure of it.

"Enough!" she said, her voice strangled.

To her amazement he dropped it, sitting back on the bed a safe distance away from her, handing her the now stale baguette. "We finished the cheese, but there are a couple of oranges left. Later on we'll get you a decent meal."

"Where? At the airport? Has the snow stopped?" She took the hunk of stale bread he offered and began to chew on it.

"I've been here with you the whole time, Chloe. Your guess is as good as mine. But we're leaving this place before long. The trick to hiding out is to keep moving. It won't take them long to find us here, and I want to be gone before they do. Fortunately the snow will have covered the taxi, so even if they use a helicopter they're unlikely to see it. But the sooner we get out of here the better."

The bread tasted like dust, but she kept chewing. "Where are we going?"

He began to peel one of the oranges. The fruit lay bloodred in his hands, even as the sweet citrus smell filled the room, and Chloe shuddered.

"I'm not sure yet. Open your mouth." He held a section of orange, but she shook her head.

He moved, one of those lightning-fast moves that always shocked her, and he'd caught her chin in one hand. "Open your mouth and eat the orange, Chloe."

She had no choice, not with his long fingers cupping her face, not with the dark eyes in his impassive face giving her no room to wriggle. "Open your mouth," he said again, softer, almost seductive, and she did, letting him place the piece of fruit against her tongue, the taste sweet and tart.

And for one mad moment she thought his mouth, his tongue would follow. Madness indeed, as he sat back, away from her, and she slowly ate the orange. He didn't want her, thank God. He would keep her safe from everyone else, and she was safe from him. She had to be grateful for that small mercy. She had to be.

"I'm sorry." Her words came as a surprise to her, but even more of a shock to him. He turned to stare at her in the tiny, candlelit room.

"What did you say?"

She cleared her throat. She could taste the blood orange on her mouth. She could taste his fingers on her lips. "I said I'm sorry. For asking you rude questions, for arguing with you, for trying to run away and not listening to you. You've gone out of your way to protect me, and all I do is whine and complain. I'm sorry. And I'm grateful."

He rose from the bed, stepping away from her, as far as he could in the tiny room. His eyes were hooded, unreadable, watching her. "Grateful? I thought you considered me a fiend from hell."

"You are," she said, her irritation bubbling up again. "But you've saved my life, at least twice, and I never said thank you."

"Don't thank me now. When you're safely back in the States you can spare a kind thought for me."

"Why do you care? I don't understand why you're going to so much trouble for me. I know you said you rescued me from Hakim on a whim, but I don't believe it. I think you're not as cold-blooded as you think you are, and when push came to shove you couldn't let Hakim kill a woman. I know deep down that you're a decent human being, even if I don't know who and what you are, or even your real name."

"You don't need to know my name. Besides, you're deluded," he said, his voice clipped. "I'm a cold-blooded bastard. I don't make a habit of rescuing women who wander into places they should keep away from. In your case it's easier to get you back to the States than get rid of you here."

"You wouldn't kill me. I know you killed Hakim, but I don't think you could kill a woman."

"Don't you?"

The faint mockery in his voice was very unsettling. Her father was right, she never could stop talking when she needed to. But she'd had to apologize, to thank him. He had saved her, was still protecting her, presumably out of the basic human decency he seemed so determined to deny. It couldn't be anything personal.

He moved closer to her, his body blocking out the candlelight, and caught her chin in his hand, drawing her face up to his. "Look at me, Chloe," he said softly. "Look into my eyes, and tell me you see the soul of a decent man. A man who wouldn't kill unless he was forced to."

She didn't want to look. His eyes were dark, opaque, empty, and for a brief moment she could almost see the blackness inside. She tried to jerk her head away, but his hand tightened, holding her firmly, and his face was close to hers. His mouth was close to hers, and she could smell the blood oranges on his breath. "Tell me I'm a good man, Chloe," he said in a soft, dead voice. "Show me just how stupid you really are."

The words were cruel, harsh, and there was no light or warmth in his face. Only pain, hidden so deep inside that no one could see it, driving, wrenching pain that was tearing him apart. She could see it, feel it, like a tangible entity in the tiny room, and she put her hands on his wrist, not to pull his harsh grip away, just to touch him.

"I'm not stupid," she said, feeling suddenly very calm and certain. He wasn't moving away, and she was going to kiss him. She was going to put her mouth against his because she wanted to. And he was going to kiss her back, because beneath that darkness was a need as powerful as hers.

And then it wasn't going to be up to her, because he dipped his head closer, and his mouth brushed hers, and her body rose to meet his mouth.

But it was no more than a featherlight kiss. "I'm the devil incarnate, Chloe," he whispered. "And you're an idiot if you can't see that."

"Then I'm an idiot," she said, waiting for him to kiss her again.

But he didn't. They stayed like that, for a long, endless moment, and then he said, "Come in, Maureen." The hidden door slid open, flooding the tiny room with blinding light.

It slid shut again, but by then Chloe had retreated to her corner of the bed, trying to make her eyes adjust to the newcomer.

"Am I interrupting something, Jean-Marc?" The woman's voice was rich with amusement. "I can always come back later."

"You weren't interrupting anything more than a little lesson in survival. Maureen, this is your charge, our little lost American." He turned his dark, opaque eyes back to Chloe. "And this, *ma chère*, is Maureen. My sometimes wife. She's a very good operative — I would only trust you to the best. You'll be in her hands from now on. She'll get you to the airport and safely on your way back home — she hasn't failed a mission yet."

"Oh, I've failed one or two in my time," Maureen said in her rich, warm voice. "But in the end I've always made it right. We'll be just fine, Chloe and me." She was an attractive woman in her midthirties, chic, well-dressed in a suit that Sylvia would have died for.

Chloe's thoughts stopped cold at the thought. She managed a stiff smile before turning her attention back to Bastien. Or Jean-Marc, as she'd called him. Or the man with no name. "You're leaving me?"

He made no effort to hide his amusement. "I'm abandoning you, my sweet, leaving you to Maureen's tender mercies. I've let my work slide for far too long, and I'm afraid I can't wait any longer. Have a safe trip home and a good life."

And then he was gone.

17

"Another one of Jean-Marc's conquests," Maureen said, moving into the room. "Poor thing. You're all alike, with your pathetic eyes and pretty faces. Jean-Marc never could resist a pretty face." She sounded affable enough, and she set the suitcase she was carrying down on the bed. She tilted her head to one side, surveying Chloe. "Though maybe you're not his usual type, come to think of it. He's never been one for the damsels in distress. I'm surprised he didn't get rid of you himself."

Her offhand words shocked Chloe into speech. "He wouldn't —"

"Oh, I assure you he would. And has. But for some reason he wants to keep you safe, so he's enlisted my help. What have you been calling him?" She snapped open the suitcase, pulling out some clean clothes.

"I beg your pardon?"

"Well, he certainly wouldn't go by Jean-Marc. I doubt that's even his real name.

He's probably forgotten what it is. Last I heard he was using Étienne."

"Does it matter?"

"No," Maureen said. "You'll want to change into some fresh clothes before we take off. And what in God's name happened to your hair? You look like you've been attacked by Edward Scissorhands."

"I cut it." There was a pair of black trousers, black shirt, even black bra and panties. Must be regulation issue for all . . . spies. Operatives. Whatever they were.

"I can see that you did," Maureen said. "Never mind — I'm sure someone can fix it when you get back home. Go ahead and change." She leaned against the wall, her arms crossed in front of her, waiting.

The last thing Chloe was going to do was strip down in front of her. "Could I have a little privacy?"

"You Americans are all absurdly prudish, aren't you? I would have thought spending a few days with Jean-Marc would have gotten you over such squeamishness."

Chloe said nothing. Clearly Maureen wasn't going to move, and she had no choice but to pull the turtleneck off.

The room was cold. She looked down at her arms, but the livid marks were almost gone. Two days ago she'd been tortured and bleeding. Now she looked nothing more than a little worn-out and a little cold.

She reached for the new shirt, but Maureen stopped her. "Take off everything," she said. "You'd be surprised at what people can trace when it comes to clothing. We don't want to give anything away."

"I have no idea what you're talking about."

"Of course you don't. Take the bra off. Though where the hell you could have gotten such a thing astonishes me. Not in Paris. It's the sort of thing nuns would wear. Don't you have any sense of style?"

"Not much. And who says those clothes will fit me?"

"Jean-Marc told me what size to get. Trust me, they'll fit. So tell me, how was he?"

Chloe was reluctantly changing her bra before Maureen's interested eyes, removing her plain white cotton one for the black lace confection that did indeed fit her perfectly. "How was he?" she echoed.

"In bed, girl," she said, impatient. "We had an affair a number of years ago, and I still remember his . . . inventiveness . . . quite fondly. You don't look as if you had the stamina to keep up with him."

She finished changing quickly, not giving Maureen any more time to catalogue her physical deficiencies. "It's none of your business."

"Of course it is. I need to know how enraptured he is. He's been acting strangely for the past few months, and falling for an innocent little bird like you is one of the oddest things he's done."

"He hasn't fallen for me. He simply felt responsible after he . . ." Her voice trailed off, uncertain as to how much Maureen really knew.

"After he killed Hakim." Maureen finished the sentence for her. "Well, at least he got that part of the mission right," she muttered. "Though why he didn't wait until after you were dead is beyond my comprehension. And why he didn't just finish you when he realized you were still alive." She shook her beautifully coiffed head.

"He hadn't planned to kill Monsieur Hakim —"

"Of course he had. That was what he was there to do, among other things. You just happened to be in the way. Don't tell me he managed to convince you he'd wasted Hakim for your sweet sake?"

"No," Chloe said bleakly.

She stood, and to her horror Maureen began examining the blanket, then stripped it from the bed. "It doesn't look like the two of you did anything while you were here, but you never can tell. We're better safe than sorry when it comes to DNA testing."

"You're way off base. Bas . . . Jean-Marc has no interest in me. I'm an inconvenience that he's passed on to you."

"So it seems. But I can't imagine he didn't at least sample the wares. He's got a strong appetite, and he'd find you attractive in a wholesome, American sort of way."

Chloe said nothing. Even with the light from the open door the room felt more claustrophobic than it ever had, probably from Maureen's poisonous cheer. "Could we leave? I'd like to go straight to the airport if we could."

Maureen snapped the suitcase shut, the discarded clothes and sheet tucked inside. "Yes," she said cheerfully. "It's time to leave. But I'm afraid you're not going to the airport."

It was getting colder by the minute. The old house was unheated, and even with the bright sunlight reflected from the snow it only seemed icier.

"Where are we going then?" she asked.

"I'm going to meet with my supervisor and tell him I finally accomplished my mission. And you, my dear, aren't going anywhere. You're going to die."

Bastien's instincts had always been infallible. He would know when a mission was going to go south, when a mole would turn, when to strike and when to abort. He would know who he could trust, and just how far he could trust them, and he would know who, in the end, would betray him.

He'd lost that skill in the past year. Either lost it, or just didn't care. His job had been simple — get rid of Hakim, keep track of the new division of territories and make certain Christos wasn't put in charge of the cartel.

But he'd stopped listening to the voices that warned him of danger. They hadn't gone away — they were whispering in his ear, insidious voices, warning him. Warning him of what?

He drove through the snow-blanketed streets of Paris with his usual suicidal speed. There was marginally less traffic than usual, but those who were out had less room to move, and the snow hadn't improved their attitude. The car Maureen had brought him was a late-model BMW, with too much power for the snowy streets, but he slid and spun his way toward the hotel with dexterity, only clipping a taxi once.

A taxi. They'd found the man he'd trussed and gagged in the basement parking garage. Found him dead, his throat cut open like Chloe's friend. He should have been prepared for that — even with all his precautions they'd managed to keep track of him. He'd grabbed the paper when he'd gone to find Maureen, and he'd spared a thought for the driver's wife the water buffalo and their four children. If he made it through the next few days he might even see about getting some money to them. It wouldn't replace their husband and father, but it would lessen some of the difficulties the work of the Committee had delivered.

It would have been Thomason who'd ordered the hit, Thomason who was having him followed and cleaning up any witnesses, any survivors. He must have seen through Bastien's usually adept lies. It was standard operating procedure — an organization such as theirs wouldn't exist for very long if people were left alive to talk and to wonder. Secrecy was the most important tenet, even more important than whatever mission they'd been assigned. They were all the same — to save the world. And yet no matter how many people he'd killed, the world never seemed to be saved.

He was nearing the hotel. A small suite was reserved for him, and most of the cartel was already assembled, awaiting the arrival of Christos. He was dressed and ready to resume his life, knowing Chloe Underwood was being taken care of by the best agent he knew. Maureen had worked on a number of missions with him, including the latest as his wife. She would get her safely on the plane, and then Chloe would no longer be their problem. His problem. In fact, by putting her in Maureen's hands, he'd already finished his part of it. He was ready to move on, concentrate on what mattered and not a momentary distraction.

Except that something wasn't right. It was gnawing at him, tickling his nerve endings, and he couldn't quite place what it was. He'd trust Maureen with his life. Their affair had matured into a deep friendship that went beyond the boundaries of the all-powerful Committee, and he knew he could count on her.

So why did he keep wanting to turn back, to make sure?

Maybe it was simply that he was having a hard time letting go of Chloe. He hadn't allowed himself to care about another human being for a long time. He wasn't sure he actually cared about Chloe, but he'd chosen to protect her, and that had put some sort of connection between them that sex hadn't.

If it was that simple — that he didn't want to give her up — then he could easily ignore that nagging little voice. Sentimentality had no place in his life. He'd lost any trace of it long ago, if, in fact, he'd ever had any. When he'd gotten news of his mother and Aunt Cecile's death in a hotel fire in Athens he'd simply shrugged. That part of his life was long over, and he'd dismissed it.

Just as he needed to dismiss all thoughts of Chloe and concentrate on finishing this last mission. She was no longer his problem, his responsibility. In fact, she never had been. He'd just chosen to make her so. And now he could forget about her.

He took the turn so quickly the car slid halfway across the snow-narrowed street, and he just barely missed hitting another taxi. He was being an idiot, and he accepted that fact, but he was going back to the old house on the outskirts of Paris. Maybe he just had to say goodbye. Maybe he simply had to make sure she was all right. Maybe he wanted to kiss her one more time. Make love to her the way she deserved.

That wasn't going to happen. If he had any sense at all he'd ignore this sense of foreboding as the extraneous bullshit it was, put it behind him and finish the job. Take out Christos, and see whether Thomason was really going to have him killed as well.

But right now he didn't seem to have much sense. And he wasn't going to be able to move on until he made sure his reluctant charge was safe.

Chloe didn't bother to say anything stupid, like "what do you mean?" She knew exactly what Maureen meant. Had known since the woman walked into their tiny, safe haven and Bastien had abandoned her, despite her talk of new haircuts and fancy underwear. The woman had no intention of letting her get on any plane. That was what the new clothing was for — so they couldn't trace her by any mark on her own clothes. Couldn't trace her body.

290

She was past the point of panic. "Is that why Bastien brought you here? Because he couldn't do it himself?"

"Ah, Bastien. This particular identity hasn't been particularly fortunate. If he were his old self you never would have left the château. As it is, I'm here to clean up the mess he made. Attention to detail is the only way to success."

She was between Chloe and the open door. She was taller than Chloe, and despite the chic clothing she looked as if she were quite a bit stronger. And Chloe was hardly at her best.

She sat on the edge of the bed in her new, perfectly fitting clothes, and looked into the eyes of her killer. She felt numb, and though she despised herself for it, unable to move. She was going to sit there like a lamb waiting for slaughter, putting up no sort of fight. . . .

The hell she was. She sat up straighter, but Maureen was already ahead of her.

"You're not going gentle into that good night?" she said with a faint smile. "That's all right. I owe you a fair amount of pain — you screwed me over and I don't like being made to look a fool in front of my superiors."

"What are you talking about?"

"Jean-Marc. Or Bastien, or whatever you call him. You're just another example of his ambivalence. You've distracted him, when he was a man who could never be distracted. Killing you will be my gift to him."

"Did he bring you here to kill me?"

"You already asked me that, *chérie*. And you may have noticed, I didn't answer. You're just going to have to wonder about that with your dying breath. Now start moving."

"Where?"

"This room has steel reinforcements, and we're directly above the bathroom. They're likely to survive a fire more than the rest of this old bundle of dry wood, and I don't take chances. One screwup is enough."

"You're going to burn the place? Then why did you bother making me change my clothes?"

"God is in the details. Except, of course, I don't believe in God. But I never count on anything. They may find enough of your body, and I don't want them ID-ing you. If you were German or English I wouldn't have to be so careful, but the Americans tend to make a huge fuss when one of their citizens is murdered overseas.

Out the door, *chérie*. We've wasted enough time as it is."

"And what if I refuse to move? Make you kill me here?"

"You won't. You'll put off dying as long as you possibly can. It's human nature. You'll do everything I tell you to do, in the hope that you'll find a weak spot, a chance to escape. You won't, but you can't believe that. So you're going to do exactly as I say, walk out that door and down the stairs to the far corner of the second floor. Where I'll cut your throat and then torch the place. I've already set the accelerants."

But Chloe's mind wasn't interested in accelerants. "You'll cut my throat?"

"It works quite well. It's quiet — no noisy gun, and you won't be able to make anything more than a gurgling noise for as long as you live. The drawback in your case is that you don't die right away, but for me that's one of the perks. I have a personal grudge this time. Not just for Jean-Marc's sake. I don't usually make mistakes, but because of you I made a major one. And I intend to make it right with a vengeance."

"What are you talking about?"

"Are you totally dim-witted? Your friend. I had the apartment number, a general description, and there she was. How was I to know you had a roommate? It was very embarrassing to be told I'd killed the wrong woman."

"Embarrassing?" Chloe echoed. The empty wine bottle was still on the table. It wouldn't be much protection against a knife or a gun, but it would be something. If she just had the nerve to dive for it.

"Though in the end there's no real harm done. I would have had to kill her anyway — it just would have been done in a different order. And this time I'll complete my mission with no more mistakes."

"You killed Sylvia?"

Maureen made an exasperated noise. "Haven't you been listening? Of course I killed her. And she put up far more of a fight than I'm expecting from you. In the dark she must have thought I was a thief, because she fought like the very devil. I still have bruises. But I know you're not going to give me any trouble —"

Chloe slammed her across the face with the empty wine bottle. The heavy glass shattered, but Chloe was already sprinting past her, running for her life, as Maureen screamed in rage behind her.

She couldn't remember much about the layout of the old house, but even in her panic she managed to find the stairs. She could hear Maureen following her, but she had a good head start, and she ran down the stairs as fast as she could.

She slid on the last flight, going down hard and losing precious moments. By the time she'd managed to scramble to her feet again Maureen was in sight on the next landing.

The stairs ended, and Chloe kept moving, running blindly, listening to the sounds of Maureen's heavy breathing as she closed in on her.

At the last minute luck was with her — she stumbled through a door that led into the murky, snow-lit outdoors. She was at the top of an outside flight of stairs leading down into the yard. She could even see the snow-covered mound of the taxi that had brought them here, but all trace of foot-prints had been covered up by the heavy snow, and it lay on each step at least a foot deep.

Chloe started down the stairs, fighting her way through the heavy wet snow, but it was too late. She was halfway down when Maureen caught up with her, grabbing her short hair and yanking her back.

"Bitch," she spat, and her face was covered in blood. No longer chic and pretty, she was murderously angry. She took her and slammed her against the snowy stairs, holding her down. The knife in her hand was small but capable, and Chloe knew a bleak, surrealistic moment of despair. Why did it always have to be a knife? Why couldn't someone just try to shoot her, cleanly and quickly, instead of carving into her flesh like a surgeon on amphetamines.

She closed her eyes, no longer brave, ready to face death, and she heard Maureen's throaty laugh. "That's the girl," she said. "No more arguments."

"Maureen! Stop!"

It couldn't be Bastien's hoarse voice — he'd set this up. Had he changed his mind, come back? Changed his mind as he had at the château, and decided to save her?

"Go away, Jean-Marc!" Maureen said in an eerily calm voice, not bothering to look away from Chloe as she lay on the snow-covered stairs. "You know this is for the best. We have no choice."

"Leave her alone!" The voice was closer, calmer now, but Maureen wasn't listening.

"Make your choice, Jean-Marc," she said. "Her or . . ." Her voice broke at the sound of the muffled gun, and she looked down in surprise. "Shit," she muttered. And fell backward, sliding down the snowy slant of the stairs until she landed at the bottom, at Bastien's feet.

There was a wide trail of bright crimson blood on the snow where Maureen's body had slid, harsh red against the brilliant white. Chloe tried to move, but Bastien's voice stopped her.

"Stay where you are," he said, sounding oddly hollow. He bent down, effortlessly lifting Maureen's limp body in his arms. For the moment he seemed to forget Chloe, as he carried Maureen toward the abandoned taxi, kicking the deep snow away, opening the door against the heavy drifts.

Chloe rose on unsteady legs, making her way down the stairs, following the trail of blood, her movements muffled by the thick snow. She should run, into the streets, and maybe he'd give up trying to find her.

She wasn't going anywhere.

He had laid Maureen on the back seat. Her eyes were open, and he reached out a hand and gently closed them. "I'm sorry, love," he whispered, before backing away and closing the door.

He seemed shocked to see her standing there, so close. She was fine, Chloe thought dazedly. She had gone past the ability to react, all she could do was stand there in the silence of the winter day, staring up at him, as the snow began to fall around them.

18

A few feet separated them, a few feet of blood and snow. She didn't even think about it, she went to him, into his arms, pressing her face against his shoulder, clinging to him, shaking so hard she thought her bones would shatter, shaking to keep from screaming.

His arms came around her, strong, safe arms, holding her tight against him. He was powerful, warm, and the faint tremor in his body had to be her imagination.

He put a hand against her head, gently stroking her hair. "Breathe," he whispered in her ear, like a lover. "Just breathe, slowly. Calm, deep breaths."

She hadn't even realized she'd been holding her breath. His hand was cupping her chin, his thumb gently stroking her throat, almost massaging her into breathing once more, and she took a deep, shuddering gasp, and then another, and then another.

"We need to get out of here," he whispered, and she wanted to laugh, somewhere near hysteria. There was no one there to hear her — Maureen was dead, the world was a whirling mass of blood and snow, and if she screamed no one would hear. . . .

But she wouldn't scream. She could absorb his heat, his strength, his breath into her bones. She stayed that way, clinging to him, and he made no effort to make her move, giving her the time she needed.

She raised her head finally. He looked the same, but then, he always did. She'd seen him kill twice, and he betrayed no reaction at all. He was a monster, not even human.

But he was her monster, keeping her safe, and she was past the point of caring. "I'm ready," she said.

He nodded, releasing her, keeping hold of her hand. She was icy cold, wet from the snow, and she clutched his hand so tightly it hurt her fingers, but she wouldn't let go. He led her away from the old house, pausing long enough to kick some snow over the trail of blood that spilled down the last few stairs. The sky was growing darker now, though she wasn't sure whether it was the storm or the hour. Or maybe her own willfulness,

closing down a life that was becoming unbearable. She might be calling the darkness in around her, so that it would
eventually close over her like a dark
blanket, shutting out everything, the light,
the horror, the pain. . . .

He was being very gentle with her, she
thought absently, as he opened the door of
a shiny car she didn't recognize, settling
her into the front seat, fastening the seat
belt. She'd left his coat behind, and suddenly it seemed terribly important, as if
she'd left her only security back in the
house.

"Your coat . . ." she said, taking in a
shuddering gasp of breath.

"Fuck the coat. I don't need it."

"I do."

He didn't move, standing there in the
open door, looking down at her, blotting
out the sky. Wondering if she'd lost her
mind, Chloe thought. The answer was yes.

After a moment he nodded. "Don't
move," he said, closing the door of the
small car.

She wanted to laugh. She couldn't move.
He'd fastened the seat belt, and her fingers
wouldn't work to unfasten it, her legs
wouldn't work to support her. It was
taking all her strength to keep breathing as

he'd told her to do, slow, deep breaths, and she concentrated on that.

It seemed as if he'd only been gone a moment. He opened her door and tucked the coat around her shoulders, then looked down into her face. "Are you all right?"

"Of course," she said.

Wrong answer, she presumed, because a frown crossed his face for a moment. But he simply nodded. "Just hold on."

What else did he think she would do, she thought, letting her head fall back against the seat and the bunched up coat. Run for it? Her running was over.

She closed her eyes as he drove fast, into the heart of Paris, listening to his calm voice with only a small part of her brain. The rest of her was drifting with the snow, snuggled inside his coat. "The airport is open again, but you're going to have to wait. I have to get to the hotel — I've let things hang for too long, and the only way to keep you safe is to keep you with me."

That was enough to make her open her eyes. "Why did you come back?" She didn't recognize her own voice — it was small and strained. What on earth was wrong with her? She felt encased in ice.

He didn't even look at her, concentrating on driving. That was the one thing she'd never done — drive on the Paris streets. She was brave enough to tackle most things, but driving in Paris was too much even for her. Sylvia had always laughed and called her a wuss. Sylvia . . .

"Breathe," he said sharply. And she did.

He drove right up to the front of the Hotel Denis. One of the very best in Paris, small and exclusive and elegant, and he was driving up to the discreet front entrance, jumping out and coming to her door before the doorman could do more than open it. He said something to the man, but she wasn't listening, and he unfastened her seat belt and helped her out, keeping the coat around her shoulders, his arm around her waist, his head low to hers like an attentive lover.

"Look sleepy," he whispered in her ear. In German, she realized without surprise. "I've told them you're just in from Australia and you're jet-lagged. They won't expect anything from you." He brushed a kiss against her temple, part of his act, and if she could she would have turned and kissed him on the mouth.

They moved through the small, tasteful lobby of the old hotel. It seemed as if a thousand eyes were upon her, watching their progress as he guided her toward the elevators, his arm around her shoulder, holding the coat around her. She was cold anyway, her chest wet from the snow, and not even the coat could warm her.

He somehow managed to get her up to his room — she was past the point of noticing. He closed the door behind them, switching on the light, and she was barely aware of her surroundings. "I'm cold," she said, her voice unnaturally loud. She dropped the coat off her shoulders, onto the floor. "I'm cold and I'm wet." She touched the front of her shirt, pulling the damp fabric away from her body. She couldn't figure out how she'd gotten snow on her front.

"You need to rest. I'll have some new clothes sent up for you. I wasn't expecting to bring you back here. The bedroom's behind you. Why don't you get under the covers and try to warm up?"

She pulled at the soft silk jersey, then looked down at her hands in sudden horror. They were streaked with red.

She looked up at him, into his impassive face. He'd wiped his hands, but she could see the brownish red traces of dried blood on them. And his shirt was wet — she could see the shiny dampness in the afternoon light.

"Have you been hurt?" she asked. "Your shirt . . ." Without thinking she put her hand against his chest. Against his beating heart.

He shook his head. "It's Maureen's blood," he said. "It's on both of us."

It was the final straw. "Get it off me!" she cried, yanking at her shirt, sobbing. "Please . . . I can't . . ." The soft knit fabric simply stretched beneath her panicked hands, and she lost whatever calm distance she'd had. She was there, in the present, covered with a dead woman's blood, as he was, and if she didn't get it off her she was going to explode.

"Calm down," he said, reaching for the hem of her shirt and yanking it over her head. Exposing her body, the lacy black bra, the streaks of blood on her pale skin.

He swore. She was past the point of speech, yanking at her clothes as she gasped for breath, and he simply picked her up, carried her through the darkened bedroom, into the bathroom. It was instantly flooded with bright light, illuminating her skin. He put her into the shower, half-dressed, and turned it on full force, getting in with her as the hot water blasted down on them both.

He stripped off the rest of her clothes,

quickly, efficiently, taking the soap and washing her as she stood there, frozen, shivering beneath the steamy downpour. His hands were fast, rough, covering her body, shocking her into action, and she pulled at his clothes, at the blood-soaked fabric, sobbing now.

He pulled his shirt over his head, his chest streaked more darkly with blood, then stripped out of the rest of his clothes, keeping a steady arm around her as he did so. She took the soap from him and scrubbed at his chest, covering him with lather, desperate to wash any trace of blood away, desperate for it all to be washed away. . . .

"Enough," he said, taking her hand, making her drop the soap onto the tiled floor of the shower, pulling her against him under the full force of the shower, her body pressed up against his, wet and naked, the both of them.

She needed it to go away, all of it. The water wasn't enough, the soap couldn't banish it. She needed more, and his erection against her belly was proof that he did, too. In normal times he might not want her, but at that moment he needed her just as badly as she needed him. Needed the oblivion.

She reached down and touched him, and he jerked in her hand, big and heavy, engorged with the same need that swamped her.

She looked up at him through the heavy downpour of the shower. "Please," she whispered, letting her fingers slip down the solid ridge of his cock. "I need . . ."

"I know," he said.

He didn't turn off the shower. He simply picked her up and carried her into the darkened bedroom, laying her down on the bed, following her, covering her, pushing inside her before she could even catch her breath.

But then, she didn't want to breathe. She just wanted this, hard and fast and deep, and she came almost immediately, hard around him, tight and clenching as her entire body suffused into heat and light and a kind of star-studded prickly darkness that went on forever, as he moved inside her, seeking his climax with mindless concentration.

It didn't take him long either. She was still shivering around him when she felt his cock thicken and jerk inside her, and her own climax began again. She tightened her legs around his hips as he spilled inside her. Hot, wet life filling her, driving away death and darkness.

She must have made some sort of noise, because he covered her mouth with his hand, silencing her. She welcomed it, letting go of the very last of her strength, sobbing against the hard flesh of his fingers, until there was nothing left of her, nothing at all.

Bastien pulled away from her, and her arms fell away. She was already unconscious. He would have liked to think he'd fucked her into oblivion, but he knew better than that. She craved the release, the forgetting, as strong as a junkie craved his drugs, and he'd given it to her, taken it for himself, and she'd found healing sleep before he even pulled out of her body.

Her body hadn't followed her mind yet — the last, stray shiver of orgasm stirred her body. He'd needed her so badly, and he still couldn't believe her need had been just as strong.

He hadn't kissed her. But then, this hadn't been about kissing. It had been about life, reclaiming it. It had been about sex and rebirth, pain and need, and he was getting hard again, just looking down at her.

He wondered if it would ever be about them. About him wanting Chloe, and

Chloe wanting him, or whether it was just a weapon, a drug, a tool. He wasn't going to find out. He was going to finish his job, tonight, and get Chloe on a plane. He was going to survive, because he had to, because he had to make sure she was safely out of there. And then he was going to wait to see what happened, if they would come for him or let him go.

The shower was still running. The Hotel Denis had unlimited hot water, as befitted an exclusive, discreet establishment. He looked down at her, envying her sleep, envying her oblivion. He had too many things to do, to keep her safe, to finish this. He couldn't crawl beneath the sheets with her, wrap his body around hers and sink into the warm, sweet pleasure of her. All he could do was pull the covers from under her, covering her body. All he could do was lean over and put his mouth against her lips.

All he could do was leave her.

Chloe opened her eyes. She didn't want to. For a brief moment she couldn't remember where she was. Her dreams had put her back in her bedroom at home, but the light coming from the open door wasn't right, and she didn't recognize the muffled voice from the other room. Her body felt strange, languorous and yet oddly tense.

And then it came back like a hammer blow, everything. Every detail, in sharp, living color, and she put her hand to her mouth, stifling a moan. What the hell had she done?

She'd had sex with Bastien. Again. But in the end that was the least of her worries. It was nothing compared to the litany of death and blood and danger.

She could only hear the distant timbre of his voice and no other. He was talking on the phone, low, calm, and maybe she should go to the door and listen in but she wasn't going to. She was going to wash off, wash him from her body, and then she was going to find some clothes and get the hell out of here.

There was no sign of their drenched black clothes on the floor of the large bathroom. He must have removed them, thank God. She washed quickly, then wrapped herself in one of the oversize towels and headed into the bedroom.

It wasn't enough. She dragged the sheet off the bed and pulled that around her instead, wrapping it like a toga before she went to the door.

She couldn't resist temptation. She paused, listening to his calm, unemotional voice.

"I've made the final arrangements. Just keep your end of the bargain. If something happens, anything, then all bets are off, you understand me?" It was a threat, in a calm, gentle voice that sent chills down her spine. There was a pause, and she held her breath, straining to hear.

"As long as you understand," he said. "I don't bluff, and she's the deal breaker."

The conversation ended, and Chloe counted to a hundred in Italian before she pushed open the door. He was sitting in an overstuffed chair, his legs stretched out in front of him, not moving. The room was dimly lit, something she was grateful for. She didn't think she could bear the bright electric light right now.

He didn't even seem to be aware of her presence, but then his voice came from his unmoving body. "Did you hear anything interesting?"

She should have realized he'd know she was listening. He seemed to have an almost unnatural awareness of her. Then again, that awareness probably stretched to include anyone around him — it was how he survived.

"Only that I'm a deal breaker." She came into the room, keeping the sheet around her. "Are you trading me for something?"

He turned his head to look at her, and there was no missing the faint light of amusement in his eyes as he surveyed her outfit. "I'm trading you for two ox and a bunch of chickens."

"You forget, I was in on those meetings. That probably means two stinger missiles and a bunch of Uzis."

The smile widened just a bit. "What do you know of stinger missiles and Uzis?"

"Not much," she admitted, moving into the room.

"Trust me, they're worth more than the life of one woman."

She grimaced. "Life seems to have very little value in your world." The moment the words had left her mouth she regretted them, but he didn't even blink.

"You're right. Which makes it even more difficult to keep you alive."

"I don't understand why. I must be a huge inconvenience."

"Inconvenience is putting it mildly. I don't know why either," he said in a cool, dismissive voice. "There are some clothes in the foyer — you'll need to dress for to-night."

She ignored the alternative of not being dressed. "Why? Are you taking me out on the town?"

"You're getting a chance to meet your old friends again. The baron and his wife, Mr. Otomi and the others. I'm afraid my unexpected departure and Hakim's unfortunate death cut our meeting short, before a major player could even get there. He's arriving tonight, and we'll be finishing up our business then."

"And you want me to come with you?" she said, disbelieving.

"You're not leaving my side. You'll do everything I say, and when I give you a signal we'll have a fight. You'll leave, head to the toilet, and I'll be there in about ten minutes. You'll stay there, no matter what you hear. You understand?"

"And what if you don't come?"

"I will. No matter what happens."

" 'I'll come to thee by moonlight, though hell should bar the way,' " she murmured.

"What?"

"Just an old poem. About a highwayman. I expect you're something of a modern equivalent," she said lightly.

"I'm not a thief. And somehow I don't see you shooting yourself in order to warn me."

She should have known he'd be acquainted with the poem — he was always surprising her. "So what am I wearing? Basic black? I finally realized why you always wear black."

"Because I'm stylish?" he suggested lightly. "Or because I'm evil?"

"Neither," she said. "Because it doesn't show blood."

There was silence in the room, so quiet that she could almost hear the snow falling outside the tall windows. "Get dressed," he finally said.

The clothes were in the tiny hallway of the suite, the name of the designer on the garment bag and boxes. If Sylvia had these she would have thought she'd died and gone to heaven. . . .

He got there so fast she barely had time to swallow the sudden gulp of pain. "What's wrong?"

She turned to look at him, managing to pull herself together. "If you try really hard you'll probably be able to guess. Your former girlfriend killed Sylvia, you know. She thought she was me."

"I know."

"Then why do you ask me what's wrong?"

"Because we don't have time for it. Once

you're back with your family you can fall apart. Right now you need to have nerves of steel."

"And if I don't? I suppose you'll kill me, right?"

He made no move to touch her. "No," he said. "You'll die, but I won't be the one to do it. And I'll die, too. I imagine that's more of an incentive than a warning, but you're not going to survive without me. And you know it."

"Yes," she said. "I know it."

"So you have to be strong. No tears, no panic. You've managed to keep it together so far, and it'll only be a few more hours and you'll be safe. You can hold out for that much longer. I know you can."

"How do you know it?" Her voice was close to breaking. "I'm a wreck."

"You're amazing," he said softly. "You've managed to stay alive this long. I'm not going to let anything else happen to you."

"Amazing?" she echoed, shaken.

"Go get dressed," he said. And he turned from her, shutting her out once more.

19

He'd thought of everything. At first she thought he'd forgotten to get her a bra, and then she realized she couldn't wear one under the slinky black halter dress. The black lace panties were only one step more generous than a thong, and the matching garter belt and stockings should have revolted her. She put them on, and thought of his hands on her legs.

He'd even ordered the right color range in the makeup — the man was unnatural. There was nothing she could do about her hair. It would have to pass muster as the latest in disarranged styles. She eyed the shoes warily — higher heels than she was used to, but they fit perfectly. He seemed to know her body better than she did, and it made her more than uncomfortable. He knew and understood her body, and yet he was an enigma to her. One she was crazy enough to long for. He'd called her amazing. For some reason she cherished the compliment. Amazingly brave, amazingly stupid, amazing curious, amazingly lucky. Amazing.

Stockholm Syndrome, she reminded herself, a silent litany to keep her absurdities in check. Once she was back home she'd remember this with astonishment. If she chose to remember it at all.

The lights of Paris were bright beyond the floor-to-ceiling windows of the living room, and Bastien stood in the center, half-dressed, fiddling with something under his open shirt. A white shirt — maybe he wasn't expecting blood.

"I need your help," he said, not turning to look at her.

"You don't strike me as someone who asks for help."

"There's a first time for everything. . . ." The words trailed off as he saw her. She'd been feeling awkward, conspicuous in the slinky black dress. That vanished when she saw the look in his eyes, one he quickly shielded. Maybe he had Stockholm Syndrome as well.

If so, he was able to ignore it far more effectively than she was. A moment later she might have imagined that surprising expression in his dark eyes. "I'm having trouble getting this right," he said.

The white shirt was open, exposing his

317

golden smooth skin. He was trying to tape something to his side, a wad of padding that looked like a bandage, when she knew his body well enough to know that he had no wound there.

She came up to him, because she had no reason, no excuse not to. And because she wanted to. "What do you want me to do?"

"I need this adhered to my skin, just below the fourth rib. I can't quite reach."

"What is it?"

He hesitated for only a moment. "It's something used to fake a gunshot wound. It has a small explosive device in it, plus an ampoule of fake blood. It'll sound and look like I've been shot, and it needs to be in the right place to be a fatal hit."

"All right." She put her hands on the piece of padding, too close to him, breathing in the scent of his cologne. Her hands touched his skin, silky smooth, hot, and her fingers trembled. "Is this right?"

"Can you feel my ribs? It should be just below the lowest one."

She tried to breathe normally. Feeling the bones beneath his flesh was unquestionably erotic, whether she wanted it to be or not. "Of course I can feel your ribs," she said in a cranky voice. "You're a skinny-ass

Frenchman. Except that I don't really believe you're French."

"Don't you?" His voice was very soft.
They were so close he barely had to speak
above a whisper, and the hush was only in-
creasing her reaction. "What do you think
I am, then?"

"A pain in the butt." Which sounded just
fine, except that she was having a little
trouble breathing with him so close. She
reached under the shirt, around his side,
and pressed the tape against his skin. "Is
that right?" she repeated.

"It should do. The powder will blow a
hole in my clothes, and there's enough fake
blood to cover any miscalculation." He
looked down at her. Her mouth was just
below his — she could close her eyes and
put her head against his shoulder, sink into
the heat and strength of him.

She stepped back, nervous, trying to
hide it. He buttoned his shirt, then
shrugged into his jacket. Black formal
dinner wear, to match her slinky dress.
He'd tied his long hair back and he looked
elegant, unconcerned as he finished dressing. Her eyes followed his hands as they
tied the black silk tie, and she found herself looking at his mouth.

"We need to talk," she said abruptly.

"About what?"

God damn him! "About what happened a short while ago. In the bedroom," she clarified, in case he was going to continue being deliberately obtuse.

"Why? There's nothing to say."

"But . . ."

"It was a normal human reaction. Survival of the species, *ma belle.* When one is confronted with violent death one reacts in a life-affirming way. It's nothing personal."

She'd been an idiot to say a word. If she'd just kept her mouth shut this weekend she might never have set off any warning flags, and everyone would still be living their normal lives.

"You're right," she muttered, not caring that she sounded sulky and graceless. "Stockholm Syndrome."

"What?"

She'd said the words out loud. It was too late to deny them, so she brazened it out. "Stockholm Syndrome," she repeated more loudly. "It's a documented psychological state where a hostage falls —"

"I know what it is." He looked both alarmed and amused at the same time. He'd stopped her before she'd said the really damning words, and she could feel faintly grateful. She hadn't managed to shame herself completely. "And you're a victim of this particular malady?"

"It's not surprising." She was getting better at keeping her voice light and unconcerned. "You've saved my life on a number of occasions, we're stuck together in a life-or-death situation, and before things got this bad there was a definite physical attraction between us." She remembered his subsequent distancing, and she felt a trace of heat rush to her face. "At least, you managed to convince me it was mutual when you needed to," she amended. "So it's only normal that I feel a bit . . . dependent at the moment. It will pass, the moment I'm safely out of here."

"Dependent?"

There was no way she was going to get out of this gracefully, so she gave up waffling. He was trying to embarrass her, but she could give as good as she got. Her eyes met his, fearlessly, and she willed the heat away from her face. Unfortunately it moved down lower. "You're my knight in shining armor," she said lightly. "My hero, my savior, at least for the time being. I'll get over it."

The amusement had vanished from his face. "No, I'm not. No hero, no savior, no knight. I'm a killer, out for my own agenda and nothing else. You need to remember that. You're nothing to me but an inconvenience."

"Then why am I here?"

"Because I can't get rid of you."

There was something going on, something she couldn't quite understand, but it was making her bolder, less vulnerable to his cold, empty words. "Of course you can," she said in a practical voice. "You can break my neck, cut my throat, shoot me. You don't seem to have any particular issues about life and death — if you simply wanted to get rid of me then why do you keep saving me?"

"Because I'm desperately in love with you and I can't help myself. I'm a prisoner to your charm and beauty, I can't bear to part —"

"Shut up," she said, stopping his mocking litany. "I'm not saying I matter to you. I know perfectly well that any . . . feeling between us is only on my side, and it's the result of trauma-induced hysteria and nothing else. I'm just saying that you're not the monster you think you are."

"I'm not?" She was standing too close to him. He simply reached out and wrapped his long, elegant fingers around her exposed neck. He pulled her closer, exerting just the slightest amount of pressure. His fingertips were just under her jaw, his thumb stroking the soft flesh of her throat. "Maybe I feed on pain and terror. Maybe I just brought you this far to kill you the moment you begin to trust me."

She swallowed. The touch of his hands on her throat was unnerving, and it took all her strength to keep from swaying against him. "And maybe you're full of shit," she said. "You may not want me but you don't want to kill me either."

His smile was wry. "Now that's where you're wrong." The pressure of his fingers against her throat increased for just a moment, and she felt dizzy, disoriented, until she realized he'd pushed her up against the wall of the damask-paneled living room, his elegant body pressed up against hers, his fingers cradling her face as he looked down into her eyes in the gathering darkness. Wrong about what, she thought distantly. Wrong about killing, or wrong about wanting?

He was about to tell her. "If this were a different time, a different place, I would take you to bed with me and make love to you for days," he said, his voice slow and deep and intent. "I would use my mouth on you, until no part of your skin went untouched, and I would make you come, over and over again until you could stand no more, and then I'd let you sleep in my arms until you were rested and then I would start all over again. I would kiss your wounds, I would drink your tears, I could make love to you in ways that haven't even been invented yet. I would make love to you in fields of flowers and under starry skies, where there is no death or pain or sorrow. I would show you things you haven't even dreamed of, and there would be no one in the world but you and me, between your legs, in your mouth, everywhere."

She stared at him, eyes wide. "Breathe," he said softly, with a self-deprecating smile, and she realized she'd been holding her breath.

"You would?" she gasped.

"I would. But I won't. It wouldn't be a very good idea."

"Why not?"

"It wouldn't be very good for you."

"Why don't you let me be the judge of what's good for me?"

He laughed then, and she realized she'd never heard him laugh before. For a moment he looked beautiful, gilded by moonlight, a perfect man in a perfect place.

And then the shadows closed down around them once more. "You have Stockholm Syndrome, remember?" he said with gentle mockery. "It won't be much longer. By midnight you'll be safely away from this, and by next week it will all be a distant nightmare. In a year you'll forget you ever met me."

"I don't think so."

But the subject was closed. He took his hands away from her throat, and she realized he'd been caressing her. "You'll do what I told you, yes? When I give you the signal you pick a fight with me, then storm out of the place and go hide in the toilet. I will come and get you as soon as I can."

"And if you don't come?"

"Though hell should bar the way," he said lightly. "You'll be seeing your old friends from the château. Such good times."

"Yeah, right," she said. "I promise to keep my mouth shut."

"You don't need to. This will all be over tonight. It doesn't really matter what you say, as long as you don't tell them about the device I'm wearing. Just keep away from Christos."

"Who's Christos?"

"You haven't met him yet. He's arriving tonight, and he makes Hakim seem like Mother Teresa. Steer clear of him if you can. Your artless prattle might get on his nerves, and he's not a man to cross."

"Artless prattle . . . ?"

He ignored her outraged protest. "If you just keep your head about you and do as I say you'll make it through the night in one piece."

"As will you?" It was a question, not a statement.

She didn't like the faint irony in his smile. "As will I," he said. "One more thing. You haven't finished dressing."

"There was no bra," she said nervously.

"I know. That's why I chose it." He might as well have been discussing orange prices. He reached in the pocket of his tuxedo and pulled out a glittering string of diamonds. "You need proper ornamentation. Turn around."

He was holding a heavy, old-looking necklace that had to be diamonds. She didn't, couldn't move, so he simply put his arms around her neck, fastening the clasp behind her. The light splintered and danced through the jewels, and the white-gold setting was oddly warm against her skin. He looked down at her, tilting his head to one side to judge the effect. "They look good on you."

"Whose are they? Stolen swag? Or the best fakes money can buy?"

"Does it matter?"

"Not really." He'd opened the door, and she knew she wasn't coming back to this place. She was never going to spend time alone with him again, and when he took her arm she held back, just slightly.

"Would you do me a favor?"

"What is it?"

"Would you at least tell me your name?"

He shook his head. "I've told you, you don't need to know. The less you know, the safer you are."

She'd expected no more. "Then would you at least kiss me? Just once, like you really mean it." If he didn't kiss her she might not make it through the next few hours. If he didn't kiss her she might not want to.

But he shook his head. "No," he said. "Once you're back home there'll be dozens of handsome young men wanting to kiss you. Wait until then."

"I don't think so." She put her arms around his neck and yanked his head down to hers and kissed him, hard. She half expected him to fight, to push her away, but he simply let her kiss him, not reacting, not participating. She might have been kissing her own reflection in the mirror.

She wanted to cry, but the tears could wait as well as the handsome young men. She drew back, a jaunty smile on her face. "For luck," she said brightly. And without another word she walked out into the hallway, leaving him to follow, closing the door behind them. Closing safety away, as he took her arm once more and slowly walked her toward destiny or disaster. She would find out which soon enough.

They were all there. Otomi and his assistant, whose tattoos showed beneath the elegant cuffs of his dinner jacket. Bastien wondered idly whether Otomi was covered with the traditional colorful tattoos sported by most Yakuza, or whether he'd always been management level. He still had all of his fingers, so he might never have been in the trenches. His silent, impassive assistant was missing only part of one digit. Obviously he didn't screw up very often.

The baron glowered at him from across the room, and Monique froze when she caught sight of them. Chloe was clinging to Bastien's arm, nervous now that it was show time, and he patted her hand reassuringly, because he could. For an hour or so, a very dangerous hour or so, he could touch her all he wanted. It was part of a show, it meant nothing, and he could indulge himself and she'd never know how damned hard it was for him.

He figured he had a fifty-fifty chance of making it through the night, but he was getting Chloe out of there if he had to gun down everyone in the room. Some of the people in the room were ostensibly on the same side as he was, assuming he even had a side. It didn't matter — he would sacrifice anyone to keep Chloe alive. Even risk her parents.

They should have arrived in Paris about now. His phone call had caught them at the airport — they were already on their way to France to find their missing daughter. Sylvia's body had been found, as well as Chloe's passport, and the gendarmes had tracked down her parents. With luck they'd be on their way to the hotel, in time to stop Chloe from getting caught in the bloodbath he knew was going to go down.

She had no idea that when he sent her out of the room he'd be sending her to her parents. And they would make sure she wouldn't come back, no matter what sounds they heard. He could only hope they'd be long gone from the hotel before the shooting started.

"Well, isn't this a surprise?" Monique cooed, gliding up to them. "We wondered where you'd gone to. We figured you'd killed Hakim, but we weren't sure whether the little American had gone with you or whether she'd left on her own. I'm glad to see you've kept track of her."

"I keep track of everything, Monique," he said, stroking Chloe's pale, cold hand.

"So tell me, why did you kill Hakim? We're all quite interested. It was unexpected, to say the least."

"And does anyone really care?"

Monique smiled. "No. He was disposable. We're simply curious." She put out her thin, bejeweled hand and touched Chloe's exposed skin. "I can see traces of his handiwork." There were the faintest of marks left from Hakim's worst wounds, and he could see the gooseflesh rise on Chloe's arm at Monique's touch.

He grabbed her strong wrist and pulled her hand away. "No touching, Monique," he said. "She's mine."

"It's always nice to share," Monique replied with an exaggerated pout. "She's very

330

pretty when she's dressed up. And where did she get those very spectacular diamonds? I haven't seen anything quite so stunning in a long time. Where did you get them, *petite?*" She turned her attention to Chloe, who jumped nervously.

"Bastien gave them to me," she said after a moment.

Monique frowned. "I had no idea he could be so generous. If I'd known you had something quite so nice in your possession I wouldn't have broken off our relationship."

Her eyes dared him to correct her, but he was already getting bored. Monique enjoyed playing cat and mouse, but she wasn't his target tonight. Compared to the man he'd come to deal with, Monique was child's play.

"Where's Christos?" he said. "Another no-show?" It would be a mixed blessing if the Greek didn't bother to join them one more time. Once Christos appeared most of the attention would be directed toward him. If he didn't, Chloe could still be a target, both of the cartel and the Committee. And while the presence of her American parents might cause the cartel to reconsider, the Committee would barely hesitate.

No, it would be better all around if

Christos showed up and things went down as planned. There was always the chance that the dummy taped to his side was the only wound he'd get, but he wasn't counting on it. As long as Chloe was safe he really didn't give a shit what happened.

"Your guess is as good as mine," Monique said. "If he doesn't show up I'm sure we'll find some way to occupy our time." She reached out to touch Chloe again, but this time Chloe jerked out of her way.

"Hands off, you skanky bitch," she said in her sweetest voice. In Monique's native German.

Monique blinked, and her smile widened. "Oh, she *is* a little treasure, Bastien. I'm going to have fun with her. And yes, I know. Over your dead body." And she blew them both a little kiss before sauntering back to her glowering husband.

"Perhaps not a wise idea, Chloe," he murmured. "Not that I blame you." She looked up at him, and in the bright light he could see her more clearly than he wanted to. The troubled brown eyes that would fill with tears when she heard he'd died. The full, soft mouth that would find someone else to kiss, someone who would kiss her back.

"Is that the worst?" she asked.

There was a commotion at the door, and he tore his gaze away from her to look at the group of men who walked in. "I'm afraid not," he said softly. "Christos has arrived."

20

Christos didn't look like the monster Bastien had painted him, Chloe thought. Compared to Gilles Hakim he seemed like nothing more than a well-dressed businessman, albeit surrounded by a small army that could only be bodyguards. Part of her had been expecting Zorba, but this was no jovial fisherman. He stood in the doorway, flanked by his men, and let his eyes scan the room, cataloguing the inhabitants. He had strong eyes — clear, almost colorless, and when they rested on Chloe's skin she felt a cold rush.

"I'm glad to see you're all still here," he said. His English was perfect though heavily accented. A good thing, because Chloe's Greek was marginal at best. "I'm sorry I couldn't join you sooner, I had business matters to attend to. But that doesn't mean I don't mourn the loss of our dear friend August Remarque and his excellent leadership skills. I gather we've lost Hakim as well. Another sorrow." He turned his gaze on Bastien, who was watching him with total impassivity. "But seeing old friends will help to make up for the loss."

"Who have you brought with you, Christos?" Mr. Otomi demanded, clearly displeased. The six men surrounding Christos's small, elegant figure trumped Otomi's lone assistant cum bodyguard.

"A man can never be too careful. What with all these sudden deaths I thought it would be wise to ensure my safety. Don't look so concerned, my dear friends and colleagues. My men are very well trained. They won't do anything I don't tell them to do."

None of the others in the room looked particularly gratified by that information, Chloe thought, moving infinitesimally closer to Bastien. He'd been right. The previous meetings had been mere skirmishes compared to this highly charged atmosphere.

"We need to discuss the disposition —" Signore Ricetti began in a strident voice, but Christos cut him off with a wave of his hand. Pale, small hands, Chloe noticed.

"There'll be time enough for business," he said. "In the meantime I'd like a drink. Some decent French wine for a change. I'm sick to death of retsina."

"Of course." Madame Lambert seemed to have taken on the role of hostess — she signaled for the waiter. "And for your men?"

"They don't drink when they're on duty," Christos purred. Chloe felt the tension in the room rise.

Bastien put his arm around her waist, steering her toward a less-crowded section of the room. It had taken all her initial self-control not to jump when he touched her, then an even stronger effort not to sink back against him. His touch was an illusion. It offered no more safety than a cobra sliding up her back. But it made her feel better.

He settled her onto the smooth pale leather banquette, then sat down beside her, close but not touching. Had he brought a gun? She couldn't remember. She'd been far more interested in his skin and his body than what kind of weapons he carried. It would serve her right if she died, she thought in disgust. Besotted little idiot.

Someone had given her a glass of champagne. She hadn't even noticed how it got in her hand, but she sipped at it for something to do, saying nothing as she watched the remaining members of the arms cartel circulate around the room with perfect party manners.

Monique was flirting with Christos — a temporary reprieve, but after a moment she turned, looking directly into Chloe's eyes. And then she came straight toward them, a wicked smile on her deep-red lips.

Chloe could feel the tension radiating from the man beside her. "Time to pick a fight," he murmured.

It should have been easy enough. He was equal parts irresistible and maddening, and she could have concentrated on the maddening part. Except that she could read the tension in the room, see Christos's phalanx of bodyguards, and she wasn't going anywhere.

"I'm fine," she said in a dulcet tone.

He swiveled on the banquette to give her his full attention. "Time to leave," he said in a low voice. "Things are getting dangerous around here."

She gave him a bright, limpid smile. "I'm not going anywhere without you," she said in a low, sultry voice that wouldn't carry beyond the two of them.

His dark, dark eyes could freeze her in her tracks, but she refused to be cowed. "Don't play this game, Chloe," he said in a dangerous voice.

"It's no game. I'm not leaving this room without you. If I do, you'll die, and I don't want that to happen."

"If you stay, you'll die."

"Probably. Which means if you're still determined to keep me alive you have no choice but to come with me." She didn't have long to feel pleased with herself for her plan — his expression was calm and faintly bored, but the look in his eyes was sheer fury.

He'd been sipping at a glass of whiskey and ice. He proceeded to dump it in her lap, leaping up in fake consternation. "Forgive me, my dear," he said loudly. "I don't know how I could be so clumsy."

The icy liquid soaked through the gown, onto her thighs, and it took all her effort to smile up at him, unmoving. Black could cover things other than blood. "It was just a drop, my love," she murmured, reaching up for his arm. "Don't worry about it."

"I really do think you should go clean yourself up," he said.

"I'm fine."

"He's trying to get rid of you, child." Monique, unfortunately, had joined them. "Go away and give us a few minutes alone. We need to renew our acquaintance."

"I don't think so," she said in a firm, pleasant voice.

"Stay, then." Monique dropped down on the leather seat, pulling Bastien down between them. "I've never minded an audience." And putting her hand behind Bastien's head, she pulled his mouth down to hers.

He kissed her back. He put his arm around Monique's slender waist and pulled her up against him, and gave her a lingering, lazy kiss. The kiss he'd refused Chloe just a short time ago.

It wasn't just her imagination that the tension in the room ratcheted up several notches. Monique's husband was watching with avid fascination and not the faintest amount of discomfort, and the others were witnessing their little soap opera with various degrees of interest. Except for Christos's bodyguards, who'd managed to station themselves around the room instead of surrounding their employer. And why wasn't Bastien paying attention to this alarming development, Chloe thought, instead of having his tongue halfway down that woman's throat?

If she was supposed to sit there looking like a fool he'd miscalculated. He probably hoped she'd storm off in tears, and while she was tempted, Christos's men were at every exit. Whether he liked it or not, she was trapped in there with them.

She put her hand on his shoulder and yanked him away from Monique. He looked down at her, his face icy. "Go away," he said, loud and clear for the room to hear. "I'm tired of you." And then he turned back to Monique.

The bitch was clearly enjoying herself tremendously, Chloe thought, taking a deep breath to steady herself. The expressionless men surrounding the room weren't paying any attention to the groping session on the banquette — their attention was glued to the man who controlled them. Christos was watching with what almost might be called amusement, but he wasn't going to be distracted for long, and when he gave the signal they would all be dead. Chloe knew it as well as she knew her own name.

As far as she knew Stockholm Syndrome might be a fatal disease. She turned, and Monique had one hand in Bastien's long, silky hair, the other on his crotch.

That was the last straw. If she was going to die, she was going down in flames. She stood up, grabbed Monique's skinny arm and hauled her away from Bastien before either of them realized what she was doing. "Get your goddamn hands off my boy-friend."

It was the most ridiculous thing she could have said. The entire room was frozen in silence, watching them, and then Monique smiled. "I don't mind a three-some, *chérie,* if you're that jealous. You may not be enough for him but I imagine I can fill in the gaps."

Chloe lunged at her, and Bastien caught her midair, hauling her against him. And then she went down, hard, on the floor, his body covering her, as all hell broke out.

She was crushed beneath him, unable to see, but the noise was hideous. The gun-shots — some of them silenced, some of them deafening, the screams and curses and sounds of a panicked stampede.

And then the smell — cordite and the heavy, coppery scent of blood. He was holding her down, but he was alive, she could tell that much. He was breathing heavily, and she could feel his heart beating against her back. She didn't move, didn't want to move. Maybe they could just lie there forever, and no one would no-tice they weren't dead.

And then he rolled off her, onto his side, taking her with him. The room was shrouded in darkness, only the spit of gunfire providing any illumination. Not that Chloe wanted to see the tangle of bodies, the writhing ones, the motionless ones, the blood everywhere.

He half-dragged, half-carried her behind the banquette, hauling her toward one of the curtained windows. He shoved her behind the fabric and slammed her up against the wall, one hand over her mouth so she couldn't speak, couldn't scream, couldn't breathe. In his other hand he had a gun — she could feel it against her skin.

"Are you hurt?" he whispered.

She managed to shake her head, just barely, he was holding her so tightly.

The windows led out on a small, snow-covered balcony. She couldn't see how many flights up they were, and she didn't care. They were trapped in the tiny alcove, and there were only two ways out. Through the gunfire. Or out the window.

"Stay put," he said, pulling away from her, turning to the enveloping curtain.

"No!" she cried out, clinging to him, but he simply knocked her away from him, so that she fell back against the wall. He opened the curtain, and she squeezed her eyes shut, put her hands over her ears to drown out the awful noise.

And then he was back. "Let's get the hell out of here," he said, his voice strained. "We might as well go." He opened the floor-to-ceiling window, and the cold air whipped inside, making the enveloping curtains billow out. He cursed, shoving the gun into his belt, and she could see the stain of fake blood on his shirt. "Come on."

She didn't have time to ask where. He simply picked her up and tossed her over the side of the balcony, dropping down after her.

It was two flights up, and she landed hard, but the snow was deep enough to keep her from hurting herself. He must have hit harder, because he stumbled as he rose, grabbing her hand and pulling her into the shadows just as people appeared on the balcony overhead, a babble of languages she didn't want to understand.

"My car's over there," he said, breathless, as he pushed her ahead of him. "I'm always prepared for contingencies. You can drive a stick, can't you?"

"I don't drive in Paris!" she said sharply.

"You do now." He yanked open the driver's side, grabbed her arm and shoved her in, and she had no choice. At least the traffic would be lighter at this hour.

He collapsed into the passenger seat beside her. "Drive," he said. "Head north."

She gave him one, assessing glance and then decided not to argue. The BMW started like a charm, when she half expected it to explode. She spun the tires backing out, slid as she started forward and stalled out.

Bastien was leaning back against the seat, his eyes closed. "If you don't get moving we're going to be dead," he said, very calm.

"I'm doing the best I can." She started the car again, shoved it into gear and headed into the street, just missing three cars and a motorcyclist. "Shit," she said under her breath. "Shit, shit, shit."

"What's your problem?" he asked wearily. "Why don't you drive in Paris?"

"The drivers are too dangerous. I'm afraid to."

He was silent for so long she thought he might have fallen asleep. "Chloe," he said, infinitely patient, "you have just been the target of some of the most ruthless people in the world today. You've survived a bloodbath, you've seen people die. One or two impetuous drivers is nothing to worry about."

She turned the corner, driving too fast,

and went up over the curb. If it were midday they'd be dead, in the middle of a twenty-car pile-up. At this hour they might have a slight chance of reaching where they were going. Wherever the hell that was.

She wasn't going to ask him. "A blood-bath?" she said after a long moment.

"What did you think that was? A parlor game? I couldn't see much before we left, but the baron was down, as was Mr. Otomi and Monique."

"Monique?"

"She was shot in the face. Does that make you happy?" He sounded so tired.

"Of course not. What about Christos and his men?"

"Christos is dead. At least that part we got right."

"How can you be sure? It was so dark. . . ."

"Because I'm the one who killed him. And in case you hadn't already realized it, I don't miss." He closed his eyes again. "Just keep driving. I need to figure out what to do next."

"Is that what you were supposed to do? Kill Christos?"

"If it came to that."

"So now I should be safe, shouldn't I?

You accomplished what you were supposed to do."

"They don't like witnesses, Chloe. You won't be safe until you're back home."

She wasn't going to argue with him — the traffic was taking too much of her concentration. The snow had melted, then turned to ice, and the BMW had too much power. She was sure that they'd survived a hail of bullets only to die ignominiously in a fender bender, but for now she didn't care. She was with him. And she knew it wasn't going to be for long.

He reached into the glove compartment and pulled out a cell phone, punching in a number. The conversation was terse and uninformative, and when he shut down the connection he simply said, "Take the next left."

She wasn't going to argue, not now. He looked pale, exhausted, for the first time almost human. Vulnerable, a thought that terrified her. Not for her own sake, but his. "Are you okay?" she said. "They didn't shoot you, did they?"

His cool smile was little comfort. "Don't you remember that device you strapped to me? It scorched me when it went off. I think I'll manage to survive."

"But if . . ."

"Hush," he said softly. "For a few minutes, just hush."

She did as he asked, a greater sacrifice than he would ever realize. She turned on the car radio, only to hear police reports of a terrorist incident at the Hotel Denis. At least eleven dead, five wounded, and others were being sought. She switched the station, finding French gangsta rap, and she turned it off. She wasn't in the mood for posturing violence. Not after the real thing.

"Take another left up here," Bastien said suddenly. She had no idea where they were. It was dark, and they were heading out of town in a direction she didn't recognize. There was a roaring noise overhead, and she suddenly realized they must be near the airport. He'd directed her via a circuitous route, but there was no mistaking where they were.

He wasn't directing her to any of the public areas, the parking areas, or the departure gates. Instead they drove on, past the main terminals to the row of airport hotels. "Drive around the back," he said, when they reached the Hilton, and she dutifully did so. At least he was taking her to a hotel before he sent her away. If one more night with him was all she was going to have she'd take it and be grateful.

"Pull up over there," he said, pointing toward a delivery entrance.

"There's no place to park."

"Just do as I say."

She had neither the energy nor the desire to argue with him. She pulled up to the curb and put the car in Neutral, pulling up the parking brake. "Now what?"

"You can get out now," he said, reaching over and turning off the car. He had blood on his hand as well. She could only hope it was the same fake blood that stained his shirt, not someone else's.

She opened the door and slid out. The snow had been scraped from the roadway, but there was still a thin coating of frozen slush beneath her slender evening sandals, and she was freezing. Her dress was ruined — it had been drenched in whiskey and dumped in snow, and the wind whipped through the night air, swirling the loose snow around her.

She saw the two figures materialize out of the darkness, and for a wild moment she wondered whether he'd simply brought her out here to have someone else kill her, when she realized the people approaching her were more than familiar. They were her parents.

She let out a shriek, running across the

snow-packed tarmac to fling herself in their arms. For a moment all she could do was cling to them, trying to catch her breath, the feel of them suddenly real and safe in a crazy world of guns and blood.

"What are you doing here?" she babbled, once she caught her breath. "How did you know where to find me?"

"Your friend was able to track us down," her father said. "We heard about Sylvia, and we were already headed to France when he called us. We were supposed to meet up with you at a hotel, but our plane got delayed."

She turned to look back. Bastien had approached them, staying just a ways back, watching them without expression. "You told them to come to the hotel when you knew what was going to happen? They could have been killed!"

He shrugged, a little stiffly. "The point was to keep you alive. I didn't particularly care what it cost."

"You son of a . . ."

"Hush, now, Chloe," her mother said. "He saved your life."

James Underwood released Chloe and held out his hand to Bastien. "I just want to thank you for looking after our daughter. She can be quite a handful sometimes."

"She was the least of my worries," Bastien said in his calm, even voice.

"Do you want me to look at the wound of yours? I don't know if Chloe told you but we're both doctors. . . ."

"I'm fine." He dismissed it. "But you should leave. Take her out of France and don't let her back for at least ten years. It probably wouldn't be a bad idea not to let her out of your sight for at least five."

"Easier said than done," her father muttered.

She could see Bastien's faint smile in the lamplight. Without another word he turned away, moving back to the car, and she stood, shivering, frozen from more than the cold, certain he was going to walk away without another word.

He opened the car door, then hesitated. He reached into the back and pulled something out, then approached her, carrying it over his arm.

She was shaking, but for some reason her mother and father had stepped back, away from her.

"Why are you limping?" she asked, trying to keep her tone light as he came up to her.

"I twisted my ankle when we jumped." He held his black cashmere coat in his arms, and he put it around her shoulders, wrapping her in the warmth and scent of it, pulling it around her. "Do as your parents tell you to do," he said. "Let them take care of you."

"I never was particularly obedient."

He smiled then, a brief, honest, heart-breaking smile. "I know. Do it for me."

She was too exhausted to fight him. She simply nodded, waiting for him to release his hold on the coat he'd pulled around her.

"I'm going to kiss you, Chloe," he said in a quiet voice. "Just a simple kiss goodbye. And then you can forget all about me. Stockholm Syndrome is nothing more than a myth. Go home and find someone to love."

She didn't bother trying to explain. She simply stood there as he cupped her face in his hands, warm, strong hands that had protected her, killed for her. His lips were whisper-soft against hers, just a touch. He kissed her eyelids, her nose, her brow, her cheeks with the tears streaming down them, he kissed her mouth again, a slow, deep, gentle kiss that held all the promise of what they would never have. It was the kiss of a man in love, and for a moment she simply floated, lost in the perfect beauty of his mouth on hers.

He released her. "Breathe, Chloe," he whispered. For the final time. And then he was gone, the BMW disappearing into the Paris night before she could do more than catch the coat as it fell from her shoulders.

"Where in the world did you happen to find such an interesting young man?" Her mother had come up to her, putting her arm around her. "You were always so traditional when it came to your boyfriends."

Boyfriend, Chloe thought dazedly. The last word she'd spoken out loud before the chaos and death had begun. "He found me," she said. Her voice sounded odd, strained.

"A good thing," her father said. "It seems as if he managed to get you out of a very dangerous situation. I just wish he'd let me look at that gunshot wound."

"He wasn't really shot," Chloe said. "It was just a fake we . . . he set up earlier this evening. Fake blood and a tiny explosive device to simulate being shot."

"Chloe, my child, I hate to correct you but I spent more than ten years as an emergency room physician in Baltimore, and I know a gunshot wound when I see one."

"It wasn't —" And then it came to her,

with an odd, sickening rush. The wound was on his left side. The fake gunshot had been taped to his right. "Oh, God," she cried, trying to pull free of her parents. "You're right! We have to find him. . . ."

"It won't do any good, sweetheart. He's long gone. I'm sure he'll go straight to the hospital. . . ."

"He won't. He'll die. He wants to." The moment she said the words she knew them to be true. He wanted to die, had been almost courting death, until she got in his way. And now that she was safely disposed of, there was nothing to stand in his way. "We have to find him, Daddy!"

"We have to catch our plane, Chloe. We promised."

There was nothing she could do. He'd driven off, speeding on the icy roads, and there'd be no way to follow him, no way to find him. He would get help or he wouldn't, but either way it was no longer any of her business. He was gone from her life, forever.

Breathe, he'd always told her. She took a deep, shaky breath, pulling his coat more tightly around her. She said nothing as her parents shepherded her through the back entrance of the hotel, over to the international departure lounge and onto the jet with surprising ease. They were in first class, but she was beyond noticing such luxuries. She leaned back in the seat and closed her eyes, refusing to surrender the coat to the solicitous flight attendant. She was past tears now, past feeling anything at all. She had blood on her hand — his blood, she realized now, not phony blood. And she had no intention of washing it off. It was all she had left of him.

Stockholm Syndrome, she reminded herself. An aberration, or a legend, or maybe just a moment of utter insanity on her part. It didn't matter, it was over. With a perfect kiss.

He shouldn't have done that. She would have been better off if he'd just walked away. Then she would have never known how sweet it could be, that there was something besides the blood-quickening need of sex.

They were halfway over the Atlantic when she opened her eyes, to see both her parents watching her, identical, anxious expressions on their faces.

"I'm fine," she said calmly, a complete lie. But her parents nodded, since their youngest child had spent most of her life being just fine. "Just one thing."

"Yes, sweetheart?" her mother said,

enough anxiety in her voice to prove that she wasn't fooled.

"I don't ever want to go to Stockholm." And she closed her eyes again, shutting out the world.

21

It was April — warm, damp, full of new spring promise. Paris would be jammed with tourists. Next to August, April was the most crowded month of all. But Bastien was nowhere near Paris, and didn't plan to be for a good long time.

He knew how to disappear, better than almost anyone. He'd had the best training in the world. And once he'd yanked the IV out of his arm and walked out of his hospital room in the private facility they'd stashed him in, he'd managed to vanish, even in his weakened condition, to a place where no one, not even the Committee, could find him.

It was the Committee he was most interested in avoiding. Anyone else would simply want to kill him, and he was still willing to face that with equanimity. The Committee didn't want to let him go, and they didn't take no for an answer. If he wouldn't come back Thomason would once again order him killed, and in retrospect he was damned if he was going to be killed by his own people. He had too much pride to accept such an ignominious fate.

He'd spent time in a tiny village in the Italian Alps, waiting for the wound to heal. The bullet had nicked his liver, and for a while it had been hit or miss whether he'd make it, particularly since it had taken them a while to discover him, passed out in the BMW in back of the deserted house. They'd found him, and they'd found Maureen, but it had been too late to do anything for her.

But the Committee hadn't been ready to allow their expensive investment to die, and he'd been brought back from death twice, fighting all the way. They weren't going to let him go, and he stopped resisting, letting them work their medical magic on him until he was conscious enough to control the pain without their drugs. Drugs to stop the pain, drugs to keep him docile, drugs to convince him to do what they wanted. He didn't need their drugs.

There'd been a guard stationed outside his room the entire time. Occasionally he'd been conscious enough to see them, though he had no idea whether they were there to protect him or imprison him. No one from the Committee had shown their face, and he wasn't about to wait for Harry Thomason to appear and give him an ultimatum. He waited until he could walk a few steps, practicing when the nurses weren't around, and then he pulled the IV out of his arm, knocked out his guard and stripped his clothes from him, taking off into the night.

The Italian Alps first, then on to Venice, a city he knew as intimately as most people knew their own home. No one could find him in the twists and turns of Venice, and he could stay lost there forever if he wanted to.

He didn't. He was restless, recuperating slower than normal, and his nerves were jumpy, dangerously so. He'd put another section of his life behind him, just as he had so many times before. The wandering years with his mother and Aunt Celeste, the selfish years when he'd gone from one woman to the next, using them and then disappearing. And the deadly years, endless, eternal, employed by and under the control of the Committee, who believed that the end justified the means, no matter how monstrous.

And now he was back to wandering, alone this time. Moving from place to place, not stopping long enough to leave any trace. He left Venice after the madhouse of Carnivale, moving west. The Azores were warm and soothing, and he only thought of Chloe once, when the liquid sound of Portuguese ran over him and he wondered if that was one more language she'd managed to conquer.

She was alive, she was well, she was immured in the mountains of North Carolina, and that was all he needed to know. She no longer had to count on him for anything — for food and warmth and sex and life itself. By now the very thought of him would have her shaking in horror. If she thought of him at all.

He could only hope she didn't. She'd been ill-prepared for those few days they'd spent together — death and violence weren't the normal lot for young girls, especially American ones. If she hadn't managed to put it all behind her he had no doubt that her efficient parents would drag her from therapist to therapist until she was cured. Cured of the memories. Cured of him.

He lay in the sun, letting his mind empty, letting his body heal. He wasn't sure where he'd go next — Greece was out of the question, and the Far East wasn't a wise idea. The Yakuza had not taken kindly to Otomi's loss, and their intelligence network rivaled that of the Committee. Once he set foot in Japan or anywhere near he'd be found and eliminated, even among millions of people. And he found he was no longer courting death, though he hadn't quite figured out why.

He wasn't going to the States, that was one thing that was absolutely certain. America was a huge country, but if he set foot inside its massive borders he'd be aware of only one, dangerous thing. One woman. He wouldn't do anything about it, but he would be unable to concentrate on anything else until he left again. Even Canada might be too close.

Switzerland might be a good choice, with its rigid neutrality. Or Scandinavia, maybe Sweden . . .

Christ, no! He was never going to be able to think of Stockholm again with anything other than . . . hell, he didn't even know what he was thinking. His world was awash in her, contaminated by her. There was no place he could run that didn't make him think of her. Maybe he did want to die after all.

Or maybe it was just part of his penance.

He was drinking too much, but what else could he do as he lay out in the sun trying not to think? Drinking and smoking, sleeping with the pretty waitress when he was drunk enough to forget. It was a good life, he told himself, settling his sunglasses on his nose and closing his eyes to the bright Portuguese sun. Maybe he could just stay that way forever.

His sun was blotted out, and he waited, patiently, for it to reappear. And then he opened his eyes to see Jensen standing beside his chaise.

He looked very different from the last time Bastien had seen him, across the room at the Hotel Denis where he'd been attending to Ricetti. His brown hair was longer and deep black, he was dressed in designer denim, and although his eyes were covered with sunglasses Bastien had no doubt they were some color other than his natural blue.

"Are you here to kill me?" he inquired lazily, not moving from his chaise. "It's a pretty public place, and I'd hate to see you get caught. We've always gotten along well — why don't you wait until I'm back in my room or alone on a deserted street?"

"You're being melodramatic," Jensen said, taking the chaise next to him. There was no visible sign of a gun, but Bastien wasn't fooled. No operative would go out unarmed. There were too many unknown, unseen enemies. "If I wanted to kill you I would have done it back in Paris, when Thomason ordered me to, instead of letting you go."

Bastien smiled faintly. "I thought it would be you. What made you change your mind?"

"Thomason is an asshole. He's not going to be around forever, and you were too valuable a commodity to simply flush away."

Bastien smiled faintly. "Sorry, Jensen. My services are no longer available. Go ahead and flush."

Jensen shook his head. "I only kill when I'm paid to," he said. "Don't you want to know why I'm here?"

"If it's not to kill me then I suppose it's to talk me back into the fold. And you're wasting your time. Tell Thomason he can go fuck himself."

"Thomason doesn't know I'm here, and he wouldn't be very happy if he did."

Bastien lifted his sunglasses to peer at his companion. "Then who sent you?"

"You and I weren't the only Committee members at the meetings."

"Tell me something I don't know. Like who else was on our payroll."

Jensen shook his head. "That's need-to-know information, and as long as you're out of the fold then that knowledge is too dangerous to spread around."

"Fine," Bastien said, pulling his sunglasses back down again. "I'm not coming back, and you can tell them that. You can either kill me or go away."

"I'm not here to bring you back, I'm here to warn you."

"I don't need warnings, Jensen. I've managed to keep myself alive for this long, I can continue as long as I'm in the mood to."

"Not you, Bastien. We both know you're always in danger. It's your little American. We think they've found her."

Spring came early to the mountains of North Carolina, but Chloe was in no mood to notice. Her parents pampered her, her brothers and sister hovered, her nieces and nephews delighted her, but the raw, torn place inside her was still bleeding. Every time she thought it had scarred over something would remind her, and she'd start shaking again.

Maureen, when she fell in the snow, the

knife flying out of her hand, the blood soaking into the heavy drifts of white. Sylvia, her eyes wide and staring at the death that had taken her. The tangle of bodies, the sounds of screams, the smell of blood at the Hotel Denis. She'd remember, and she'd start shaking, and there was no one there to remind her to breathe.

They were all dead — she'd been able to ascertain that much. The police had broken in on the scene just moments after she and Bastien had jumped from the balcony, and those who survived the bloodbath died in the hospital shortly thereafter. Convenient that no one was left to tell the truth. Monique had died on the scene, shot in the face, Bastien had told her. The baron had succumbed a day or two later, and the rest of them were already gone.

The one thing she didn't think about was Bastien. For all she knew he was dead — he'd been careless and courting it long enough, and he'd been shot. Then again, he was someone who didn't die easily. Maybe he was off on a new assignment, or maybe . . .

Anyway, she wasn't going to think about him. He was in the dark, mixed-up past, and there was no way she could make sense of it, no matter how hard she tried. So she let go, moving through her days in a calm, even state of mind, while her parents looked on with worried eyes.

They were beginning to relax by mid-April. She'd signed up for courses at the university. Chinese would be enough of a challenge to keep her mind totally occupied, and she would start doing some volunteer work at the hospital in a week or so. By the fall she'd be ready to find a real job, even move out on her own despite her parents' protests. She was healing, and she refused to even consider what she was healing from. She only knew it took time.

For now she was safe. The Underwoods owned two hundred acres on the side of a small mountain, and their sprawling house was casual, comfortable and nicely isolated. The old farmhouse had been renovated, added on to, torn down and fixed up for a hundred or so years, and its current state was rambling, cluttered and completely cozy. Her mother made no pretensions at being neat, and while a weekly housekeeper kept the place clean, order was a lost cause. All the Underwoods had too many interests. Books and projects, fishing rods and sewing machines, microscopes and telescopes and seven working computers pretty much took up any available space.

Even the guest house wasn't immune, mainly because Chloe was doing her best to keep her mind busy. She read constantly — television was too ephemeral to keep her mind occupied. She knitted, she played Tetris on her Game Boy with single-minded concentration whenever she had to be in a public place. It even went with her into the bathroom. The little blocks falling into place gave her a Zen-like sense of security, and she played till her hands went numb.

She was cheerful, calm and pleasant, and her parents were almost deceived into thinking she was well on her way to being healed. Chloe knew it was going to take longer, but there was no rush. As long as she had her parents' place to hide in she could take all the time she needed.

"I think you should come with us," her mother said, shoving a pile of papers to one side of the breakfast counter and setting down a tall glass of orange juice. "You've been isolating too much."

"I haven't been isolating," she said calmly, taking the orange juice that she didn't want, knowing an argument would be futile. "I'm just . . . on vacation. If I'm in the way I can always —"

"Don't be ridiculous!" It was hard to annoy her easygoing mother, but Chloe was the one most likely to manage. "There's always room for you here, as well as the entire family. Why do you think we built the guest house? In fact, you know I wish you'd stay in the main house. I'd feel more comfortable knowing you were under the same roof."

Chloe drank her orange juice, saying nothing. She knew that was one of the things that worried her family the most, her unnatural quiet, but there was nothing she could do about it. Idle chatter was totally beyond her at that point, even if it meant reassuring her mother.

"I know this conference is going to be a total bore for anyone not in the medical profession, but your brothers and sister will be there, as well as their families. It's being held in a charming resort on the coast, and I know you'd have a lovely time. . . ."

"Not yet," she said, her voice so quiet her mother had to lean forward to hear her. "You go on and have fun. I'll be fine here. You haven't gone anywhere since I came back, and I know how you like to travel. Trust me, it's perfectly safe. No one's going to bother me, and I'll just enjoy a few days' solitude."

"You've been enjoying too much solitude." She turned to her husband who'd just entered the kitchen. "James, talk her into coming with us!"

James shook his head. "Leave the girl alone, Claire. She'll be fine. She's just tired of having us hanging around all the time. A few days of quiet will be the best thing for her. Right, Chloe?"

Chloe managed to rouse her voice for that one. "Absolutely. There's nothing to worry about."

Claire Underwood looked between her husband and youngest child, equally frustrated. "I can't fight the both of you," she said. "Just make sure you have the security system on, you understand?"

"We never use the security system," Chloe protested.

"We paid a huge amount of money for it, we might as well use it," her father said, the traitor. "That sounds like a good compromise. Promise to leave the security system on and I'll make sure your mother comes with me."

Chloe had never considered that her mother might refuse to go at the end. The very notion of a weekend of mother-daughter bonding gave her cold chills. Not that she didn't love her mother, but

Claire's attempts at bonding were notoriously inept. "I'll use the security system," she said. "I'll even go buy a gun and a pack of guard dogs if you think it's necessary."

"Don't be ridiculous, Chloe." Her mother had given up at this point. "Besides, I think your father has an old twenty-two somewhere up in the attic."

"Great. I'll go make sure I know where to find the weapons when the Mongol hordes attack."

"Very funny," her mother muttered. "I know the two of you think I worry too much. . . ."

"And we love you for it," James said. "But in the meantime we've got to go. You've got a paper to deliver and I've got grandchildren to see." He glanced over at Chloe, sitting on the stool with both hands clasped around the glass of orange juice. "Speaking of which, I wouldn't mind some more eventually. No hurry, of course, but you might just keep it in mind. I hear Kevin McInerny's back from New York, setting up a law firm in Black Mountain. You used to date him, didn't you? Nice young man."

"Yes, he was nice," Chloe said. She couldn't even remember him.

"Maybe I'll invite him out to dinner when we get back," her mother said. "You wouldn't mind that, would you, Chloe?"

She'd rather have her toes eaten by lizards. "That would be fine."

Her mother swallowed it whole, and by that time her father had reappeared with the luggage. "Have a good time," Chloe said brightly. "I'll be fine."

Her mother gave her a quick hug, pulling back to search her face one more time. She didn't like what she saw there, Chloe thought, but there was nothing she could do about it.

"Be careful," her mother said.

Ten minutes later they were gone, blissful silence filling the huge old house. She dutifully set the security system, once she knew they were off the grounds, and then forgot about it. There was an odd chill in the air. The soft ripe scent of spring had been temporarily halted. She should have paid attention to the Weather Channel, but scenes of snowstorms in more northerly climates tended to make her shake, so she usually avoided it completely. The sky was overcast, threatening, and the wind had picked up, laced with an edge of ice. A cold front must be coming through, she thought, trying to still her instinctive nervousness. It wouldn't affect her traveling family — they were well ahead of whatever storm was blowing in. And it wouldn't affect her — she had no intention of going anywhere. Instead she was planning on pampering herself while they were gone — taking long, leisurely soaks in the Jacuzzi, watching old musicals on the television. She used to have a fondness for martial arts movies, but since she'd returned from Paris she found she had a low tolerance for artificial violence. But Judy Garland and Gene Kelly calmed her into believing in a happy place where people woke up singing and dancing. For the next few days, she was going to live in that place, no matter what the weather outside.

It was growing dark by the time she emerged from the hot tub, and she wrapped herself in a thick terry robe and wandered down into the kitchen. The security panel was blinking, the green lights telling her all was safe and secure, and she realized for the first time in months she was hungry. Probably because her mother wasn't there nagging her to eat. She opened the massive refrigerator that was always kept overstocked, found herself some leftover apple pie. She pulled it out, closing the door behind her, only to look directly into Bastien Toussaint's dark, merciless eyes.

22

She dropped the pie. It was in a Pyrex dish that shattered at her bare feet, but she didn't move, looking up at him in shock.

"You look like you've seen a ghost, Chloe," he said, his voice that familiar, mesmerizing sound. "Surely you didn't think I'd died?"

It took her a moment to find her voice. "I wondered," she said. He looked different. Thinner, his face lined from pain or something else, and his hair was even longer, though streaked with sunlight that matched his tanned skin. Odd, because she never would have thought of him in the sunlight — only in darkness and shadows.

"It takes a lot to kill me," he said. He was standing too close, and she started to step back, away from him, when he caught her arm in an iron grip. She fought back, instinctively, but he simply lifted her up, setting her down out of the way of the broken glass. She'd forgotten that her feet were bare.

"You might want to get dressed," he said. "I'll clean up the mess while I wait."

"I don't need to get dressed," she said. "I'm not going anywhere, you are. You can leave, right now. I don't know why you suddenly appeared out of nowhere, but I don't want you here. Go away."

"The necklace."

"What?"

"I came for the diamond necklace," he said in a calm voice. "You left Paris wearing it, remember? It has a certain value, and I came to get it."

She stared at him in shock. "Why didn't you come sooner?"

"I was . . . incapacitated."

"Why didn't you just call me and ask me to send it to you?"

"It's not something I would trust to the mails, or even to a courier. I'm sorry if my presence distresses you, but I had no choice but to come myself."

She felt nothing, Chloe told herself. It was like prodding a wound, only to discover it had healed. She looked into his dark, unreadable eyes and was certain she felt nothing at all.

"All right," she said. "I'll go get it, and then you can leave. I really have nothing to say to you."

"I didn't expect you would," he said, leaning back against the counter. "Just get me the necklace and I'll be on my way."

She stared at him for a moment longer. He didn't belong in her mother's kitchen. He didn't belong a few feet away from her, while she was wearing nothing but a loosely tied terry robe. She didn't feel a thing for him, not hatred or passion — she was totally numb, the blessed numbness that had protected her during those last few days in Paris. And she had to get him out of there, fast, before that numbness faded.

"Stay right there," she ordered, moving past him, holding herself out of reach as she headed toward the kitchen stairs. He made no effort to touch her, and she felt stupid, but she couldn't help herself. The closer she got to him the shakier she felt.

Most of her clothes were in the guest house, but there was some clean laundry in the dryer upstairs. While the selection didn't provide her with much choice, she managed to find a pair of old gray sweatpants, a baggy gray T-shirt and a thick pair of wool socks. Her hair had begun to grow again, and she'd pulled it back in a low ponytail, refusing to look at her reflection in the mirror. She knew what she looked like and she didn't care.

She'd actually forgotten about the necklace. She'd taken it off, halfway across the Atlantic, and her father had locked it up in the safe once they got home. If only she'd remembered she could have figured out some way to send it back to him.

Or could she? She didn't know his name, who he worked for, where he lived. She knew absolutely nothing at all about him. Except that he killed.

The evening light was an eerie blue-gray, and she glanced at the window, wondering where his car was. Wondering how he'd managed to get past the alarm system. Silly question — he could probably materialize through stone walls if he wanted. A commercial security system would be child's play for him.

She watched with stunned disbelief as a few flakes of snow began to fall. It shouldn't snow in April, not with the daffodils and the rest of the beautiful landscape about to bloom. He must have brought the storm with him, like the coat of black ice surrounding his heart.

He'd cleaned up the broken pie dish by the time she arrived back in the kitchen, and he'd made coffee. It annoyed her, but not enough that she refused the mug he handed her, rich with cream and no sugar, just the way she liked it. She wondered how he knew. In their time together she couldn't remember having time for a leisurely cup of coffee.

"Here," she said, dumping the diamonds into his outstretched hand, careful not to touch him.

He put the necklace in his pocket. Black, he was always wearing black, and today was no different. Whose blood was he hoping to hide?

She was being ridiculous. She took a sip of the coffee and couldn't quite stifle her soft sigh. She hadn't had as good a cup of coffee since she'd left Paris.

He was sitting at the breakfast bar, looking oddly at ease among the clutter. He didn't belong there, she reminded herself, and she took another sip.

"How did you get past the security system?" she asked.

"Do you really need to ask?"

She shook her head. "I suppose that means it won't be any protection at all if someone wants to come after me?"

"And why would they?"

"I don't know. But then, I never understood why they wanted to kill me in the first place."

"They're all dead, Chloe. No one wants

to hurt you anymore. And the security system is very good. Just not good enough." His eyes ran down her body, and there was just the faintest trace of a smile at the corner of his mouth. "You look well."

"Do we have to do this? You got what you wanted. Why don't you get on a plane and go back to France and we can forget we ever knew each other."

"I'd like to," he said with his customary lack of flattery, "but there seems to be a small problem."

"What's that?" she said. She should sit. The hours in the hot tub, followed by the spring chill of an open window and the shock of seeing Bastien once more made her disoriented. If she blinked maybe he'd disappear.

"I don't want to blink," she said out loud, her voice sounding peculiar. Bastien looked odd as well — prettier than she remembered, which was certainly unfair of fate, and she would have said as much but she seemed to have lost the ability to speak.

"Then don't blink, *chérie*," he murmured. "Just close your eyes." And the blackness closed in around her.

He caught her as she fell. He'd lied to her — nothing new. She didn't look well at all. She'd lost weight, and she had circles under her eyes as if she hadn't been sleeping well. It shouldn't have been a surprise, but he'd hoped . . . he'd hoped to find a healthy, buoyant American female ready to hand him his head on a platter. She'd had time to recover, to move past things.

But she hadn't.

He picked her up, carrying her into the living room. The big old sofa was covered with books and newspapers, and he swept them on the floor before laying her down. He'd probably given her too much — he'd calculated the sedative in her coffee based on her Paris weight and she was down at least ten pounds from that.

Still, it would just keep her quiet longer. Maybe long enough to deal with the problem and then leave, with her none the wiser about her close call. She didn't need to know that there was an unexpected survivor of the Hotel Denis debacle. And that particular survivor would risk anything to get to Chloe.

There was no mistaking the expression of shock and horror on her face when she saw him, and he couldn't blame her. She would have counted on him being out of her life forever, and to have him show up was undoubtedly a nightmare come true. Fortunately he'd had the excuse of the old necklace, and she'd believed him. He just had to hope his luck would hold, as it had so many times before.

He'd hoped to leave it with her — the necklace. He'd had it for years, the first step on his self-determined road to hell. He'd been twelve years old, old enough and tall enough to be an embarrassment to his mother and Aunt Cecile, who liked to think of themselves as at least a decade younger. It was Monte Carlo, they'd been gambling unwisely, and his mother had had to sell her diamond necklace. She'd raged and cried and stormed, and young Bastien had never seen her so upset, and like a child he'd resolved to do something about it. He couldn't get her necklace back, but he could replace it with another necklace.

It had been easy enough — people don't suspect a child, even a tall, gangly one. And he was agile as a monkey and totally fearless. The woman who owned the necklace was so old and so fat that the wrinkles in her neck covered it. His beautiful mother deserved it far more.

She was lying in her bed at the hotel when he came in. He waited until her partner for the night left, a middle-aged wine importer whom he sincerely hoped wouldn't become her next husband, and then he tiptoed in.

The curtains were pulled against the cruel daylight, and the room stank of cigarettes and perfume and whiskey. And sex. She was passed out, her artfully streaked blond hair flowing down her narrow back, and he whispered, *"Maman?"*

She didn't move. He tried it again, but she simply let out an inelegant snore. He reached over and touched her shoulder, tugging at her, and she turned over, blinking up at him before her eyes focused.

"What the hell are you doing in here, you little brat? I've told you to keep a low profile when I'm having friends over."

"I brought you something." She'd lost the ability to frighten him when he was about nine, but the anger in her ragged voice almost made him turn around and leave.

"What?" She sat up, not bothering to cover herself with the sheet. He was used to his mother's body. She had no modesty, and he surveyed her dispassionately. She was getting older. "What did you have to wake me up for?"

He held out his grubby little hand, the

diamond necklace glittering even in the shadowy light. "It's a present. I got it for you."

She sat up farther still, reached for her cigarettes and lit one. "Give it to me."

He put the necklace in her hand, and she examined it for a moment, then let out a little laugh. "Where did you get this?"

"I found it. . . ."

"Where did you get this?"

He swallowed. "I stole it."

He wasn't sure what he expected. Rage. Tears. Instead she laughed. "Already embarking on a life of crime, Bastien? Maybe your father was that pickpocket after all, and not the American businessman." She put the necklace back in his hand, stubbed out her cigarette and lay down once more.

"Don't you want it? You were so sad when you lost your diamonds." It was perhaps the last vulnerable thing he ever said to her.

She turned and looked at him out of slitted eyes, her makeup caked around them. "Those belong to Gertruda Schondheim, and she has some very nasty connections. I would never dare wear them. They're far too recognizable. Besides, Georges has already redeemed my own, and I expect he'll be good enough for a few other trinkets as well. Now go away and let me sleep."

His hand closed around the diamond necklace. He turned and walked toward the door, when her voice stopped him. "You might as well leave it," she said. "I don't know if I can find a fence around here, but sooner or later I can find someone to cut it down and sell it stone by stone."

He looked down at the necklace. It was a beautiful thing, very old, very elegant, and he'd chosen that one on purpose for his mother's beautiful neck.

He turned back, ready to pour all his rage and love and hurt out, but she'd fallen into a drugged sleep once again, her son forgotten.

So he'd pocketed the diamond necklace and walked out of the room, and she'd never mentioned it again.

He never knew for certain whether she even remembered the useless gift. It didn't matter. He had no intention of giving it to her, or even his marginally more affectionate Aunt Cecile.

Nor was he going to return it. It had become a symbol, an icon of power and independence. As long as he held the necklace he had something of value, and he was no longer dependent on his mother's whims.

Oddly enough, he'd kept it for all those years. There'd been times when he could have sold it, should have sold it, but instead he'd kept it with him.

It should have been easy prey for a thief, as it had been in the first place. But the shadowy world of criminals was far too close to the Committee, and no one would attempt something so dangerous, no matter what the prize. In the twenty years since he'd stolen the damned thing he'd never seen it on anyone's neck until he fastened it around Chloe's.

He went through the house swiftly, efficiently, checking the doors and windows, the vulnerable entryways. The security system was state-of-the-art, which meant it would hold off a determined operative for approximately five minutes. He'd had enough time to boost the outside defenses, and he worked quickly, doing what he could on the inside of the house. Locking them in.

He glanced at his watch. There was no guarantee that Jensen's detailed information was accurate, though his infallible instincts told him he could trust him. But plans could change, transportation could be delayed, as he knew far too well from the debacle of the Hotel Denis. If the Underwoods had landed on time Chloe would have been out of harm's way long before the shooting began.

He might be dead, but that was a small price to pay. Life and death had stopped mattering a long time ago.

He came back to the cluttered den, where Chloe lay in a deep sleep on the sofa. There was a brightly colored quilt tossed on a chair, and he picked it up and covered her with it. Her hair was longer now, but no one had given it any kind of professional styling. His trained eye knew it was still the same ragged cut she'd performed on herself while he'd watched from a distance. And damned if he didn't still like it.

Then again, he'd accepted the fact that he liked far too much about her. Which was why coming back into her life was the last thing he'd wanted to do. But he'd had no choice.

He moved to the window, looking out through the gloomy afternoon. In his preliminary scouting he'd found she'd been staying at one of the guest houses off to the side. He'd turned on the lights, the television, closed the blinds and arranged a little surprise for them. It wouldn't slow them down for long, but every extra minute of warning could make the difference between life and death.

They'd landed in Canada — five of them, including their leader. Jensen had managed to get that much information to him before he'd gone in, but now he was officially cut off. He was going to have to wing it from here on in.

There were countless computers all over the place, but he was wise enough not to touch them. Without the proper defenses in place anyone in the world could find him. His mobile phone was safer, though not completely, but after a few moments it looked reasonably certain that they weren't going to arrive for another eight hours at the least. The kind of people he was fighting wouldn't be deterred for long by the unexpected forces of nature.

Time enough to get her out of there? That was always the question — they were probably safer in this mini-fortress, particularly with his modifications to the security system. Out on the road was a different matter, and they could only run for so long. Her family would return sooner or later, and while he didn't give a crap about them, she did. So for her sake he had to keep them alive as well. And that meant dealing with the problem here and now.

The den was too vulnerable, and she was going to be out for hours on end. Maybe, with extreme luck, she'd stay unconscious until all this ended, and she'd never have to know a thing about it. By the time she came to he'd be long gone, the danger passed.

The only drawback was that he'd have to take the necklace, and for some reason it was important to him that she have it. But if she kept it, she'd always be wondering when he was going to show up again. Too much to risk on a sentimental gesture.

Their best spot was a second-floor bedroom near the back of the house. The windows on the sloping site were close enough to the ground if they had to jump, but it gave him a decent vantage point of the overgrown grounds surrounding the house. It was a slim advantage, but the only one they had. He picked her up off the sofa, marveling again at how damned light she was, and carried her upstairs. The light from the hallway illuminated his way, and set her down on the king-size bed before he went to open the window a crack. She looked pale, cold, even in the shapeless, bulky clothes no Frenchwoman would ever wear, and he pulled back the covers and slid her under them, tucking her in.

He stood there, staring down at her for a long moment. And then, on impulse, he pushed her tangled hair away from her forehead. She looked the same — stubborn, pretty when there was no room in his life for pretty, and on impulse he leaned down and kissed her, softly, while she slept.

And then there was nothing he could do but keep watch. And wait.

Until Monique came to kill her.

23

When she opened her eyes she was disoriented, confused. The room was dark, only bright moonlight coming through the uncurtained windows, and for a moment she didn't know where she was. Slowly it came back to her . . . she was in the back guest room, the one her older brother and his wife usually used. She was tucked up in bed, in the darkness, and she'd dreamed she saw Bastien once more.

Someone was sitting in a chair by the window. She could only see his outline, but she knew it hadn't been a dream.

She didn't sit up, didn't move. Her voice was very quiet when she spoke. "Why are you really here? It wasn't the necklace, was it?"

He must have known she was awake. He always seemed to have an instinctive awareness of everything about her. Oh, God, she hoped not everything. She hoped he didn't know the mixed, crazy tangle of emotions he brought out in her. For a moment he didn't answer, and it was long enough for him to fantasize all sorts of things, that he couldn't live without her, that he had to see her one more time, that he loved . . .

"Someone wants to kill you." His voice was calm, dispassionate.

It was no more than she'd expected, and that one crazed moment of hope hadn't lasted long enough to make it hurt. Much. "Of course they do," she said. "Why should anything have changed? And you're here to save my life? I thought you'd already done your duty. You got me safely out of France — the rest should be up to me. And presumably the American cops or CIA or whatever."

He didn't say anything, so she sat up, frustrated. "And why in hell would anyone want to kill me? You're a much more likely target. I didn't do anything to anybody — I was just in the wrong place at the wrong time. I'm no threat to any of your insane plans for world domination."

"You've been watching too much television," he said. He had less of an accent now, along with his different look. She wondered if he had a different name as well.

"Who wants to kill me and why? And

why should you care?" *Please,* she thought. *Just say something, anything that I can keep with me. Something to let me know I'm more than a hindrance.*

But she knew what he was going to say. He'd said it far too many times. He didn't care — he simply felt responsible, and she didn't want to hear it.

He rose, silhouetted against the moonlit window, and for a moment she was afraid someone would shoot him. But the light was much too murky — the snow must have picked up while she was unconscious, and even if she could see out, as long as the lights were out no one would see in. He moved toward her, out of range of the windows, and to her astonishment he sat down on the floor next to her bed.

"Monique survived," he said softly.

"You told me she was dead. That she was shot in the face."

"That's what I saw. But the night was chaos — I must have been mistaken. All that I know is that she survived, and she's coming after you."

"Well, you can protect me from one single woman, can't you? You've done it before." The memory of Maureen's body, facedown in the snow, leeching blood, was still etched in her brain, and she shuddered.

"She's not coming alone."

He was leaning against the bedside table, hands propped on his knees, seemingly at ease. "But why?" Chloe asked. "If she wanted to kill someone, why wouldn't she want to kill you? I was just an innocent bystander."

"You still are. And she has every intention of killing me when she can find me. I'm just a little harder to track. So she's having to make do with you."

"Lucky me," she muttered. "Always someone's second choice."

"I'm sorry, would you rather have half of Europe after you? It's easy enough to arrange."

"And how would you do that?"

"Simply by staying with you."

She turned to look at him. He'd said the words offhandedly, and she knew he had no interest or intention of being around her a moment longer than he had to. If it had been up to him he wouldn't have seen her again. Hadn't he said that earlier?

"So why does she want to kill me? Apart from the fact that I think I called her a skanky bitch. Why should she bother, I don't matter to her."

"No," he said, "you don't."

"Then why?"

392

"Because you matter to me."

His face was hidden in the moonlight, his words without inflection, and she almost thought she'd misheard him. "I don't understand."

"What's to understand? Monique knows me well enough to recognize that the best way to hurt me is to hurt you. Simple logic. She'll be here in a few hours."

"A few hours? Then why don't we leave?"

"For one thing, the snow is piling up, shutting down the highways. It won't stop Monique, but it might slow her down a bit. Anyway, this is the safest place we can be, for now. I've improved the security system, and we have the advantage. They're coming into unknown territory, whereas I've had time to check things out thoroughly. I've even managed to set a few surprises to welcome them. I was considering sneaking you out of here ahead of time, but you're safer with me."

"So you've always told me."

"I have, haven't I?" he said wearily. "Once Monique is finished you won't have to see me again. Consider it a reward for following my orders."

"Are you going to kill her? If you have to?"

"I'm going to kill her whether I have to or not," he said. "And then I'll be gone."

"Where?"

He shrugged. "Where I belong, I suppose. Back to the Committee. It's all I know how to do, and I've been well-trained to do it. It would be a shame to waste such expensive education and talent." His voice was light.

"It would be a shame to waste you," she said. "Don't you think you matter more than a few highly specialized skills?"

He turned to look at her, and the murky light fell across his face, revealing his faintly ironic smile. "No," he said. "Go back to sleep. I thought I gave you enough to knock you out for twelve hours at least, but you always were a stubborn woman."

"You drugged me?"

"It wasn't the first time. And I can do a lot worse if you annoy me. Be quiet and let me think. I'll keep watch, and you'll be safe enough. Believe me, they won't come without warning."

"When are they coming?"

"If it weren't for the storm they would have been here by midnight. As it is, I expect they'll be here sometime between four and five in the morning. It will still be dark enough to cover their movements. They've probably planned a simple assault — get in fast, complete their mission and out again in no more than twenty minutes. Monique would only hire the best."

"And you're enough to stop them?"

"Yes. Now go back to sleep."

"What time is it now?"

"Just after eleven."

"And they won't be coming for another five hours?"

"Six if we're lucky, four if we're not."

"Then why don't you lie down and try to get some rest? It's a huge bed. You won't have to worry about accidentally touching me." She hadn't expected anything more than a cutting response, but without a word he rose, moving around to the other side of the huge bed, and lay down on it, kicking off his shoes. He didn't get under the covers, but he was there, within reach.

"Have you been having trouble sleeping since you got back?" His voice was just a whisper on the night wind, closer than she realized.

"Yes. And you?"

"I never have trouble sleeping. I'll sleep for exactly one hour now, and wake up feeling rested and alert. Don't forget, what happened in Paris was nothing new for me."

She was nothing new for him, she thought. And she was an idiot to be thinking about such things, when she could be dead in a matter of hours, but somehow the imminent possibility of dying only made living more important. Made loving more important. And all the psychobabble and rationalizations didn't mean a thing when it came right down to it.

"It wasn't Stockholm Syndrome," she said in a muffled voice, turning her back on him in the vast expanse of the king-size bed. There might as well be an ocean between them.

"I know," he said, and he sounded oddly gentle. "I told you, Stockholm Syndrome is a myth."

She turned over to look at him, and he was much closer than she'd realized. So close she could reach out and touch him. "Then why do I still feel this way?" she whispered.

He said nothing, but for the first time his face looked unguarded in the moonlight. "Are we going to die in a few hours?" she asked.

"Quite possibly," he said. "But not right now." And he reached out and touched her face, his hand incredibly gentle. She stared at him, frozen, as he leaned over and kissed her with heartbreaking tenderness.

"What's this?" she asked, trying to sound cynical and failing miserably. "My reward?"

"No," he said. "It's mine." He caught her face with his hands, cradling it, looking down at her. The stillness was complete, magical, and she felt everything seem to fade away, the blood, the pain, the danger. For a moment there was just the two of them, alone in the night, and there was no barrier, no cool defenses in his dark eyes. She could see past the calm, dispassionate surface, to something deep and hard and frightening inside him. Something he felt for her.

She closed her eyes, reaching up to slide her arms around his neck. He moved over her, a heavy, warm weight that kept the monsters at bay, and began to kiss her, slowly seducing her with his mouth, his lips, his teeth, his tongue. She'd never been kissed like that, with such dedicated concentration, as if kissing her was all that mattered in the world, an end in itself, and she gave herself up to it, opening her mouth for him, kissing him back with single-minded concentration that was slowly turning into a kind of panicked fire.

Then she reached for his shirt, her fingers fumbling at the buttons.

He caught her hands in one of his strong ones, holding her still. "Shh, Chloe. This time there's no need for rush. No need for fear or pain. There's all the time in the world to just enjoy yourself. Pleasure — that's all you need to think about. Close your eyes and let me bring it to you."

His voice was low, hypnotic, soothing her sudden uprush of tension, and she lay back against the pillows, staring up at him.

He held her hands, more as a reassurance than a restraint, as he brought his mouth down the side of her neck, and he was reaching under the baggy sweatshirt, to touch her skin, his fingers cool against her heated flesh. She was so lost in his kisses, the taste of his mouth, that she barely noticed when he pulled the sweatshirt over her shoulders and tossed it away, when he slid the baggy pants down her legs and off her. He'd left her underwear on — the French bra and lace panties that her well-meaning parents had gotten her for Christmas. She hadn't even paid any attention when she'd put them on, but when his hand slid up her body to cover her breast she knew she'd done it on purpose. He followed with his mouth, sucking at her through the lace, and her body trembled as the need blossomed through her body in a rush of heat. He'd released her hands, and they lay beside her on the wide bed, where he'd placed them. She felt strange, filled with a dreamy lassitude, able to only lie there and let him touch her, kiss her. It must be the hangover from the drug, she thought dizzily, as he put his mouth on her hip bones, just above the lace band of the panties. That, or he'd managed to hypnotize her with his mouth, his eyes, her own longing.

She felt as if they were in a snow globe — roughly shaken, but now all was still and silent with the flakes drifting down around them in their safe little glass jar. She could always try to fight her way out of that strange surrender, but she didn't want to. He was right. They could be dead in a matter of hours. She could have what she wanted, needed, right now, and there might be no consequences to live with. No life to live with. And if she was going to die she wanted to spend the last hours of her life in bed with a man whose name she didn't even know.

He unfastened the bra with a flick of his fingers, the same bra she'd struggled to fasten a short while ago, and he pulled it from her body and tossed it. He moved slowly, touching her nipple with his tongue, and she felt it stiffen immediately into a hard, tight knot that matched the hard, tight knot between her legs. She'd never thought her breasts were particularly sensitive, but he seemed to know just how to touch them, suck them, slide his tongue over them until she was shaking with reaction. Just when she thought she was going to climax simply from the feel of his mouth tugging at her breast, his tongue swirling around the tip, he moved down, his mouth dancing across her flat stomach, and his hands slid under the lace straps of the panties and pulled them down her long legs. His mouth followed — on her hips, her legs, the insides of her knees, moving up again, and when he put his mouth between her legs she trembled, reaching for him, threading her hands through his long, thick hair as it fell over her hips.

He cupped her hips, pulling her thighs apart, and his mouth was like nothing she'd ever felt, an invasion, a branding, a claiming that felt so total and absolute that she could do nothing but let him touch her, lick her, bite her, using his mouth in ways she hadn't imagined, until he slid his fingers inside her, and she arched off the bed in sudden, rigid climax that was fast and hard and like nothing she'd ever felt.

It was fast, it was short, and she sank back, breathless, only to have him start it all over again, building slowly, gently, into a greater intensity so that when he slid his fingers inside her she cried out this time, and the orgasm held for longer. As long as he seemed to want to hold it.

She collapsed back on the bed, panting, shaken, and reached out to touch his face. "No more," she whispered. "I can't . . ."

"Of course you can," he whispered between her thighs. This time the simple touch of his tongue sent her into spasms, and the shocking feel of his fingers finished her. She thought she screamed, she who usually made love in discreet silence, but it didn't matter, since he was prepared, covering her mouth with his hand, so that her cries fell into his skin and nowhere else.

And that final freedom made it complete. She didn't have to hold anything back, she could scream, she could cry, and could simply let go of her body and let it happen, let him do whatever he wanted, and she gave in willingly, ready to vanish into a thick maelstrom of unimaginable power.

When she fell back on the bed in a

mindless, boneless heap he moved his hand from her mouth, falling back beside her, his heavy breathing matching her own, as she slowly started to come down from the inexpressible power of her climax. She lay on her back, eyes closed, listening to him, feeling him lying beside her, exactly where he should be, as her racing heart slowed infinitesimally.

"Sleep now, Chloe," he whispered, his voice soft, soothing.

The lassitude vanished. Her eyes shot open, and she turned her head to look at him. He lay on his back, seemingly at ease, still fully dressed, the murky light drifting across him.

She spent one moment considering the possibilities. That he didn't want her, had no need of her or her body, had only given her what he'd promised without giving anything of himself. And then she ignored it. If they were going to die, she wasn't going to waste another moment on a rash of stupid insecurities.

She rose on one elbow, looking at him. Her muscles trembled slightly under her, but she ignored her unexpected weakness. "What are you doing?"

He didn't open his eyes, the rat bastard. "Sleeping," he said.

"No," she said. "You're not." And she reached over and began unfastening the row of black shell buttons on his shirt.

One hand came up and caught hers, stopping her once more, but she wasn't about to be distracted. "Let go of my hand," she said. "We're not finished here."

"I am."

She pulled her hand free, slid it down his stomach to touch him. Hard, pulsing, through the black pants. "No, you're not," she said, as she began to unbuckle his belt. "And neither am I."

"Chloe . . ."

"Shut up," she said ruthlessly, and she freed him, leaned over and put her mouth on him.

He was cool and smooth and silken, hard as ice in her mouth, and she had no idea where the pleasure came from that filled her as she let her mouth learn him. She only knew it made her tremble with its strength.

He'd stopped arguing. She reached a hand up to blindly rip at his shirt, but he was helping her now, unbuttoning it and pulling it off, and then his hands cupped her head, and he talked to her, whispered words in gutter French as she slowly sucked and pulled at him with her mouth, and she was sweating, shaking with the power of the response she was drawing from him, when he suddenly pulled her away, moving back against the head of the huge old bed, kicking the rest of his clothes onto the floor so that he was now as naked, as ready as she was.

"If you really want me, Chloe, you have to take me," he said.

She sat back on her heels to look at him. And then she put her hands on his shoulders, the smooth, strong skin, and climbed on top of him, straddling him as he sat there on the bed.

She felt momentarily self-conscious. "I've never done this . . ." she said.

"Good." He pulled her the rest of the way, positioning her over him, moving so that she could feel the head of his cock just touching her. "Now it's up to you."

She moved, just enough to let him enter her, and a look of almost exquisite pleasure crossed his face, and his quick intake of breath was so erotic that she pushed down, so that he filled her, so deep, so tight that she almost climaxed again.

He'd closed his eyes, but his long fingers were clutching her hips, and only the slightest pressure made her move, rise up, then slowly down again, and his guttural groan seemed to vibrate inside her own body. She rested her forehead on his shoulder as she moved, he moved, together, the rise and fall, deep and hard, and he was talking to her, telling her lies that she wanted to believe, all in French, words of praise and love and sex and the dark, spiraling need that suddenly flamed out of control as he exploded inside her. And without expecting it she lost the last tiny bit of self-control, following, and she was sobbing quietly against his skin, shaking with the force of their joining, until she collapsed against him, gasping for breath.

She didn't know what she expected. Not that he would turn, with her still tight in his arms, stretching her out beneath his strong body, and she knew that even though he'd climaxed inside her he was still hard, getting harder, and she didn't think she could bear it, as she wrapped her legs around him, pulling him in deeper still, the words long gone.

She didn't need to speak, he was kissing her again, fucking her again, and she simply gave into it, a holy wash of sin and redemption, and the snowy darkness closed around her, and time lost its meaning.

And there was nothing left between them but love, neither pure nor simple, but love it was.

24

Chloe lay sprawled across his body, drained, exhausted, in a deeper, more abandoned sleep than he'd given her with his cocktail of drugs. She was practically boneless, so relaxed that he doubted even gunshots would wake her.

He couldn't afford to test that theory. He'd lived to the ripe old age of thirty-four always being aware that failure was an option, and looking out for it. If a stray bullet managed to hit him then she was doomed, and he wasn't about to let that happen. She was sexually infatuated with him, he accepted that with a strange combination of fatalism and gratitude, and he'd given himself over to her with single-minded dedication and a total lack of restraint. The result was that she was half-dead with pleasure and his own body still trembled occasionally from the aftermath.

She'd get over it. She was a practical young woman, a born survivor, and once he disappeared, either into the murky netherworld of the Committee or the more solid answer of a grave, she'd be able to move on.

But she was never going to get better sex in her life.

It was the one selfish bastard thing he'd kept for himself. He hoped and prayed he'd spoiled her for anyone else. She'd sleep with other men, she'd marry and have children and orgasms with someone other than him. But no one would ever be able to make her body sing as he did, and no matter how ruthless that was, he rejoiced in it.

He let his hand trail down her arm. Her skin was smooth, flawless, with Gilles Hakim's brutality nothing more than a distant nightmare. If he ever returned to the Committee, Thomason was going to scream bloody murder that he'd wasted that liquid platinum on a civilian. Fuck him. He'd give Chloe anything he could get away with giving her.

Including the safety and freedom that could only come from his complete absence in her life.

Monique was the last danger. He still didn't know how she'd managed to survive, but she was the most unstable of anyone he'd dealt with while he was working for the Committee. The most unstable of those still alive, that was. People like her didn't last long in the business — you don't let personal feelings get in the way of the mission, you didn't kill for anything other than a job, you didn't hate, you didn't love.

But Monique was so eaten up with hatred that she'd managed to survive when no one else had. And instead of rebuilding her power base, she was hunting for Chloe Underwood, simply because she knew it would hurt him. Lure him out of hiding, so that she could kill him as well.

Once Bastien had stopped Monique there would be no more problem, at least for Chloe. Even if he had to go and cut Harry Thomason's throat to make sure of it.

He knew when her heartbeat shifted, the faint shiver across her skin, and he knew her eyes fluttered open, even though her face was turned away from him. He was strangely attuned to her — they'd slept together only a few times and yet he knew her body, her pulses, the rhythm of her heartbeat and her breathing so well that his own matched hers. He let his hand dance along her arm, just the faintest of caresses, and he could feel her instant response. She wanted more. And, God help him, so did he.

"They're coming soon," he said gently. "We need to get dressed."

She turned her head to look at him, and he could see the dried trace of tears on her face, the mussed hair, the total lack of makeup. She looked younger than ever, innocent in a way that had nothing to do with the inventive hours they'd just shared. Innocent deep in her heart, where he was nothing but an empty core.

"Do we have to?" Her voice was low, husky, sexy. He couldn't believe he could be wanting her again, so quickly. It was a good thing he was going to be either dead or gone in the next few hours. Now that he'd let down his guard it was more and more difficult to build it up again. And their lives depended on his well-honed talents, that had nothing to do with vulnerability at all.

"We have to," he said, pushing her hair away from her face. She reached up and caught his hand, bringing it to her mouth, her lips. He had bite marks on his wrist, where he'd had her use her teeth rather than make the noises he was drawing from her, and she'd drawn blood. It gave him a deep, strange satisfaction. "If we're to have any chance of survival we need to be ready."

"Any chance? How likely is it?"

He shrugged. "Stranger things have been known to happen."

"You could always lie to me."

"Why?"

She pushed away from him, sitting up in the bed. She looked beautiful in the moonlight, no longer self-conscious. He'd marked her as well — love bites at the side of her breast, the roughness of his beard scratching her thighs. It would heal. They would both heal.

"If we're going to die there's no harm in telling me pretty lies," she said. "In the end it won't matter, and I'll die happy."

"I have no intention of letting either of us die. And then where would the lies get us?"

"If you manage to keep us alive then I promise I'll forget. Just tell me you care about me. If we're going to die then how important is the truth?"

"It's because we might die that the truth is particularly important," he said, making no effort to touch her. "And telling you that I care about you is a waste of time. I wouldn't have crossed the ocean, come out of hiding and tracked you down if you didn't matter to me."

Her smile was tentative, so sweet that if

he had a heart it would have broken in it. "Then come up with a better lie. Tell me you love me."

"You don't need lies, Chloe," he said. "I do love you."

It took a moment for his words to sink in. And then, of course, she didn't believe him — he could see it in the doubtful expression in her beautiful brown eyes.

"I shouldn't have asked you," she said unhappily, starting to move away. "Just forget it . . ."

He pulled her back, off balance so that she fell against him, and he took her face in his two hands and held it very still while his eyes looked down into hers. Somber, truthful, painfully honest. "I love you, Chloe," he said. "Which is the most dangerous thing I could do."

"I'm not the one who wants to kill you," she whispered.

"Maybe not today," he replied with a faint smile. "At least that's a change from our usual relationship." He kissed her, lightly, and then pushed her away.

He didn't give her a chance to say anything more, to ask more questions. He couldn't be sorry he told her — if he died he'd regret that he'd held that back from her. She didn't believe him. He didn't know if he was relieved or annoyed. She probably believed it was his soft heart that made him lie to her and tell her that he loved her. Even after the days they'd spent together, the things she'd seen him do, she still thought he was capable of kind lies. When kindness had no part of his being, and lies were only to get what he wanted.

They dressed quickly, in the dark. He couldn't tell if the sky was beginning to turn light — sunrise was sometime after six, but before long it would soon be spreading over the hilly countryside. He wondered if the snow had stopped. Monique would want to be in and out before the full light of dawn, and he could tell they were nearby. Not by any kind of proof, just his instincts at full force.

He'd left the light on in the hall — the usual light an absent house owner would leave to scare off burglars. It went out, and a moment later he heard the muffled explosion with a kind of cold satisfaction.

"They're here," he said. "And they should be down one."

"What do you mean?" He couldn't see her in the newly minted darkness, but he recognized the faint thread of fear in her voice, one she was trying to hide from him.

"I sabotaged the security system. I knew

they were going to try to cut the power, but whoever actually did it isn't going to survive to do anything more. Which leaves Monique and four others at most."

She didn't ask him how he knew that — she accepted it. If she continued being that unnaturally docile then they might have a fighting chance.

She was dressed in that shapeless outfit again, and yet he could see the clean, strong lines of her body beneath the soft fleece as if he could see through cloth. No woman should look that sexy in sweat clothes. No woman should look that sexy when people were trying very hard to kill him.

There was another muffled explosion, and the bright glow sent a rosy shadow into the room. He could see her face again, the doubt and worry that he wanted to kiss away. "What was that?"

"The guest house. Their information is top of the line — they'd know you were supposed to be there, and they would have gone there first. I'm hoping it took at least one more of them, but I can't count on that."

"The guest house is burning?" she said, moving toward the window. "Everything I care about is in there. . . ."

He caught her around the waist, pulling her back into the shadows. Monique and her cohorts would be stationed around the house, watching the windows for any sign of occupation. It wouldn't take much to tip them off. "Things can be replaced," he said. "I need to go."

She stared at him, uncomprehending. "You need to go? You're leaving me?"

"You'll just hold me back. You're going to need to hide while I go hunting. I can work better if I don't have to worry about you at the same time. If I succeed I'll come back for you."

"And if you don't?"

"Then, my sweet, *au revoir*. I'll be going straight to hell, and I don't expect to see you there," he said, his voice light.

"Then you're not leaving me."

He should have known that was coming. She was fully dressed except for her shoes, and she had a stubborn expression on her face, and he knew that he had one chance and one chance only of keeping her alive.

In the shadowy darkness of the bedroom it was easy enough for him to pick up the supplies he'd stashed there earlier. He knew her better than she knew herself, knew she'd object, and he was ruthless enough to do what needed to be done. He came up to her in the darkness, and for the first time she didn't flinch, didn't back away. She would kiss him if he asked her to, she would take her clothes back off and lie down on the bed once more, and he only wished life could be that simple. But it never was.

"I'm sorry, love," he said, cupping her face with one hand. Slapping the duct tape over her mouth before she had any idea what was happening, capturing her hands as they flew up to fight him, wrapping the rope around them. She was struggling now, but he was much bigger and stronger than she was, and he had her down on the floor, tying her quickly, efficiently despite her struggles. He didn't need to see her eyes to know they were blazing with fury. Maybe it would help her get over him. Especially when she was faced with the worst part of this.

He hauled her upright, and she tried to hit him with her bound hands, but it threw her off balance, and he caught her before she fell. He should have just hit her, knocked her out, but he couldn't bring himself to do that to her again. Even if, in fact, it would have been a kindness.

"Don't fight me, Chloe," he whispered in her ear. "I have no choice. When I'm finished with them I'll set you free. Either that, or someone will find you before long. As long as it's not Monique."

She wasn't in the mood to listen, and he didn't expect it. He picked her up, tossing her over his shoulder like a sack of potatoes, and left the room, nothing more than a shadow on the edge of dawn.

She'd stopped fighting, a small grace, until she began to realize where he was taking her. Down two flights of stairs, into the pitch-dark confines of the basement. He could feel the tremors begin to run through her body as the claustrophobia took hold once more, but he ignored it. There was always a price to be paid, and when he opened the crawl space he'd broken into earlier that day her struggles became so fierce that he could no longer hold her, and she fell onto the concrete floor with a muffled cry.

He couldn't afford to waste time with gentleness. He pushed her into the tiny crawl space — there was just enough room for her, none for him, but he could touch her, put his hand on her cold, damp forehead, run his thumb against her temple in a useless, soothing gesture. "It's the best I could come up with, Chloe," he whispered. "Close your eyes and don't think about the darkness. Think about how you're going to kick my ass when you get out of here."

She was trembling, and he doubted she even heard his words. He could see just enough to know her eyes were wide with panic, and there was nothing he could do about it.

Instead he leaned down and put his lips against the silver tape that covered her mouth, a strange, muffled kiss that he couldn't resist. And for a moment her shaking stilled, and she leaned toward him, into the kiss.

"I'm sorry," he said. And moving back, he put the solid door back in place, closing her in there, in the coffinlike space with no light, closing her into her worst fear.

He half expected to hear her kicking at the panel, struggling. The silence was deep and cold as death. He kissed the wood, a soundless goodbye, and went out into the predawn air, ready to kill once more.

She couldn't breathe, couldn't think. She didn't dare move, terrified that she would do something that might endanger Bastien. She sat huddled, trussed and gagged in the dark, tiny space and tried to keep from screaming. Knowing that no scream would be heard.

She moved, and through her panic she heard something hit the floor, something metallic against the cold, hard concrete. If her hands had been bound behind her she wouldn't have been able to find anything, but with them in front she could hunt around, trying to concentrate on that rather than the inky darkness. It had sounded hollow and metallic, like a bullet, but she knew that was ridiculous. It had to be something else.

Her bound hands curled around the slender metallic cylinder, and for a moment she had no idea what it could be. She could feel the bubble of hysteria at the back of her throat. Was he French enough and crazy enough to give her lipstick? And then she knew.

Such a bright light, flooding the cramped space, all from a tiny little flashlight. She felt the clawing panic begin to recede, slowly, and she leaned back against the hard wall, trying to control her breathing. It took her a moment to realize she could also pull the duct tape from across her mouth, and she did so, not even wincing in pain as she yanked it from her skin. He would have known she'd figure it out sooner or later. But by then she'd be calm enough to know that any sound she might make would only endanger them both.

She jerked at her wrists, but that was the limit of his concessions. The rope held firmly, and she could do nothing about her ankles. She was trapped there, but not in the darkness. She could survive anything if she had even a tiny beacon of light. And if enough time passed, and he didn't come back for her, if her parents returned she could call out, and someone would come and rescue her.

The very notion seemed bizarre, but Bastien had been prepared for all contingencies. Now all she had to do was stay calm and wait. Wait for him to come back to her.

Because he would. Though hell should bar the way, hadn't they both said? She had to believe that, or even the security of the tiny flashlight wouldn't be enough to keep her from crying out.

It must be sometime after four. She had no idea how long they'd been in bed together — time had lost all meaning. He'd told her he would kiss every part of her body. He had. He'd made love to her with such exquisite tenderness, such fierce possessiveness, such mind-shaking intensity that even now she felt shaken, shocked. Aroused.

The light was strong and bright, but the battery wouldn't last forever. She had no idea whether any stray light would filter through the solid covering to the crawl space, but she didn't want to risk it. Because if they found her, they'd have a weapon to use against Bastien, and she couldn't let that happen.

She moved the tiny cylinder down in her hand and pushed the button at the tip. The thick, suffocating darkness closed around her like a smothering blanket, and she took a deep, shaky breath. She closed her eyes, refusing to be a victim of the darkness. She huddled there, silent, alone, and waited.

She almost thought she might have slept, though such a thing seemed impossible. She jerked suddenly, as the unmistakable sound of footsteps on the old stairway brought a surge of crazed hope.

She started to call his name, then bit her lips before anything more than a soft intake of breath could be heard. It wasn't Bastien. Whoever was moving around the basement was very quiet — she could barely hear the softest sound of footsteps.

With Bastien, there would have been no sound at all.

Either her eyes had grown accustomed to it, or the darkness of the tiny cubbyhole had lightened slightly. She could see her hands in front of her, bound by rope and duct tape, but she couldn't see the flashlight. She moved, just the tiniest amount, careful not to make a sound, when she felt something roll across her stomach, and a moment later it hit the concrete with a clang as loud as a pair of crashing symbols.

She held her breath, praying, panicked. Please, God, don't let them hear. Let it be Bastien, let it be anyone but the crazy woman who wanted to kill her for reasons so obscure that she wouldn't have believed it if the smell of blood from the Hotel Denis hadn't stayed with her all these months later.

She had no warning. The door to the crawl space was pulled open, and someone stood there, silhouetted by the dim light coming from the cellar door. It wasn't anyone she knew — the person was tall, painfully thin, bald. She didn't move — maybe Bastien had brought help.

"So there you are, *cherie*." Monique's voice came from the cadaverous figure, sounding eerily cheerful. "I knew I'd find you sooner or later. Come out and play." She put a thin, painfully strong hand on her bound wrists and dragged her out into the basement, letting her collapse at her feet.

Monique knelt down by her, and Chloe could see her more clearly now. She wasn't bald — her head had been shaved. And Bastien hadn't been wrong — she had been shot in the face. The left side of her jaw had been blown away, and after four months she had only begun the healing process. Four years wouldn't help.

"Pretty, aren't I?" Monique cooed.

"I didn't do that," Chloe said in a shaky voice.

"Of course you didn't. I doubt you could even shoot a gun, you useless little idiot. I have no idea who did — whether it was the Greek's men, or Bastien's people, or even my own. It doesn't matter. I'm just clearing up a few loose ends. And you're the very final one. There's no one else."

A cold, sick dread filled Chloe's throat. "What do you mean?"

"What do you think I mean? Bastien's dead."

25

"No!" Chloe said, hating the sound of fear in her own voice.

"But yes. Did you think he was some kind of superhero? He bleeds red blood, just like everyone else. I will admit he's harder to kill than most men, but in the end he's only mortal. Or was."

"I don't believe you."

"Of course you do. I can hear it in your voice. I think you knew all along that it was hopeless. I never expected to find him here in the first place. Why didn't he try to run with you? He wouldn't have gotten far, but at least it would have been better than waiting here like a cornered deer. Then again, maybe he decided he'd rather be dead than have a wet little creature like you hanging around his neck for the rest of his life."

From somewhere deep inside she pulled the last of her resources. "He wouldn't have come to save me if he didn't want me."

Monique shrugged. The daylight was growing brighter — it must be a little after six. Chloe's sleep had been so erratic that she'd become far too familiar with how the sky looked at different times during the endless night. "Our mutual friend has a death wish — I've known it for quite a while. I'm merely the instrument to deliver his salvation."

She didn't say she'd already delivered that salvation. Surely she would have changed tenses if, in fact, he was already dead.

But then, English wasn't her first language, and Chloe couldn't place her hopes on the grammatical nuances of a crazy woman.

"So if you've done what you came for, why are you still here? Bastien is dead — what else do you want?"

"*Chérie!*" Monique said, mocking. "Haven't you been listening to me? Killing Bastien, while enjoyable, wasn't what I came for. Besides, my men found him first, trying to escape. He would have abandoned you to my tender mercies, but Dmitri was too fast for him. If we hadn't killed him now I would have found him in Europe sooner or later. No, I came here for you."

"Why?"

425

Monique shrugged. "Because you annoy me. Because Bastien seemed willing to risk everything, including me, for some ridiculous notion of honor."

"Honor? You think that's why he saved me?"

"Of course. What other reason could he possibly have?"

"He loves me."

Monique hit her so hard she fell back on the rough floor of the basement. She'd been holding a gun, a fact that had managed to escape Chloe's attention, and the solid metal had connected with her face, her mouth. She could taste her own blood, but she was well past the point of caring. If Bastien was dead then she would be as well, but she'd make her last few minutes as painful for Monique as she could. She was willing to pay the price.

"Jealous?" she asked sweetly. "I'm sorry he preferred you to me, but I think he was tired of older women."

Monique kicked her in the ribs, so hard that the breath was knocked out of her. The pain in her side was excruciating, and Chloe thought her rib might have snapped. In a while it wouldn't matter. "Or maybe he just tired of you," she managed to choke out.

Monique squatted down beside her, catching Chloe's shirt in her fist and jerking her upright. The pain in her side was agonizing, but she managed to meet Monique's furious gaze with stony unconcern, even when she felt the cold steel of the gun barrel against her forehead. "Would you like to see what it's like to have part of your face blown away, little girl? I know exactly what to do — where to shoot you so that you won't die right away. You'll lie there writhing in misery, praying for it all to end. . . ."

"I don't really care," Chloe said, wishing she could manage a convincing yawn. "If you've already killed Bastien then why would anything matter?"

"Oh, Christ, you're in love with him!" Monique cried in disgust. "Of course you are. How absolutely pathetic! I will admit he's very good in bed — one of the best I've ever had, even if he had a faint aversion to some of the games I like. But he's hardly a romantic hero. He died begging for his life. As you will."

"Don't count on it." She didn't see the second blow coming. A flash of blinding pain, pure white, and Chloe wondered if Monique had shot her. And then the darkness followed, and there was nothing left.

★ ★ ★

The spring storm had finally stopped, leaving the landscape blanketed with white. Bastien had hoped the explosion of the burning guest house had taken more than one of them, but only one charred body lay in the melting snow. There might be another inside, but he couldn't count on it. He'd already circled around to check on the security system, and the second man was down there, electrocuted.

He broke the third one's neck behind the garage, but not before he'd been stabbed. The knife had missed anything vital — he'd moved fast enough before his attacker could turn and pull the knife up, cutting through major organs. He recognized the shape and the style of the attack even before he turned the body over. It appeared that Fernand had gotten tired of running that little bar in the Marais and decided to pick up a little outside work. He was good, but no match for Bastien.

Still, he'd managed to prick him. He'd also been well briefed — the knife went in close to the recent bullet wound. Obviously he was hoping his target would be more vulnerable, but he'd grown enough scar tissue that it had deflected some of the blow.

Bastien stepped back. He was still bleeding freely, and it was soaking into his pants, but he put Fernand's knife into his belt. He was well armed, but at that point he still wasn't sure how many he had left to face. Jensen had told him Monique had entered the country with five men. Had she picked up anyone else along the way, or did he only have the two left to deal with?

He was better off assuming there were more. He skirted around the garage, as the sky slowly grew lighter, streaks of iridescent peach spearing across the sky, and he stopped for a moment. The snow was already melting as the temperature began to climb. In the midst of death and danger it was very beautiful, and he could hear the faint noise of birdsong. What kind of morning birds did they have in America? It was a random thought, quickly dismissed. He would never know. But it gave him some kind of peace, to know that Chloe would wake to skies of that brilliant color, to the songs of unknown birds.

He headed for the house — Monique would have sent her cohorts through the grounds but she'd head straight for the house. Her instincts had always been strong — he could only hope they weren't strong enough to lead her straight to

Chloe. The crawl space would be hard to find in the darkness, and if she just stayed there, quiet and unmoving, she might have a chance.

Leaving her the flashlight had been a stupid idea, but he couldn't stand the idea of sealing her into the dark that terrified her so much. He could only hope that tiny gesture didn't kill her.

He heard them coming from a distance. They were making no effort to keep silent, and moving through the fresh snow was cumbersome going. Presumably they were hoping to lure him out. He vanished into the shadows, waiting, as Monique came out of the cellar, accompanied by a couple of men. One of them had Chloe's limp body slung over his shoulder.

She was unconscious, but not dead. If she were dead they would have left her there. He could see the blood on her pale face, matted into her hair, and it took everything he'd ever learned not to move, not to make a sound. He couldn't risk taking them in the darkness. If he failed, Chloe would die. He had to wait.

Monique opened the door, and he got his first good look at her. In the dawn light he couldn't see much, only enough to know that the skeleton-thin figure was his former lover. The bullet could have done major damage — no wonder she wanted to kill. Her logic in choosing Chloe was twisted but undeniable. If Chloe hadn't been there, everything would have been re-solved at the château, not in a blood-splat-tered night in Paris. She'd let her anger at Chloe lower her defenses, and she'd almost died because of it.

She would die because of it, as soon as he got a clear shot. In the meantime he couldn't do anything but follow and watch until the moment was right. He'd put Chloe in danger too many times. This would be the last.

The spring morning was clear and calm, the snow melting beneath their feet and the new leaves on the trees rustled with the barest trace of wind. It only took him a moment to realize where they were taking her — he should have known that Monique's intel would be infallible.

The old, boarded-up mine.

The possibilities were simple. Either she was dead, and their previous scouting had found the perfect place to dump a body where it wouldn't be found, particularly if they torched the main house. Or they could know her fears, and be taking her there to torture her.

Knowing Monique, it was more likely to be the latter. She wouldn't care who found Chloe's body — she'd be long gone. And she wouldn't be dumping Chloe in an abandoned mine with nothing more than a gunshot wound. He doubted she'd leave her in one piece. Monique's insane rage would require more of a punishment, either before or after death.

The gun was smooth in his hand, cold, as his hands were cold, as his blood ran cold in his veins. The rising sun was hitting the snow, but the chill in his heart was untouched. Don't think about her, he told himself. Concentrate on the target, and don't let sentiment get in the way. The only way to save Chloe was not to care one way or the other. He needed to pull that sheet of calculating ice over him so that he was nothing more than a machine.

But Chloe had melted the ice that held him. His armor had vanished, and for the first time in his life he was afraid he might lose.

He moved through the woods silently. Even the fallen leaves soundless beneath his feet. Once he knew where they were going it was easy enough to circle around, find a good position before they even got there. The entrance to the old mine was just beyond the first hill, overgrown now, boarded up, chained up and locked.

But not anymore. When he'd done his initial surveillance, while her parents were still here, the place had been impenetrable. Now it was a dark, yawning hole. Monique had done her research — it was just what would terrify Chloe the most.

They made no effort to muffle the noise they made as they approached. The two men were speaking some middle-European language — possibly Serbian. He only understood every few words, and he wished to God that Chloe were awake, alert, there to translate for him. She seemed to understand every language under the sun.

In the daylight it was still hard to even recognize Monique. She'd shaved her head, though he didn't know whether it was a fashion choice or because of surgery. One side of her face was ruined — they'd had to remove a cheekbone when they'd removed the bullet, and there hadn't been time for any reconstructive surgery. She looked like a gruesome ghost of her former self — dangerously thin, dangerously mad.

One of the Serbians dropped Chloe's body on the hard ground, and the sound of her muffled groan was music. She was alive, coming around, and all he had to do was get between her and Monique. The Serbians were no problem — he could take care of them in a matter of moments. He was a very good shot, and neither of them had weapons out. The second one would be dead before the first even hit the ground.

Chloe rolled over on her back, groaning, struggling to sit up. Bastien didn't make a sound when Monique went over and kicked her, hard, with her heavy leather boots. Chloe's muffled cry was enough.

"You have a choice to make, *petite*," Monique said. "I can put a gun to your head right now, blow your feeble little brain to pieces. That might be the kindest move, and I expect you know I'm never kind. Vlad and Dmitri certainly deserve some kind of reward for making it this far, and they've both expressed a certain interest in . . . having their way with you before you die. You American girls are so oversensitive about rape — that might be the most fun. I could watch, and you'd never know when I was going to shoot you. The boys wouldn't either, which would make it even more exciting for them."

"Sick bitch," Chloe muttered. Her mouth was bloody — someone, probably Monique, had hit her hard enough to split her lip.

"Or you can join your reformed hero. He might not even be dead yet. You have a chance, a slight chance, of survival, if you're willing to take it."

"You think I'd trust you for even a moment?" This time when she tried to sit up Monique didn't stop her. She merely smiled a horrible parody of a smile.

"Of course you don't trust me. It's a simple shell game. Under one shell is a quick, merciful death. Under another, rape and a slower death. And the third is to join Bastien in his watery grave."

Watery grave? What kind of mind games was Monique playing? Something was wrong here — why was Monique concentrating on Chloe when he was her main target, why was she lying about already killing him . . . ?

"Dmitri was kind enough to take care of our mutual friend, weren't you, Dmitri? I think he should have first crack at you — after all, he's earned it."

Interesting, Bastien thought. Dmitri had lied to Monique — the woman believed he was dead. He knew her well enough to know she wasn't bluffing. So had Dmitri lied to help Bastien, or to save his own butt?

He didn't look at all familiar, and

Bastien knew most operatives. The question was, could he trust him for help, or should he simply take him and his companion out, hoping he could get to Monique before she could do anything more to Chloe?

"I think I prefer the watery grave," she said, her voice husky. "I'd just as soon not give you the satisfaction of killing me yourself."

"I'd still count it as my accomplishment. He's at the bottom of the mine shaft. There's water down there, so you might drown before you starved to death. Or you might hit your head as you went down, making it very merciful. But I don't think you want anything to do with it. You're not very fond of close, dark places, are you? I think you'd rather die out in the open, on your back, spread-eagled."

Oh, Christ, he knew what she was going to do. She was going to dive for the mine shaft, anything to get away from Monique. She thought he was down there, and she was going after him, even if it killed her.

It was no choice, Chloe thought. Bastien was dead, dumped like so much garbage at the bottom of the old shaft. She could barely remember where that particular en-

436

trance led, she only knew it was steep and dangerous. It didn't matter. She wouldn't believe Bastien was dead until she saw him, and if she was going to die she wanted it to be with him. Stupid, romantic, ridiculous. He'd laugh at her if he was still alive. I'll come to you by midnight, though hell should bar the way. Except it was past dawn, the day growing brighter and brighter, the snow melting around her, the mine shaft a suffocating tunnel of death.

She moved so fast Monique barely had time to draw her gun. She scrambled across the clearing, ready to dive headfirst, anything to get away from that scrawny, demented bitch and her two rapacious goons, when the explosive sound of gunfire shattered the stillness, and she heard a scream that wasn't her own.

It didn't matter. She made it as far as the broken barricade when a heavy hand clamped down on her shoulder, whirling her around to face one of Monique's goons. Dmitri, the one who killed Bastien.

Something inside her snapped. She went for him, kicking, scratching, biting, screaming, pounding at his huge, heavily muscled body. He brushed her hands away like he'd brush away a fly, putting his burly arms around her and holding her motionless against his sweaty body.

And then she realized that all was chaos in the clearing. A shouting noise, the hideously familiar sound of gunfire. The other man lay on the ground, a bullet hole in his forehead, his eyes staring sightlessly into the bright blue sky. And somewhere out of sight came the sounds of a struggle.

She twisted around, just enough to see Bastien on the ground, blood flowing from beneath him, and Monique's thin body straddling him, her shaved head tipped back as she laughed. "I'm glad you're not dead, *chére*," she said. "I did so want to do the honors myself." The gun in her hand was huge, enough to blow his head off, and Chloe shrieked, unable to stop herself.

Monique turned at the noise, a minuscule mistake, but enough. The volley of bullets tore through her, so that her body jerked in a spastic dance, and she squeezed the trigger in her hand.

The gun exploded in the snow, and Monique splayed out on the ground, twitching slightly. And then she went still, lying on top of Bastien's still body.

And then, to Chloe's horror, she began to move, to sit up, and she wanted to scream, until she realized that Bastien was simply shoving her blood-soaked body off him, onto the ground.

Dmitri released her, and she panicked, grabbing at his arm, certain he was about to shoot Bastien, but he simply swatted her away. "Are we done here, Madame?" he called out.

The woman who strolled out of the woods was as elegant as ever, her silver-blond hair beautifully coiffed, her makeup perfect. Wearing designer black, and the armed men with her were wearing black as well. So perfect for hiding the blood.

Chloe tried to move, to get to Bastien, but Madame Lambert was ahead of her, holding out her elegant hand to him. He stood, wincing slightly, not even looking in Chloe's direction.

"I take it Dmitri is one of yours?" he said in a calm voice.

"One of ours," Madame said. "You should have come to us. The Committee could protect you. There was no need to go haring off like this. Haven't we always worked well together? Even when you weren't quite certain we were on the same side. The moment Jensen told me I put together a team to come after you. It was almost too late," she said sternly.

Bastien's smile was ghostly. "The Committee is never too late, Madame Lambert. And if Harry Thomason knew he would have let Chloe die. He never had much use for her." He said her name, but he wouldn't look at her. And there was nothing Chloe could do but stand there in the early-morning sunlight, with the smell of blood all around, poisoning the beautiful clearing.

"Harry Thomason has taken early retirement. His decisions have been a bit rash recently, and it was decided that he should work in merely an advisory capacity."

"Should I ask who's taken his place?" He might have been discussing the price of oranges. But oranges were hand grenades, weren't they? Chloe wanted to laugh, but she was afraid she would sound hysterical, and she didn't want to do anything to draw attention to herself. Not when he was making such a concerted effort to ignore her.

Madame Lambert's smile was cool and elegant. "Who do you think? We need you back, Bastien. The world needs you. You're not fit for anything else, and you're very, very good at this. I have no doubt you'd have managed Monique even without our help."

"Do you?" His voice was expressionless,

440

and Chloe was going to faint. She absolutely didn't want to — the pain in her side was so overwhelming she wasn't sure how much longer she could stand there. But if she fell over he'd have to look at her, and she couldn't bear it. She had to let him go, since that was what he so clearly wanted, and if she had to make herself stand perfectly still so he could safely ignore her then she'd do so for the next twelve hours.

"I can promise you complete autonomy, Jean-Marc. I need your help on this one. Do you have a reason to stay?"

Still he didn't look at her. He was bleeding, not badly, but she knew. She was probably in worse shape, and she was still standing, although with Dmitri's grip she probably had no choice.

"No reason," he said.

Madame nodded. "Then I suggest we get out of here. Dmitri can clean up the mess and join us later. You need to have that wound looked to."

"Are you going to kill her?" He seemed no more than casually interested.

"Of course not. I told you, Thomason's era is over. I don't think she'll discuss this with anyone — it would put your life in danger, and I know how you are with women. All you have to do is smile at them and they'll defend you to the death."

"Monique being a perfect example of that," he murmured.

"If Miss Underwood causes trouble we can deal with it when it happens. Unless you'd rather tie up loose ends right now? It's your call."

He turned and looked at her, at last. She stood perfectly still, determined not to betray any weakness. She looked into his face, his eyes, and saw nothing. Just the emptiness she thought had gone.

He shrugged then. "I don't think she'll cause any trouble," he said finally. "As you said, we can always deal with the situation later if need be. And we mustn't discount my powerful effect on women."

Madame Lambert ignored his sarcasm, nodding. "That's the Jean-Marc I know. I was afraid he was gone forever. Your midlife crisis is over?"

"Completely. I know who I am and where I belong."

Madame's satisfied smile hinted at the beauty she once was. Even she wasn't immune to his effect on women. Probably one of the first in a long line of suckers, culminating in silly little Chloe Underwood. "Thank God," she said, putting a hand on his arm and starting to draw him away. "Together we can make the Committee what it always should have been. I can't tell you how happy you've made me. The difference you'll make in our war against terrorism and oppression."

He paused at the edge of the clearing, pulling his arm free of Madame's possessive grip.

"I'm afraid not," he said in a cool voice. "Jensen can take my place. I've lost the killer instinct."

"Not from what I've observed," Madame said, eyebrows raised. "The world needs you, Jean-Marc."

"Fuck the world," he said succinctly.

The silence in the small, blood-soaked clearing was suffocating. Chloe didn't dare move, didn't dare breathe.

"You can let go of her, Dmitri," he said, moving toward her in the bright sunlight. The snow was almost gone now, a bright new day dawning.

Dmitri released his crushing grip, and she felt her knees begin to buckle. She let out a muffled cry as Bastien caught her. He put his arms around her, gently, and turned her bruised face up to his. The light was back in his eyes, and he smiled down at her, a slow, sweet smile that she'd seen only once before.

"Don't look so shocked, Chloe," he said, touching her bruised mouth with his finger and then bringing it to his own lips. "I told you I wouldn't lie."

"I don't suppose you'd consider just taking a short sabbatical, Jean-Marc?" Madame asked in a resigned voice.

"I'm retired," he said, looking into Chloe's eyes, and everything else faded into nothingness. "And my name is Sebastian."

About the Author

Anne Stuart has written over sixty novels in her twenty-five-plus years as a romance novelist. She's won every major award in the business, including three RITA Awards from Romance Writers of America, as well as their Lifetime Achievement Award. Anne's books have made various bestseller lists, and she has been quoted in *People*, *USA Today* and *Vogue*. She has also appeared on *Entertainment Tonight*, and, according to her, done her best to cause trouble! When she's not writing or traveling around the country speaking to various writers' groups, she can be found at home in northern Vermont, with her husband, two children, a dog and three cats.